THE TEMPTATION
OF ANGELIQUE

The Jesuit Trap

BOOK ONE

By the same author in Pan Books

ANGELIQUE I: THE MARQUISE OF THE ANGELS
ANGELIQUE II: THE ROAD TO VERSAILLES
ANGELIQUE AND THE KING
ANGELIQUE AND THE SULTAN
ANGELIQUE IN REVOLT
THE COUNTESS ANGELIQUE I:
IN THE LAND OF THE REDSKINS
THE TEMPTATION OF ANGELIQUE II:
GOLD BEARD'S DOWNFALL

SERGEANNE GOLON

THE TEMPTATION
OF ANGELIQUE

The Jesuit Trap

BOOK ONE

Translated from the French by
MARGUERITE BARNETT

UNABRIDGED

PAN BOOKS LTD : LONDON

Originally published 1969 as *La Tentation d'Angélique* by
Editions de Trévise.

© Opera Mundi, Paris 1969

First published as one volume in Great Britain 1969 by
William Heinemann Ltd.
This edition published 1971 by Pan Books Ltd,
33 Tothill Street, London, S.W.1

ISBN 0 330 02594 5

© Opera Mundi, Paris 1969

Translation © William Heinemann Ltd 1969

*Made and printed in Great Britain by
Cox & Wyman Ltd, London, Reading and Fakenham*

CONTENTS

PART ONE

The Dutchman's Trading Post

PART TWO

The English Village

PART THREE

The Pirate Ship

PRINCIPAL CHARACTERS

Angélique, Countess Peyrac: an aristocratic French lady of the seventeenth century; after an early marriage to the Gascon nobleman, Joffrey de Peyrac, by whom she had two sons, Florimond and Cantor, she becomes separated from her husband whom she believes has been executed for sorcery. She herself regains favour at Court as a result of her second marriage to her cousin Philippe du Plessis-Bellière, who is killed shortly afterwards. In order to escape the King's attentions she flees the country and is captured on the Mediterranean by the Berbers and imprisoned by the Sultan Mulai Ismail at Meknès in North Africa. There she is rescued by her fellow-captive, Colin Paturel, who accompanies her across the desert to Ceuta. She is taken back to France by the King's agents but escapes and leads the people of her native province, Poitou, in their uprising. She is condemned to death and once more obliged to flee France with her youngest child, Honorine, and a party of Huguenot refugees. On reaching America she is reunited with her long-lost husband, Joffrey de Peyrac, and with Florimond and Cantor. Together they survive their first winter in the inland fort of Wapassou, in the mountainous country of Upper Kennebec near the Canadian border. When spring comes they set off down river to visit their settlement of Gouldsboro at the mouth of the Bay of Fundy, then known as Frenchman Bay.

Joffrey de Peyrac: a high-born Frenchman. His great learning and considerable fortune arouses the envy of King Louis XIV, who contrives his ruin and has him condemned as a sorcerer. After many adventures, he is reunited with his family and disembarks on the shores of Maine where he founds the colony of Gouldsboro. By setting up inland mining communities to exploit the vast mineral resources of the region, he established a claim to a large part of the territory of Maine, then known as Acadia, the sovereignty over which was disputed between France and Britain.

Colin Paturel: often referred to as the King of Slaves at Meknès, Angélique's rescuer from captivity in North Africa. (See above.)

7

Florimond and Cantor: Joffrey's and Angélique's sons, aged seventeen and fifteen respectively at the time of the action.
Honorine: Angélique's four-year-old illegitimate daughter.
Yann le Couennec: Joffrey de Peyrac's equerry.
Kurt Ritz: a Swiss mercenary in Peyrac's employ.
Rose-Ann: an English child whose life Angélique has saved.
Piksarett: chief of the Patsuikett Indians.

French Canadians:
Baron Saint-Castine: a friend of Peyrac's.
François Maupertuis and Romain de l'Aubignière: trappers.
Adhemar: a buffoon.

Settlers in Gouldsboro:
Gabriel Berne: leader of the Protestant community.
Abigail Berne: his young wife.
Monsieur and Madame Mercelot: paper-makers.
Bertille: their daughter.
Monsieur and Madame Manigault.
Madam Carrère: the innkeeper.

PART ONE

The Dutchman's Trading post

CHAPTER ONE

FROM THE forest rose the sound of an Indian drum, a muffled, rhythmic roll vibrating through the oppressive heat that hung heavily over the trees and the river.

Joffrey de Peyrac and Angélique stood quite still on the river bank and listened for a moment to the low yet distinct pounding of the drum. It came to them through the branches, in full soft notes, firmly tapped out like the beating of a powerful heart. Nature, sweltering in the steamy haze of a torrid day, was recalling the presence of man in her midst.

Instinctively Angélique caught her husband's hands, as he stood at her side.

'That drum,' she said, 'what is it saying?'

'I don't know. Wait.'

Night had not yet fallen, but the day was drawing to an end. The river lay spread out like a huge sheet of tarnished silver before Angélique and her husband the Comte de Peyrac as they stood at the water's edge, beneath the arching alders.

A little farther on towards the left, a number of canoes made of birch bark caulked with resin had been drawn up on the sandy shore of a small cove to dry out.

The line of the cove curved round, half enclosed by a narrow promontory, while, at its innermost point, the tall black cliffs, crowned with elms and oak, had retained a welcome coolness.

This was the spot they had chosen to pitch camp. They could hear the crackle of branches, snapped off for the building of huts and the lighting of fires, and already a blue pall of smoke was beginning to rise and spread out slowly over the calm waters.

Angélique tossed her head vigorously to drive off a cloud of buzzing gnats which had suddenly begun to eddy around her. And she tried to shake off at the same time a vague sense of apprehension caused by the throbbing of the drum in the forest.

'That's strange,' she said, almost without thinking. 'There were hardly any braves in the few Abenaki villages we passed on our way down the Kennebec. Only women, children and old men.'

'Yes, all the natives have gone off to the south to sell their furs.'

'It isn't just that. The travelling parties we met on our way south consisted mainly of women. It looks as if it is they who are doing the fur trading. But where are all the men? . . .'

Peyrac threw her a swift, inscrutable glance. He too had asked himself this question, and he, like her, suspected that he knew the answer. The menfolk of the Indian tribes must have gone off to some secret meeting to plan a war . . . But what war, and against whom?

He hesitated to put his fears into words, and decided it was better to remain silent.

It was a peaceful, carefree hour. For several days now they had journeyed without let or hindrance. The thought of returning to the coast and the more thickly populated areas filled them all with childish excitement.

'Look!' said Peyrac with a quick gesture, 'That must be what set the drums beating. Visitors!'

Three canoes had rounded the promontory opposite them and were heading into the cove.

From the way they had so suddenly appeared, it looked as if they must have been paddling up the Kennebec instead of slipping downstream like most craft at this time of the year.

With Angélique close behind, Peyrac strode forward to the very edge of the water, where ripples stained with foam were leaving brownish lines on the fine gravel of the shore. He screwed up his eyes a little and scrutinized the newcomers.

The Indians in the three canoes showed every sign of pulling in. They lifted their dripping paddles from the water, then slid overboard to push their canoes in towards the bank.

'At all events these are men, not women,' Peyrac commented. Then, breaking off abruptly, he grasped Angélique's arm.

In one of the canoes a dark shape in a black soutane had risen up and then slipped down into the water to make its way to the beach under the willow trees.

'The Jesuit,' murmured Angélique.

A wave of panic swept over her so powerfully that she almost yielded to the impulse to run off and hide in the depths of the forest.

But the Count checked her by laying his fingers on her wrist.

'What have you to fear from a Jesuit, my love?'

'You know what Father d'Orgeval thinks of us. He considers us dangerous usurpers if not agents of the devil.'

'As long as he comes to us only as a visitor, we must keep calm.'

Meanwhile, on the other side of the water, Black Robe had begun to pace swiftly along the bank. His long thin shadow moved across the shimmering emerald reflection of the trees with an alacrity which seemed strangely out of keeping with the heat-wearied landscape, which was already sinking into the mists and torpor of the evening. The figure was that of a young man, brimming over with vitality, a man who went straight for his goal, heedless of all obstacles, refusing even to see them.

He vanished for a moment on reaching the camp, and a heavy silence seemed to settle around the campfires, then they heard the approaching thud of the Spanish soldier's knee boots, and the tall black shape reappeared just behind him, between the leafy drapery of the willows.

'It's not he,' said Peyrac between his teeth. 'It is not Father d'Orgeval.'

He almost felt disappointed.

The visitor was tall and thin and looked very young. Inasmuch as his Order required a very long novitiate, he could not have been under thirty, and yet he seemed to have all the inconsequential grace of a man ten years younger. His hair and beard were blond and his eyes of an almost colourless blue. His face would have been pale had it not been for the large red patches where the sun, so harsh to people of his complexion, had burned him on the forehead, the cheeks and the nose.

He halted as he caught sight of the Count and his wife, and scrutinized them for a brief moment, standing a few paces off; one of his slender, delicate hands was laid across his chest on the crucifix that hung round his neck from a purple ribbon, while the other clasped his walking stick topped with a silver cross.

Angélique thought him astonishly distinguished looking, like a knight errant or one of the warrior archangels portrayed in stained-glass windows in French churches.

'I am Father Philip de Guérande,' he stated in courteous tones, 'coadjutor of Father Sebastian d'Orgeval. My superior heard that you were travelling down the Kennebec, Monsieur de Peyrac, and sent me to present his compliments.'

'Please convey my thanks to him for his kind thought,' Peyrac replied.

He motioned to the Spaniard, who, overwhelmed by the presence of the Jesuit Father, was holding himself almost at attention, to withdraw.

'My apologies for being able to offer you nothing better than the rustic hospitality of an encampment, Father, but I imagine

13

you must be used to this kind of discomfort. Shall we move closer to the fires? The smoke will afford us some protection from the mosquitoes. It was one of your Order, I believe, who said that in America the hair shirt was superfluous as the mosquitoes and gnats more than adequately fulfilled its function of chastising the flesh.'

The priest condescended to smile.

'Blessed Father Bréboeuf was indeed responsible for that quip,' he admitted.

They sat down not far from the groups of people who were busy preparing the meal and making ready for the night, but at a certain distance.

Angélique made as if to leave them but Joffrey held her back with a scarcely perceptible pressure of his hand, for he wished her to be present at the interview. So she took her place beside him on a large moss-covered rock. She had already noticed, with a woman's quick intuition, that Father de Guérande was behaving as if he had not noticed her presence.

'May I introduce my wife, the Countess of Peyrac de Morens d'Irristru?' Joffrey went on in the same serenely urbane tones.

The young Jesuit bowed his head in Angélique's direction in a stiff, almost perfunctory gesture, then turned away to gaze over the smooth, gradually darkening surface of the water in whose depths were beginning to appear the scarlet reflections of the numerous camp fires that crackled along the shore.

On the opposite side of the cove, the Indians who had accompanied the priest were preparing their encampment.

Peyrac suggested that they be invited to share the venison and turkey already roasting on the spits, and the salmon caught only an hour before and now baking in the hot ashes, closely wrapped in leaves.

But Father de Guérande shook his head, explaining that the Indians were Kennebas, an unsociable tribe that did not care to mix with strangers.

Angélique suddenly remembered the little English girl, Rose-Ann, who was accompanying them, and she looked around for her but failed to see her. Later she was to learn that Cantor had whisked the child away out of sight as soon as the Jesuit had arrived, and was sitting patiently in some thicket, strumming his guitar to amuse her, until the conversation should come to an end.

'I gather,' continued Father de Guérande, 'that you spent the winter in the depths of the Appalachians. Did you suffer scurvy, or famine? Did you lose any members of your colony? ...'

'No, not a single man, God be praised!'

The priest raised his eyebrows and gave a surprised little smile.

'How delighted we are to hear you praise God, Monsieur de Peyrac. It has been rumoured that you and your band were scarcely what one might call pious people, indeed, that among your recruits were heretics, men of no particular religious belief, free thinkers, and even headstrong men whom pride had so misled as to indulge in blasphemy and in cursing God – blessed be His Holy Name ...'

He waved aside the goblet of cold water and the bowl of roast meat offered him by Yann le Couennec, the young Breton who served as Count Peyrac's equerry.

'What a pity,' thought Angélique irreverently, 'we shan't be able to get at these Jesuits through their stomachs any more ... In the old days Father Masserat was more sybaritic.'

'Do take some refreshment, Father,' Peyrac insisted.

But the Jesuit shook his head.

'We ate at noon. That is enough for one day. I eat little, like the Indians ... But you did not answer my question, Sir. Do you deliberately recruit your men from among those in rebellion against the authority of the Church?'

'To tell the truth, Father, what I ask above all of those I employ is that they should be skilled in the use of arms, axes, and hammers, that they should be capable of withstanding cold, hunger, fatigue, and battle, in a word, adversity, without a word of complaint, that they should remain faithful and obedient to me for as long as they have contracted to work for me, and that they should give of their best in all the tasks I set them. But if they happen to be pious and devout as well, that I do not expressly regard as an obstacle.'

'And yet you have never set up the Cross over any of your settlements.'

Peyrac made no reply.

The sheen on the glittering water, suddenly afire from the light of the setting sun, seemed to kindle a tiny mocking light in his eyes – a light that Angélique knew well – but he remained patient and uncommonly friendly.

The priest persisted in his questioning.

'Do you mean to say that there are men among you whom this sign, this wonderful sign of love, of sacrifice – may God bless it – that this sign, I say, might shock or even antagonize.'

'Possibly.'

'And what if there were among your men some – like that young man, for instance, with the frank, open face who offered me food just now – who might, remembering a pious childhood, still feel some affection for the sign of redemption? Would you deliberately deprive them of the succour of their Holy Religion?'

'One is always more or less obliged to forgo something when one undertakes to live in a mixed community, under harsh conditions, and sometimes in very cramped quarters. It is not for me, Father, to remind you how imperfect a thing is human nature, or that mutual concessions are essential if one is to live in harmony.

'It would seem to me that to give up paying tribute to God and seeking His mercy should be the last concession one should make; that it is indeed a sinful one. Is this not an indication Monsieur de Peyrac, of the very slender importance you attach to spiritual succour? Works done without the life-giving divine force count for nothing. Works undertaken without sanctifying Grace are null and void. They are empty shells, a mere puff of wind; they are as nought. And this Grace can only be given to those who recognize God as Lord of all their actions, who obey His laws and who offer up to Him, in the prayers they utter every day of their lives, the fruits of all their labours.'

'And yet the Apostle James wrote: "Faith without works is dead ..." ' Peyrac straightened his shoulders that had been bowed as if weighed down by his thoughts. From a slit in his leather jerkin he drew forth a cigar made from rolled tobacco leaves which he lit at the burning brand the young Breton lad passed him almost instantaneously before withdrawing discreetly again.

On hearing the Count quote Scripture, Philip de Guérande gave the cold, thin smile of an adversary acknowledging a shrewd thrust. But the smile in no way indicated he had been won over.

Angélique kept silence, gnawing irritably at her little finger nail. Who did this Jesuit think he was, to dare to talk like this to Joffrey de Peyrac? Yet at the same time her convent upbringing came back to her with sudden force, recalling the feeling of painful dependence she had felt as a child before all clergy, particularly Jesuits, who feared nothing, neither King nor Pope. Their Order had been founded to teach and admonish the powerful of this world. She gazed thoughtfully with her wide eyes at that emaciated face, experiencing through the unaccustomed presence of this visitor, in the heart of the American forest, all the ancient fears that belonged to the Old World: the fear of the priest, the possessor of mystical powers. Then she looked again at her husband's face and breathed a sigh of relief. For he was free – and would ever be free of such influences. He was a son of Aquitaine, an heir to a liberal philosophy of existence, handed down through time immemorial from pagan civilizations. He was not of the same essence as her or this Jesuit, both of them irrevocably involved in unshakeable creeds. He escaped this attraction, and because of it she loved him passionately. She heard him reply in measured tones:

'Father, anyone who works for me is free to pray if he so chooses. As for the others, do you not consider that work well done sanctifies men?'

The Jesuit appeared to reflect for a moment then slowly shook his head.

'No, sir, I do not. And I recognize in what you say foolish and dangerous heresies propounded by philosophers who wish to free themselves from dependence upon the Church.

'You are from Aquitaine,' he continued in a different tone. 'Men from your province are both numerous and active in Canada or Acadia. At Pentagouet Baron de Saint-Castine has utterly cleared the English from along the Penobscot river. He has had the chief of the Etchemins baptized, and the Indians of that area treat him like one of themselves.'

'Yes, Castine is my neighbour at Gouldsboro. He is a man I know and esteem,' Peyrac replied.

'Now, what other Gascons have we in our colony?' Father de Guérande continued with studied affability. 'Why, yes, there is Vauvenart on the St John river ...'

'A pirate of my ilk!'

'Granted! But he is utterly devoted to the French cause and an excellent friend of the Governor of Acadia, Monsieur de Villedavray. In the north we have Monsieur de Morsac at Cataracoui. Not forgetting of course our dearly beloved Governor Monsieur de Frontenac.'

Peyrac, puffing quietly at his cigar, nodded his agreement. Angélique herself could read nothing from his expression. The evening light falling through the shining leaves of the enormous oaks that overhung the cliff, and filtering through the dense masses of verdure, had taken on a greenish tinge that made their faces look pale, and deepened the shadows. Now a golden sheen lay on the river and the little bay had darkened to the colour of copper. Thanks to the reflection of the sky in the waters, there seemed to be more light about than a little earlier. Soon it would be June, when the evenings encroach upon the kingdom of night, a time of the year when both human beings and animals devote but few hours to sleep.

Someone had thrown big black mushrooms, round and desiccated like cannon balls, on to the fires, where they burned giving off a bitter, woody smell which had the beneficial effect of driving the mosquitos away, and this smell now mingled with that of tobacco rising from the pipes of the men. The tiny cove was full of mist and goodly fragrance, a cosy refuge beside the Kennebec.

Angélique passed her hand over her brow and from time to time ran her fingers through her heavy, golden hair, drawing it back from her moist temples, in an attempt to enjoy a momentary sensation of coolness, while she unconsciously strove to cast off her anxiety. Her eyes travelled backwards and forwards between the two men with the keenest interest, while her lips remained parted, so closely was she following the conversation. But what she was really listening to was all that lay hidden behind the words they exchanged. Then suddenly Father de Guérande came in to the attack:

'Can you explain to me, Monsieur de Peyrac, by what chance, if you are in no way hostile towards the Church, every single member of your colony in Gouldsboro is a Huguenot?'

'Yes indeed, Father. The chance, to which you refer, was that one day I cast anchor off La Rochelle, just as this handful of Huguenots, destined for the King's prisons, was fleeing from the Dragoons who had been ordered to apprehend them. I took them on board my ship to save them from what looked to me like certain doom when I saw those musketeers draw their swords. Not knowing what to do with them, once I had them on board, I brought them over to Gouldsboro, so that they could pay for their passages by cultivating my lands.'

'But why did you remove them from the jurisdiction of the King of France?'

'I'm not sure,' Peyrac replied with an offhanded gesture and his habitual sardonic smile. 'Possibly because it is written in the Bible: "Preserve Thou those that are appointed to die!" '

'Are you quoting the Bible?'

'Yes, that phrase occurs in the Holy Scriptures.'

'Dangerously tainted with Judaism, it seems to me.'

'It seems to me to be rather obvious that the Bible is tainted with Judaism,' Peyrac replied, with a burst of laughter.

And to Angélique's surprise Father de Guérande began to laugh too, this time appearing quite relaxed.

'Yes, obviously,' he said, willingly admitting the ineptitude of the dictum he had just uttered, 'but you see, Monsieur, nowadays Holy Scripture is so often mingled in people's minds with the most disturbing heresies, that it is our duty to view with suspicion anyone quoting it recklessly.

'Monsieur de Peyrac, from whom do you hold the charter giving you rights over the lands of the Gouldsboro? From the King of France?'

'No, Father.'

'From whom then? From the English of the Bay of Massachusetts who claim improperly to be the proprietors of these shores?'

Peyrac sidestepped the trap.

'I have made alliance with the Abenakis and the Mohicans.'

'But all those Indians are subjects of the King of France, most of them have been baptized and they should never, under any circumstances, have entered into any such agreement without consulting Monsieur de Frontenac.'

'Go and tell them so then . . .'

A note of irony was beginning to creep into the conversation. The Count had a way of swathing himself in his own cigar smoke that betrayed his impatience.

'As for my Gouldsboro people, they are not the first Huguenots to set foot on these shores. There was Monsieur de Monts, for instance, who was sent over by King Henry IV.'

'Never mind the past. At this present time here you are without a charter, without a chaplain, without a creed – without the backing of any nation, laying claim to these lands, and you alone already possess more outposts, more trading posts and a greater number of people than the whole of France, which has held possessions here for a very long time. You alone, quite alone, claim ownership of all this, am I right?'

Peyrac made a gesture that could have been read as acquiescence.

'In your own right,' the Jesuit repeated, his agate eyes suddenly lighting up. 'Pride! pride! that was Lucifer's unpardonable sin. For it is not true that he attempted to be like God; but he did claim to be the source of his own greatness which he attributed to his own intellect. Is that your creed?'

'I would hesitate to associate my own creed with so formidable a figure.'

'You are being evasive, Monsieur. He who sought to achieve Knowledge unaided and to his own glory, what a fate was his! Like the sorcerer's apprentice, he lost control over that Knowledge and brought about the destruction of the Universe.'

'And Lucifer and the wicked angels fell in a shower of stars,' Peyrac murmured. 'And now they and their secrets are mingled with the earth, are become tiny grinning gnomes and goblins that men find in the depths of mines, where they keep watch and guard gold and other precious metals.

'You must know, Father, for you must undoubtedly have studied the secrets of the Cabbala, what name the Hermetic philosophers gave to the legions of demons made up of these little kobolds, gnomes, and genii of the earth.'

The priest stiffened and threw him a piercing glance that was at once a challenge and the recognition of a fellow initiate.

'I follow you perfectly,' he replied slowly and thoughtfully. 'We all too readily forget that certain names which we have come to accept as part of our everyday language, once served to describe the hordes of the infernal powers. Thus it was that the genii of Water, the undines, formed the legions of the Lustful. Those of the Air, the sylphs, were the legions of Sloth. The spirits of Fire, symbolized by the salamander and the will-o'-the-wisp, were the cohorts of Wrath. And those of the Earth, the gnomes, were known as . . .'

'The Rebels,' Peyrac replied with a smile.

'True sons of the Evil One,' the Jesuit murmured.

Angélique's eyes travelled backwards and forwards in dismay between the two participants in this strange dialogue.

She laid her hand impulsively upon her husband's as a warning to take care.

A warning, a protection! To restrain him . . . Here in the heart of the American forests they were suddenly menaced once more by the very same perils that had beset them in their palace in Toulouse. The Inquisition! And Joffrey de Peyrac was smiling that same sardonic smile accentuated by the scars that had remained on his face.

The Jesuit caught Angélique's eye.

Would he say tomorrow, when he had returned to his Indian mission station: 'Yes, I have seen them! They are indeed as they are reported to be. He is a dangerous man, a subtle man, while she is as lovely and sensual as Eve, with strange, incomparable grace in her every movement. . . ?

Would he say: 'Yes, I saw them standing by the river, reflected in the blue waters of the Kennebec, standing amid the trees; he was black, hard, and sardonic, and she was dazzling; they leaned the one upon the other, the man and the woman bound by some pact ..? Ah but what pact could it be?' he would say to Father d'Orgeval with a shudder ...

And once again the marsh fever that so often racked the missionary would set his limbs quivering wretchedly ... 'Yes, I saw them, and I spent a long time with them, and I did as you asked me – I sounded the heart of this man ... But now I am exhausted.'

'Is it gold you have come to seek?' asked the Jesuit in measured tones. 'Gold you have found! You have come to enslave all these pure, primitive lands to the idolatry of gold.'

'I have never been called an idolater before!' Peyrac replied with a merry guffaw. 'Are you forgetting, Father, that 150 years ago the monk of Tritheim taught at Prague that gold represented the soul of the first man?'

'But he also laid down that gold contained in substance Vice and Evil,' the Jesuit replied with alacrity.

'And yet wealth gives power which can serve the Good. Your Order realized that from the time of its foundation, it seems to me, for it is the richest Order in the world.'

As he had already done several times before Father de Guérande changed the subject:

'If you are a Frenchman, why are you not an enemy of the English and the Iroquois who are seeking to destroy New France?' he asked.

'The quarrels between you go back such a long way that it is more than I can manage to take sides. I shall do my best to live on good terms with everyone. And who knows? I might even be able to establish peace.'

'You could do us a great deal of harm,' the young Jesuit replied, in a strained voice, in which Angélique caught a ring of genuine distress. 'Oh why,' he cried, 'why did you not set up the Cross?'

'It is an emblem of conflict.'

'Many a crime has been perpetrated in the name of gold.'

'And in the name of the Cross too,' Peyrac replied looking hard at the priest.

The Jesuit drew himself up to his full height. He was so pale that the sunburned patches looked like raw, bleeding wounds on his chalky face.

In his thin neck, rising above his white bands, the sole

adornment of his black soutane, a vein pulsated violently.

'At last I have heard your profession of faith, Monsieur,' came his gruff reply. 'In vain will you protest that your intentions towards us are friendly. Every word that has fallen from your lips was tainted by that abominable spirit of revolt which characterizes the heretics with whom you associate – rejection of the external signs of piety, scepticism about revealed truths, indifference to the triumph of Truth, and little do you care if the very image of the Word made Flesh is wiped off the face of the globe along with the Catholic Church, and if darkness descends on men's souls!'

The Count stood up and laid a hand on the Jesuit's shoulder, a gesture full of indulgence and a kind of compassion.

'Very well!' he said. 'And now, Father, listen to me and make sure you repeat my exact words to the man who sent you here. If you have come to ask me to show no hostility towards you, to help you in time of famine and poverty, that I will do as I have done before since I settled on these shores. But if you have come to ask me to go away along with my Huguenots and my pirates, then I will reply: *No!* And if you have come to ask me to help you to massacre the English and fight the Iroquois as a matter of sheer principle, without any provocation, then I will reply: *No!* I am not one of your men, I owe allegiance to no one. I have no time to waste and I regard it as pointless to transfer the metaphysical wrangles of the Old World to the New.'

'Is that your last word?'

Their glances met.

'No doubt not my last,' Peyrac murmured with a smile.

'Well, it is ours!'

And the Jesuit strode off under the shadow of the trees.

CHAPTER TWO

'Is THAT a declaration of war?' Angélique asked, looking up at her husband.

'It looks like it to me.'

He smiled and laid a hand on Angélique's hair, stroking it slowly.

'But these are only the preliminaries. We must discuss things with Father d'Orgeval and that I shall try to do. And then ...

well, every day gained is a victory for us. The *Gouldsboro* should be back from Europe by now and I have some small coasting vessels due from New England which are well armed, and further reinforcements of mercenaries. If necessary I shall sail right up to Quebec with my fleet, but I am determined to face next winter in peace and in strength, that I swear. After all, however hostile and antagonistic towards me they may be, they are only four Jesuits in a territory that is bigger than France and Spain put together.'

Angélique brooded. In spite of Count Peyrac's optimism and reassuring logic, it seemed to her that the battle would be fought on a plane where numbers, arms and men were of little account in comparison with the mysterious, nameless forces pitted against them.

And she sensed that he felt as she did.

'Why, oh why did you talk all that nonsense to him?' she complained.

'What nonsense, my love?'

'All that talk about little demons at the bottom of mines and the theories of some monk or other long ago in Prague ...'

'I tried to talk to him in his own terms. He has a fine brain and he's a born scholar. He must have a sheaf of bachelor's and doctor's degrees; his head is stuffed with every scrap of theological and occult science known to this day and age. What on earth does he think he's doing in America? ... The savages will put paid to him.'

Peyrac, who seemed inwardly cheerful and not at all upset, raised his eyes towards the dark leafy vault, where some invisible bird was flapping its wings. Night had come, deep purple, velvet night, spangled by the firelight from the bivouacs. A voice called through the branches, summoning the company to dinner.

Then in the silence that followed, the bird gave a sudden cry, so close to them that Angélique shuddered.

'An owl,' said Joffrey de Peyrac, 'the sorcerer's bird.'

'Oh! my love, please don't,' she cried, throwing her arms around him and burying her face in his leather doublet. 'You scare me!'

He laughed softly and, gently yet passionately, stroked her silky hair. He would have liked to say something, to talk about the words that had been exchanged, to bring out the meaning of the conversation they had had with the Jesuit. But suddenly he found it unnecessary to speak, knowing that both he and

Angélique had sensed, guessed, and understood exactly the same things at each stage of the dialogue. They both knew that this visit was nothing other than a declaration of war. A means too, perhaps, of obtaining a pretext for war.

With the extraordinary skill characteristic of members of his Order the young Jesuit had forced him to say much more than he had intended. One had to admit that the Jesuits knew how to handle human beings. And they had other weapons too, of a particular kind, whose power Joffrey did not entirely discount.

Almost imperceptibly Joffrey de Peyrac's cheerfulness evaporated and in some inexplicable way he found his anxiety centring upon his wife.

He clasped her closer. Every day, every night, he felt this need to hold her close to him, to encircle her with his arms to reassure himself that she was really there, and that nothing could touch her while the shelter of his arms was about her.

He would have liked to speak to her, but feared that in so doing his own anxiety might be communicated to her, so he decided to remain silent.

All he said was:

'I do miss little Honorine, don't you? . . .'

She nodded her bowed head, drawn closer by the tenderness his remark had inspired. A little later she asked:

'She is safe at Wapassou, isn't she?'

'Yes, my love, she is safe,' he replied.

CHAPTER THREE

FATHER DE GUERANDE bivouacked for the night with the Indians, and declined to share the white men's meal when an invitation to do so was sent across to him.

He set off at dawn, without bidding farewell, which in a man of his breeding constituted a slight of the first order.

Angélique alone caught sight of him as he carried his pack down the shore on the far side of the water. A handful of Indians were moving lackadaisically around the beached canoes. Early mist hung over the ground up to the height of the trees but was thin enough for her to make out the shapes of people and their reflections. The heavy dew was beginning to glisten in the faint light, while the still invisible sun struggled to overcome the mists of night.

Angélique had slept but little, although their tent was by no means lacking in comfort: if the bed of pine branches strewn with furs was not exactly the softest she had ever slept on, she had known many worse. But the events of the previous evening had left her with a feeling of uneasiness.

Now, enjoying the coolness of early morning, she stood brushing her long hair in front of a small mirror propped up against a branch, telling herself that she must find some means of softening the heart of the Jesuit, of easing the tension that held him as taut as a bow drawn and ready for war.

Thus it was that she caught sight of him preparing for departure, and, after a moment's hesitation, laid down her brush and comb and shook her hair out over her shoulders.

The previous evening, as they talked, a certain question had been constantly on the tip of her tongue, but she had been unable to find the right moment to ask it in the course of such a serious conversation, full of veiled meanings and threatening hints.

Now she really wanted to know the answer, so she made up her mind.

Holding up her skirts to avoid contact with the dead ashes and the pots of lard that littered the camp, she picked her way through the customary untidy muddle left by the Indians and followed the path along the edge of the cove; then, disturbing two tawny dogs gnawing at the entrails of a doe, she approached the priest as he was about to set off with his sorry gear.

He had caught sight of her a few moments before emerging from the thinning, golden mist of the morning. The same sheen that dawn had laid upon the leaves, played likewise over her fair, streaming hair.

Father de Guérande was a man of delicate constitution and often, on first rising in the morning, his mind felt dull and empty. Then bit by bit the memory of God came back to him and he would begin to pray. But it always took him a certain time to pick up the thread of his thoughts. Seeing Angélique approach, at first he did not recognize her, and began to ask himself anxiously who this apparition might be.

Then he remembered with a sensation like a stab of pain in his side that it was She, the Countess of Peyrac. She saw quite clearly, in spite of the impassiveness of his expression, his inner start of fear and repulsion, a stiffening of his entire being.

She smiled in an attempt to win an answering smile from the young, stony face. 'Father! Are you leaving us already?'

'My duties oblige me to, Madame.'

'Father, I wanted to ask you one question that has been bothering me.'

'I am listening, Madame.'

'Could you tell me what kinds of plants Father d'Orgeval uses to make his green candles?'

The Jesuit had obviously been prepared for anything but this. So taken aback was he that he quite lost countenance. At first he looked for some hidden meaning in Angélique's words, then when he realized that the matter was indeed a practical, domestic one, he lost his bearings. For an instance he thought she must be making fun of him, and the blood rushed to his face, but he took a hold on himself and made a desperate attempt to call to mind the details he needed to give a precise answer.

'His green candles?' he muttered.

'People say that the candles are very beautiful,' Angélique went on, 'and give a delightful white light. I understand they are made with some berries the Indians pick in late summer, but if you could tell me at least the name of the bush they grow on – you who know the native tongue so well – I should be most obliged . . .'

'No. I am afraid I can't ... I have never noticed the candles ...'

'The poor man has no practical sense,' she told herself. 'He lives in his own dream world.' But she liked him more thus, rather than when hiding behind the breastplate of a mystical fighter. She glimpsed a point of contact between them.

'It does not matter,' she went on. 'Do not let me delay you, Father.'

He gave her a brief nod.

She watched him climb into the Indian canoe with ease of long custom, bringing in 'neither sand nor stone' as Father Bréboeuf had instructed his missionaries. Father de Guérande's body had bowed to the necessities of primitive life, but his mind would never accept its intolerable disorder. 'The savages will prove too much for him,' Peyrac had said. America would prove too much for him. This long frame with its lean backbone visible through the threadbare black robe, this body would be martyred. They all died a martyr's death.

Father de Guérande glanced one last time towards Angélique,

and what he read in her eyes brought a sarcastic smile to his lips.

With an ironical phrase he defended himself against the inexplicable pity which he sensed that she felt for him.

'If you are so anxious to get an answer to the question you asked me, Madame, why not ask it yourself of Father d'Orgeval? . . . Why not go to see him at Norridgewock?'

CHAPTER FOUR

THREE SMALL craft, their sails billowing in the wind, were making their way down the Kennebec. At the last halt, the baggage had been transferred from the Indian canoes into bigger and more comfortable boats prepared and fitted out by three of Count Peyrac's men who, after wintering at the Dutchman's trading post, had returned to their duties at a small silver mine the Count had staked the previous year. He had agents and allies everywhere, and a whole network of miners and settlers had grown up imperceptibly, under his name in Dawn-East.

Yann, after accompanying Florimond de Peyrac as far as Lake Champlain with Cavelier de la Salle's party, had got back just in time to reoccupy his former position as Count Peyrac's equerry on the journey to the Atlantic. He brought good tidings of Peyrac's elder son, but thought that the expedition to the Mississippi was unlikely to succeed because of the difficult personality of its leader, the Frenchman Cavelier.

The little wooden boat, boasting only a mainsail and a forestay sail, carried scarcely more passengers than the Indian canoes which always seemed miraculously expansible when it came to accommodating numbers, but it was more comfortable.

Yann le Couennec managed the sails while the Count steered with Angélique sitting beside him.

A warm, gusty wind played with her hair, and she felt happy. She felt that a boat drifting downstream was in utter harmony with the very momentum of a man's soul, exemplifying freedom, fluidity, and at the same time control, self-possession, despite an intoxicating sense of temporary liberation from earthly contingencies. The river was very wide and its shores distant and hazy.

She was with Joffrey, her whole being suffused with emotions that were both tranquil and acute. Ever since Wapassou, ever since they had won the battle with the winter, she had ceased to be in a state of conflict. She was happy. No longer could anything disturb the even tenor of her life. All that mattered to her now was the knowledge that he was there beside her, and that she had become worthy of his love. He had told her so, beside the Silver Lake, while the polar dawn crept up over the trees. She was his companion, she was the fulfilment of his great heart and his boundless spirit, she, who knew so little, she who had for so long drifted weak and helpless in a world without haven. Now she was truly his. They had acknowledged the kinship of their spirits, she and this frighteningly virile and pugnacious, exceptional man. They were bound together now, and no one would ever be able to loosen the bonds that held them linked.

She glanced at him occasionally, taking in his image, his tanned, scar-lined face, and his eyebrows drawn together over his half-closed eyes as a protection against the dazzling shimmer of the water. Sitting there beside him like this, without touching him, her knees close to his, without a single gesture passing between them, so intensely did she feel her physical union with him that the colour came and went in her cheeks. Then he would glance at her impenetrably, almost casually.

He noted the smooth line of her profile and the downy curve of her cheek caressed by her wind-blown golden locks. The spring had revitalized her: the lines of her figure were full and rounded, and she had an animal grace that was as apparent in her stillness as in her every gesture.

There were stars in her eyes, and a sparkle on her soft, moist, parted lips.

Then suddenly, as they rounded a sharp bend in the river, a landing place appeared beside a deserted village. An Indian called out something from one of the other boats.

Joffrey de Peyrac pointed towards a line of trees, their colours softened by the heat haze.

'Over there!' he said, 'that's Norridgewock ... the mission station ...'

Angélique's heart began to flutter but she braced her resolution, knowing in her heart that they must not leave the area without meeting Father d'Orgeval face to face and trying by diplomatic means to dispel the misunderstandings and difficulties which had grown up between them.

While the three boats leaned to one side and steered for the shore, she drew towards her the soft leather bag in which she had brought some of her belongings.

It would not be fitting for a member of the French nobility to meet so redoubtable a Jesuit in clothes that appeared casual.

She carefully arranged her hair beneath a starched but becoming coiffe, and completed the effect with her wide felt hat stuck with a red feather. A touch of flamboyance was also a necessity. For had she not been to Versailles and been presented to the King? She needed to remind the proud ecclesiastic of that fact, for he was in the habit of using his connexions with the court somewhat freely in order to impress those around him.

Then she slipped on a long-sleeved mantle which she had made for herself at the fort from some blue Limburg cloth, to which she had contrived to add a white lace collar and cuffs.

The boat grounded, and Yann caught hold of a trailing branch and drew it up on the sand.

To save his wife from wetting her shoes and the hem of her dress, Peyrac lifted her and carried her in his arms to the shore, and while so doing gave her a smile of encouragement.

The shore was deserted and hemmed in by sumac trees overhung by huge slender elms. The inhabitants appeared to have abandoned the village several years before, for the whole area was overgrown with a thicket of hawthorn bushes.

One of the Indians informed them that the mission station was farther back from the river.

'We simply must talk things over with that difficult man,' Peyrac grumbled.

'Yes, we must,' Angélique agreed, although she felt highly apprehensive. God would not allow them to leave the area without taking with them a promise of peace.

As they advanced, strung out in single file, along a path that cut through the undergrowth, the smell of the flowering hawthorns accompanied them, heady and delectable.

As they left the river bank behind, the wind dropped, and the heat came down, heavy and breathless. They found the smell of flowers and pollen oppressive, and a kind of febrile agitation took hold of them, a vague nostalgia for they knew not what.

Two of the Spaniards headed the column while two others brought up the rear. They had left some of the armed men to guard the boats.

The path wound its way through the forest full of the growth of spring, narrowing here as it squeezed between clusters of thick bushes, widening there as it passed through a coppice of cherry or hazel trees.

They walked on for nearly an hour, then, when they were in the very thickest part of the forest, they heard the sound of a bell. Its pure, limpid notes rang out across the forest in rapid succession.

'It's a chapel bell,' said one of the party, coming to a halt in astonishment. 'It can't be far now.'

And the Wapassou column moved forward again. The smell that hangs around the approaches to a village was beginning to reach them now, a smell of wood smoke and tobacco, of fried fat and boiled maize.

No one came out to meet them, a most surprising fact considering the habitual curiosity of the Red Indian, always avid to witness the most trivial spectacle.

The bell rang again, then fell silent. Then suddenly they came upon the hamlet, which consisted of some twenty rounded wigwams with roofs of elm and birch bark, surrounded by tiny gardens full of ripening gourds and pumpkins growing from long coiling shoots. A few scraggy hens were pecking here and there, but apart from them the village appeared to be deserted.

The visitors walked right down the central avenue in a silence that was almost palpable ...

The Spaniards had placed the barrels of their heavy muskets on wooden forks, so as to be ready to fire at the slightest suspicious movement, and their eyes were everywhere at once.

They held the fork in their left hand, while the index finger of their right rested on the flintlock, and they moved forward with the gun butts firmly clasped under their arms.

Thus they made their way slowly through to the far end of the village, where Father d'Orgeval's little chapel was situated.

CHAPTER FIVE

SURROUNDED BY flowering shrubs that made it look like a street altar, the chapel was an attractive wooden building, constructed by no mean craftsman. It was widely known that the Jesuit father had built it with his own hands.

There was a bell tower over the main part of the building in which the silver bell hung still vibrating.

In the silence Joffrey de Peyrac stepped forward and opened the door.

Almost immediately they were dazzled by a brilliant, flickering light. Four silver candelabra with flat, circular bases each held innumerable candles that burned with a faint rustling sound giving the impression of some hidden presence. But there was no one inside, only the dancing light from the soft green candles that banished every shadow.

The candelabra stood in pairs on either side of the main altar, and towards this Joffrey de Peyrac and Angélique walked.

Above their heads a lamp shone in a holder of silver-gilt open work lined with crimson glass. It held a little oil in which trailed a lighted wick.

'The Blessed Sacrament is present,' Angélique murmured, crossing herself.

The Count removed his hat and bowed his head. A fragrant smell filled the air, warmed by the glow of the candles.

On either side of the altar, copes and chasubles hung exposed to view, dazzling in all their silk and gold work, with their embroidered faces of saints and angels, hieratic and sumptuous; 'robes of light' as they were called by the Indians, who greatly envied the priests on their account.

The banner was there too, and for the first time they saw it as it had been described to them, stained with English blood, with the four red hearts at the corners, and a sword drawn diagonally across the battle-stained silk.

Extremely fine sacred vessels, reliquaries, and silver-embroidered corporals were on display beside the tabernacle, above which stood a magnificent silver processional crucifix.

The reliquary was an ancient piece, a gift of the Queen Mother, and consisted of a small coffer fashioned of Fatimite rock crystal encircled by six gold bands studded alternately with pearls and rubies. It was said to contain a splinter of one of the arrows which had killed Saint Sebastian in the second century AD.

On the altar stone itself lay something difficult to identify until they drew closer and saw that it was a musket. It was a long, glistening, handsome warlike object laid there on the altar, as an offering, in homage – a categorical declaration.

They both gave a shudder, and seemed to hear the prayer

which had risen so many times, in this very spot, from the lips of him who owned this weapon:

'Accept, O Lord, in expiation of our sins, the blood we have shed for You . . .

'The unclean blood of the heretic, the blood of the sacrificed Indians, and my own blood which has been shed for You, for Your glory, for Your greater glory . . .

'Accept, O Lord, the trials and tribulations of war, so that Justice may reign, and Your enemies be wiped from the face of the earth. Let the idolater who knows You not, the heretic who flouts You, the indifferent man who ignores You, be crushed. Let those alone who serve You have the right to live, may Your Kingdom alone come, and Your name alone be honoured!

'I, Your servant will take up arms and offer my life to Your greater glory, for You are all in all to me.'

This passionate, violent prayer echoed through their hearts, so clearly that Angélique felt a strange dread creep over her.

She understood him. She understood perfectly well that this man should regard God as the one and only being that mattered.

Would he fight for his own life? . . . What a mockery! To protect his possessions? How petty!

But for God! What a death, what high stakes!

The blood of the Crusaders, her ancestors, rose to her heart. She understood what kind of spring it was at which the man who had laid this weapon here quenched and intensified turn and turn about his thirst for martyrdom and sacrifice.

She saw him in her mind's eye, with bowed head and closed eyes, far away, remote from his wretched, mortified body. Here he had offered up all the toils of war, the weariness of battle, of massacre, that left the arms broken from striking too often, the lips dry from never having had time to draw breath during the fighting, he had offered up the joys of triumph, the prayers for victory, the sacrifice of pride, giving to the angels and the saints the credit for the strength and valiance of the warriors . . .

'Musket of the Holy War, faithful servant, keep your vigil at the feet of the King of Kings, until the time comes to ring out for Him!

'Blessed weapon, sanctified and blest a thousand times over, lovely in honour of Him you serve and defend, watch and pray, and let not those that gaze on you prevail against you.

'May those who gaze on you today understand your symbolism and the message that I cry to them on your behalf!'

Anguish gripped Angélique by the throat.

'It's terrible,' she thought. 'He has the angels and the saints on his side, while we . . .'

She glanced distractedly towards the man who stood beside her, her husband, and already an answer had formed in her heart.

'We . . . we have Love and Life . . .'

On the face of Joffrey de Peyrac – the adventurer, the outcast – the dancing light of the candles revealed what looked like expressions of bitterness and mockery.

Yet he was, at this moment, impassive. He did not wish to frighten Angélique, did not wish to give the incident its precise, mystical interpretation; but he too had understood the message of the exposition of the musket.

Such power! Such an admission! Between you and me there will be forever total war.

Between him, the solitary soul, and them, blessed by love, war . . . forever war!

And no doubt out there in the forest, prostrated on the ground, he had a precise image of them within himself, that warrior priest, that Jesuit could see those who had chosen the delights of this world, the couple standing before the sign of the cross, as they stood, their hands close and ready to grasp one another, as they in fact grasped one another in silence . . .

Peyrac's warm hand clasped Angélique's cold fingers, then once more he bowed respectfully before the tabernacle, slowly retreating, and led her from the glittering, perfumed chapel, barbarous, mystical, burning and fiery . . .

Once outside they had to stop in order to find their bearings once more in the unaccustomed light, to return to the world once more with its white sun, its humming insects, and village smells.

The Spaniards remained anxious, on the alert . . .

'Where is he?' thought Angélique, 'Where is he?'

And she sought him with her eyes beyond the hedges and the trembling trees, limp with the heat, grown pale in the fine, dancing dust.

Count Peyrac gave a signal indicating that the company should set off on the return journey.

When they were about halfway back to the river, rain began to fall gently, murmuring through the trees.

To this sound was added the throbbing of a distant drum.

They quickened their pace and when they reached the boats the river was spattered with the sudden shower and the banks had faded from view.

But it was only a shower, and soon the sun came out once more, brighter than ever across the rain-washed landscape, and the sails filled softly in the wind.

Followed by the flotilla of Indian canoes heading downstream to trade their goods, the boats set off once more and soon the Norridgewock mission station vanished behind a promontory of cedars and huge, dark, densely-growing oaks.

CHAPTER SIX

AT THEIR next halt, while they were setting up camp, Angélique caught sight of an Indian woman running, carrying something unusual on her head. She sent someone to run after the woman, who, when she had been brought back, readily agreed to show the object in question, which turned out to be a huge wheaten loaf. She had purchased it that very day at the Dutchman's trading post for six black otter skins and had also obtained a pint of brandy for two silver foxes. She was on her way back to her camp where she had more furs. She told them that the Dutchman's trading post did a brisk trade.

The trading post proclaimed its presence by the appetizing smell of baking bread. The Indians were extremely fond of wheat bread, and during the bartering season the trader's assistant was kept constantly busy loading batches of bread into a huge brick oven.

The trading post was built on an island, in the hope, probably a vain one, that this would save it from suffering the fate of previous establishments which had been founded over the past fifty years round the big village of Houssnock,* and which had on many an occasion been pillaged, burnt, or razed to the ground on one pretext or another.

Houssnock no longer even merited the title of township. The name alone remained, and a tradition among nomadic

* Now the city of Augusta.

34

tribes heading south to make halt at this point

From this point on, in fact, where the river became tidal, they were approaching the mouth of the Kennebec, and in spite of the clarity of the water, which flowed calm, vast and powerful between forest-clad banks, there were many reminders of the proximity of the sea.

There was a salty tang in the moisture-laden air, and the Indians of the region, the Wawenokes and Kanibas, instead of covering their bodies with bear fat, plastered themselves from head to foot with the oil of seals, which they called sea wolves, and which they hunted during the winter months along the shores of the Atlantic. Thus a strong fishy smell mingled with the smell of new bread and the rank odours of piles of skins, creating about the trading post a powerful symphony of smells, hardly appreciated by those with delicate noses. Angélique had long since ceased to worry about details like these, and the antlike activity that blackened the river around the island seemed to her a promising sign. It should be possible to find untold treasures of merchandise there.

Once landed on the island, everyone went off bargain hunting. Joffrey de Peyrac was almost immediately approached by someone who appeared to know him and who began to talk to him in a strange tongue.

'Come,' said Angélique to Rose-Ann, the little English girl, 'let us first get something to drink, for I imagine we shall find some good cold beer here. Then we shall go shopping, just like in the Galerie du Palais.'

They were managing quite well together as far as language was concerned, since, over the past few months, Angélique had been practising English with some occasional tuition from Cantor. And in any case her charge was not very talkative; her smooth, pale face, with its rather prominent jaw, wore an expression of dreamy good behaviour far beyond her years. She sometimes had a lost, almost doltish look.

But she was a sweet child; when they had set out from Wapassou she had unhesitatingly left Honorine her doll, the doll which Rose-Ann had skilfully and lovingly hidden in the bodice of her dress lest it should fall into the hands of the Indians when she had been held captive by them and was on the point of dying.

Honorine had been delighted with the gift; with this marvellous toy and her tame bear, she would manage to wait not too impatiently for her mother's return.

But in spite of this fact, Angélique still wished Honorine had accompanied them, for the little creature would so have loved the bustle of the trading post where the bartering season was in full swing.

The Dutchman, manager and agent of the Massachusetts Bay Company, lorded it over everyone in the middle of the yard, dressed in black petticoat breeches, with billowing, dusty skirts.

At that moment, musket in hand, he was busy measuring a pile of beaver skins. The height of the gun barrel measured forty skins.

The store itself was a modest building, constructed of weatherboards stained with walnut juice.

Angélique and Rose-Ann made their way into a big room, which was adequately lighted by two windows with diamond-shaped leaded panes but sufficiently dim inside to remain cool. In spite of the fact that Indians were perpetually coming and going in and out of the building in order to trade their wares, it remained more or less clean and tidy, which spoke volumes for the drive and organizational powers of the man in charge.

On the right stood a long counter furnished with scales, balances, receptacles, and various measures for the sale of beads and ironmongery.

Above the counter, wooden shelves had been fitted one above the other along some of the walls to hold various wares, among which Angélique had already noted blankets, woollen bonnets, shirts, and underlinen, brown and white sugar, spices, and biscuits. There were also kegs of peas, beans, prunes, salt pork, and smoked fish.

A large brick fireplace surrounded by kitchen utensils held nothing on this very hot day but a low fire over which stood simmering a frugal meal for the storekeeper and his assistants.

A range of beer mugs and pewter goblets stood along the edge of the chimney hood, for the use of customers who wanted to drink the beer that stood in an imposing barrel, open to all, that dominated everything else. Capacious ladles hung from the edge of the barrel, thus enabling people to help themselves as they wished. Part of the room was arranged like a tavern, with two huge wooden tables flanked by wooden stools, and a few up-turned barrels to serve as extra seats in case of need or to accommodate solitary drinkers. Groups of men were sitting in this part, swathed in clouds of blue smoke.

When Angélique entered, nobody moved, but heads turned

slowly in her direction, and eyes began to glow. After greeting the assembled company she took two pewter goblets from the chimney hood; for she felt an urgent need for some cool beer.

But in order to reach the barrel she had to disturb an Indian chieftain, who, wrapped in his embroidered cloak, sat drowsily puffing away at his pipe at the end of one of the tables.

She addressed him in the Abenaki tongue with all the customary circumlocutions and respect due to his rank which was manifested by the eagle feathers stuck in the coil of long black hair which he wore plaited at the nape of his neck.

The Indian appeared to awaken from his nebulous dream and sprang to his feet, his eyes grown clear and sparkling. For a moment he examined her in astonishment and delight, then, laying one hand on his heart, held forward his right leg and gave the most impeccable courtly bow.

'Madame, how can you forgive me?' he replied in excellent French. 'Such an apparition was so totally unexpected. Allow me to introduce myself: Jean-Vincent d'Abbadie, Lord of Rasdacq and other places, Baron of Saint-Castine, Lieutenant of the King in his fortress of Pentagouet, for the government of his possessions in Acadia.'

'Baron, I am delighted to meet you. I have heard a great deal about you.'

'And I too, Madame . . . No, you do not need to tell me who you are. I recognize you, although I have never seen you before. You are the lovely, the most lovely Madame de Peyrac! And although I have heard time and time again how lovely you were, reality far exceeds anything I could ever have conjured up in my imagination . . . You took me for an Indian? How can I explain my discourtesy? Seeing you suddenly appear before me, realizing in a flash who you were and that you were present before me, I was overcome, petrified, made dumb like those mortals who receive the visit of a goddess moved by some incomprehensible whim to call upon them in their sombre earthly dwellings. For, to tell the truth, Madame, I knew that you were infinitely beautiful, but I did not know that such graciousness and charm went hand in hand with your beauty. Furthermore, what an extraordinary sensation it was to hear the Indian tongue I love so dearly fall from your lips and to see your smile suddenly light up this crude, dismal den! This I shall never forget!'

'And you, Sir, now I know that you are a Gascon!' she replied in a burst of laughter.

'Did you really take me for an Indian?'

'Indeed I did.'

She scanned his copper-coloured face, in which shone two brilliant black pupils, his hair, and his general bearing.

'And like this?' he asked, throwing off the scarlet cloak embroidered with beads and porcupine quills in which he had been wrapped.

He appeared in the blue, gold-braided jerkin of the officers of the regiment of Carignan-Sallières, with its white lace ruffle. But this was the sole item of his regulation uniform; for the rest, he wore high Indian-style leggings and moccasins instead of breeches and knee boots.

Then he stood, one hand on his hip, with all the haughtiness of a young officer in the King's service.

'What about that? Am I not the perfect courtier from Versailles?'

Angélique shook her head.

'No,' she replied, 'your fine words come too late, Sir. In my eyes you are an Abenaki chieftain.'

'In that case, so be it!' the Baron replied gravely. 'And you are right.'

He bent down to kiss her hand.

This brisk and lively exchange of compliments and courtesies in the French style, had taken place beneath the bold, unblinking gaze of the drinkers in the smoke-filled room. As for the handful of Indians in the warehouse, busy with their bartering, for once they paid not the slightest attention to the scene. One of them was busy counting out needles one by one with a magnet, another testing the blades of jack-knives on the edge of the counter, while a third, stepping back to measure a piece of cloth, bumped into Angélique, and in his displeasure, gave her an unceremonious shove to get out of his way.

'Let us go elsewhere,' the Baron suggested. 'There is a room next to this one where we can talk in peace and quiet. I shall ask old Joshua Higgins to bring us something to eat. Is this delightful child your daughter?'

'No, she's a little English girl who . . .'

'Ssh!' the young Gascon officer broke in. 'An English girl! . . . If anyone heard that, I would not stake much on her scalp, and certainly nothing on her freedom.'

'But I bought her back officially from the Indians who had captured her,' Angélique protested.

'Your status as a Frenchwoman enables you to do certain things,' Saint-Castine replied, 'but it is well known that Monsieur de Peyrac does not buy back English citizens in order to have them baptized, and this fact is not viewed favourably in high circles. So above all let no one suspect that the child is English.'

'And yet there are foreigners here. Is not the head of this trading post a Dutchman? And his assistants look as if they came straight from New England.'

'That proves nothing.'

'But they are here, aren't they?'

For how long? Believe me, play for safety. Ah, my dear Countess,' he exclaimed, kissing the tips of her fingers once again, 'how charming you are, and how exactly you resemble the reputation you have acquired!'

'I thought that the French considered me rather diabolical.'

'That you are,' he retorted. 'Diabolical for those who, like me, are too easily moved by the beauty of women ... diabolical, too, for those who ... I mean that you are exactly like your husband ... whom I admire and who scares me. I must confess that the reason I left my outpost of Pentagouet and travelled across to the Kennebec was to meet him, for I have grave news for him.'

'Has anything gone wrong in Gouldsboro?' Angélique asked, growing pale.

'No, rest assured, it has not. But I imagine that Monsieur de Peyrac is with you; I shall send word to ask him to be so kind as to join us.'

He pushed open a door, but before Angélique, still holding Rose-Ann by the hand, could enter the neighbouring room, someone clattered noisily down into the main room and rushed towards Baron Saint-Castine.

It was a French soldier, musket in hand.

'This time, this is it, lieutenant,' he wailed. 'They are preparing their war cauldrons ... There is no mistake about it. It's a smell I would recognize anywhere. Come here, come and smell it!'

He grasped the officer by the sleeve and dragged him outside almost forcibly.

'Smell it! Just smell it!' he went on, lifting up a nose that was both long and turned up at the end, a nose that gave him the look of a fairground entertainer, 'It smells of ... it smells of maize and boiled dog. Can you really not smell it?'

'There are so many smells,' Saint-Castine replied with a grimace of distaste.

'But it doesn't fool me. When it stinks like that, that means they're all out there in the woods, feasting before setting off to battle. They eat maize and boiled dog to give themselves courage! And they drink water on top of it all,' he added with a look of loathing that made his eyes stand out still farther from his head like those of a startled snail.

This soldier had the face of a real buffoon, and any mountebank who had engaged him to appear on his stage would have been sure of raising a great laugh.

It was a fact that the wind was blowing a sickly smell across the water from the depths of the forest, the smell of Indian feasting.

'It's coming from there, from there, and from there,' the soldier went on, indicating various points along the left bank of the Kennebec. 'It doesn't fool me!'

What a queer looking man he was, with his ill-fitting blue coat and clutching his gun with alarming awkwardness. He was wearing neither leggings nor moccasins, but heavy shoes which seemed to add still further to his clumsiness, and his thick cotton stockings, inadequately tied beneath the knee, hung down his legs in folds that would hardly have passed as regulation dress.

'Why get into such a state, Adhemar,' said Baron Saint-Castine with feigned solicitude. 'You should never have joined a colonial regiment if you were so frightened of Indian warfare.'

'But I've told you over and over again that it was the recruiting sergeant in France who got me drunk, and I came to again on board the ship,' the man wailed.

At that moment Count Peyrac arrived, in the company of the Dutchman and the Frenchman who had approached him as they landed.

They had heard what Adhemar had said about the war cauldrons.

'I think the lad is right,' said the Frenchman; 'there is much talk of the Abenakis being about to attack those insolent English. Will you be joining them, Castine, with your Etchevemins?' The Baron appeared put out and did not reply, but bowed to the Count who held out his hand to him affectionately.

Then Joffrey de Peyrac introduced his two companions to his wife.

The Dutchman's name was Pieter Boggen.

The other man was Monsieur Bertrand Defour who, with his three brothers, was joint proprietor of a cookhouse on the Isthmus at the far end of Frenchman Bay.

He was a Picard with broad shoulders and heavy features carved from what looked like wood seasoned by the sun, and it was obvious that it had been a very long time since he had last had the opportunity of greeting a pretty woman.

At first he appeared embarrassed, then, pulling himself together, and helped by the courage of his natural simplicity, he gave a low bow.

'This is something we must celebrate,' he said. 'Let's go and have a drink.'

A kind of gasp from behind the group of men made them turn their heads.

Adhemar the soldier had collapsed against the door frame, and was staring hard at Angélique.

'The She-Devil,' he stammered, 'it . . . it's her! You never told me. That was not fair. Why did you not tell me right away, lieutenant?'

Saint-Castine let out a roar of exasperation.

He seized hold of the man and sent him sprawling head over heels in the dust with a firm, accurately placed kick.

'Damn that imbecile!' he said, panting with fury.

'Wherever did you dig up a creature like that?' Peyrac asked.

'Heaven only knows! That's the sort of thing they send you from the recruiting centres in Quebec nowadays. Do they imagine we want soldiers in Canada who spend their whole time sweating with fear?'

'Please do not upset yourself, Monsieur de Saint-Castine,' said Angélique, laying a calming hand on his arm. 'I know what the poor man meant and' – she could not help laughing – 'he was so funny with his eyes popping out of his head like that. It was not his fault. Ugly rumours have been going around Canada, rumours I am powerless to combat – and they have terrified him. It is not his fault.'

'So you are not offended, Madame? Truly not?' Saint-Castine insisted, ringing his hands with typically southern exuberance, 'how I curse those imbeciles who, taking advantage of your absence and of the mystery that surrounds your name, have spread these nonsensical and insulting tales.'

'And now that I have come out of the woods it is up to me to do my best to destroy them. That is why I am accompanying my husband down to the sea; for when I return to Wapassou I want the whole of Acadia to be convinced not that I am a saint – heavens, no! – but at least that I am harmless.'

'As for me, I am already convinced of it,' the powerfully built Frenchman Defour affirmed striking his heart with his open hand.

'You are both wonderful friends,' said Angélique with gratitude. And as she put an arm round each of the two men's shoulders, she gave them each one of her enchanting smiles. She knew that she could encompass them both in her friendship: the very aristocratic Baron Saint-Castine and the worthy Picard peasant, made brothers through their common citizenship of this crazy, wild land of Acadia. Peyrac watched as she drew them both away towards the door laughing and joking with them as she went.

'You might not believe it, my friends,' she said, 'but it is not altogether displeasing for a woman to be regarded as diabolical. There is something about the notion that suggests a kind of grim homage to some power which has all too often been denied. Poor Adhemar did not deserve so rough a handling ... But now I beg you, let us talk of the matter no more, and let us go and have a drink; I am dying of thirst.'

They seated themselves round a table in the second room of the outpost, where they laughed and joked about all kinds of serious matters, which to many others might have appeared dramatic.

The Dutchman recovered, in the company of the French, the innate joviality of the Flemish, and set on the table glasses, tankards and pitchers, beer, rum, brandy, and a flash of Spanish wine, red and burning, that a Caribbean corsair who had wandered into the mouth of the Kennebec by mistake, had recently bartered for some furs.

CHAPTER SEVEN

PEYRAC SAT smiling and listening to the conversation with one ear, his eyes glued to Angélique. He remembered how, in the old days in Toulouse she would captivate all his friends with a single smile and a few words, so that from that moment on they would have given their very lives for her. Once again he discovered all the varied aspects of her feminine character, her quick, vivacious wit, her incomparable elegance of movement and the charm of her repartee, each matured now by a woman's experience of life.

Then suddenly he remembered her as she had been the previous year when she and he had reached this land together, after that strange voyage on board the *Gouldsboro* during which they had recognized and discovered each other.

Then she had worn a look of sadness, she had behaved like a woman on the run; it was as if an aura of unhappiness surrounded her.

And now after less than a year she had recovered her gaiety, the zest of a happy woman. This was the effect of love and happiness, in spite of the trial of winter, this was his doing!

He had helped her to come alive once more, and as his eyes met hers he gave her a tender, possessive smile.

The little English girl, pale and silent in the midst of this exuberant crowd, kept on looking from one to another.

Baron Saint-Castine told how the Marquis of Urville, the commanding officer of *Gouldsboro*, had, with the help of the Huguenots from La Rochelle, held off two ships belonging to the pirate Gold Beard. The thing that had finally turned the tide of victory had been the firing of salvoes of red-hot cannon balls. When the pirate ships found their decks were on fire they had retreated to the far side of the islands, since when they appeared to be lying low, but everyone had to keep on the alert.

The Count asked whether the two ships he was expecting, one from Boston and the other the *Gouldsboro* on its way back from Europe, had yet appeared. But it was still too early in the year. As for the little yacht from Boston which had dropped Kurt Ritz's men at the mouth of the Kennebec, it had been forced to do battle with Gold Beard and had put back into harbour considerably damaged.

'That brigand will have to pay me a hundred times over for that,' Joffrey de Peyrac declared. 'He is losing nothing by waiting, and if he does not let me have my Swiss back alive, I'll have his skin for it; I'll chase him right to the Antipodes.'

Defour said that Frenchman Bay was infested with the worst pirates and filibusters from the tropical seas. Knowing that in the summer months both the French and English in the north were visited by ships from Europe laden with goods, they prowled about the area in the hope of intercepting these, which was less risky than setting upon Spanish galleons. Moreover, their attacks drew the British warships up towards Acadia when they should have been protecting the fishing fleets off Boston or Virginia.

'And in any case, Monsieur le Comte, these Englishmen have no right to be in Frenchman Bay, where they think they can behave exactly as they like.

'You supplied me so generously with provisions last year, Monsieur de Peyrac,' Defour continued, 'when I was about to die of hunger for lack of supplies, that I wanted to do something to repay your generosity. So when I passed the mouth of the Saint John river on my last trip along the coast I rounded up all six soldiers who formed the garrison of the little fort of Sainte-Marie, and brought them down here to place them at your disposal.'

'So it is you we have to thank, Defour, for the presence of that yokel in uniform Adhemar!' the Baron exclaimed.

To which the other rejoined:

'He was forced on me. It appears that from Montreal to Quebec, from Lake Superior to Chaleur Bay, everyone keeps passing him on in order to get rid of him. But the others are tough chaps who know how to fight.'

Peyrac laughed, quite delighted.

'Thank you, Defour. I welcome the presence of a few more good shots, but what did Monsieur de Vauvenart and the Chevalier de Grandrivière have to say about your theft?'

'They were at Jemseg, waiting for the visit of the Governor of Acadia, Monsieur de Villedavray. That, incidentally, was why I set off across the bay; it seemed more prudent. My brothers can take charge of this nuisance,' he concluded with a great burst of mocking laughter.

'But why did you not drop the soldiers off at Gouldsboro?' asked Castine.

'I was driven right down to the Matinicus Islands by a storm,' the other man replied simply. 'And then I was completely fog-bound for four days. The Gouldsboro harbour channel is not an easy one to navigate, and I might have run into Gold Beard. But we always seem to meet up in the end.'

Peyrac got up to go and see the soldiers and his companions followed.

Angélique stayed behind in the shady room. The Spanish wine was delicious but a little heady. Rose-Ann had drunk some beer and was hungry. Scarcely had Angélique and her young charge had time to convey to one another the fact that they both needed some food in their stomachs, when an amiable old man suddenly appeared and put two plates on the table covered with huge slices of hot bread spread with a preserve made from huckleberries, which the Europeans called bilberries, and which in America cover vast areas of the countryside.

With a smile he urged them to take some refreshment. He had a tiny white beard and his face wore an expression of great kindness. He was austerely dressed in a black doublet and somewhat old-fashioned breeches that puffed out above the knee, and his white pleated collar reminded Angélique of the clothes her grandfather habitually wore in the days when the goffered ruff was still in fashion. He told them his name was Joshua Pilgrim.

When little Rose-Ann had eaten her fill, he sat down beside her and asked her some friendly questions in English.

He seemed very moved when she told him that her parents were called Williams and had come from Biddeford-Sebago.

He told Angélique that Rose-Ann's very own grandparents lived fewer than thirty miles away on the Androscoggin river, at a place the Indians called Newehewanik, which means land of spring. Some ten years back they had founded a settlement, which had grown and prospered and which was known in English as Brunswick-Falls. They were enterprising folk, these Williamses, always heading farther and farther inland. John Williams, the son, had left Biddeford on Lake Sebago, and had been taken away captive to Canada. But villages on the coast were not much safer when the red tide of Indians poured down from the woods upon the English. Still if you lived along the shore you could always escape to the islands.

As for himself, Joshua, he understood people like the Williamses, for he had never liked cod nor did he enjoy the turbulence of the sea. He preferred reflections on rivers and lakes beneath the trees and the meat of wild turkeys.

He himself had been ten when his father, a merchant from Plymouth on Cape Cod, had founded this trading house at Houssnock. That was why he was known as Joshua Pilgrim, for he had been among the Pilgrim Fathers and as a small child had come ashore from a ship called the *Mayflower* on a deserted stretch of land where half the settlers had perished during the first winter.

After telling his tale in measured and somewhat schoolmasterly tones, the old man went to fetch something from a

45

shelf and came back with a goose quill pen, an ink horn and a sheet of thin birch bark resembling a piece of parchment, on which he began to draw some lines. It was a plan to enable them to find the English trading post of Brunswick-Falls where Rose-Ann's grandparents, old Benjamin Williams and his wife Sarah, lived.

He went on to explain to Angélique that if they crossed on to the right bank of the Kennebec and went on heading west they would arrive in less than a day.

'That's wonderful,' she cried.

She and her husband had always intended to take the child back to her own people, but there had been difficulties involved. Since they were going to Gouldsboro, that is to say towards the east, they were heading right away from the main Anglo-Saxon community. But the region in which they found themselves at that moment, called Maine by the English, Acadia by the French, was in fact a frontier region whose shifting boundaries were more or less mapped out by the Kennebec, a no-man's land without masters or laws.

And Providence had willed it that their protégée's family should live fewer than ten leagues from Houssnock ...

CHAPTER EIGHT

THAT EVENING, they all returned to the trading post at the invitation of the Dutchman, who wanted to hold a banquet for his most important visitors, and they first discussed ways and means of getting the child back to her grandparents.

Their host brought them maps of the region.

Taking into account detours, trails and hills, they would have to reckon on three days there and back to Houssnock before heading off towards Gouldsboro with the caravan. But Joffrey de Peyrac soon hit upon another solution. Brunswick-Falls was on the Androscoggin river, which was navigable and swift flowing and would enable them to reach the mouth of the Kennebec in a few hours. So Count Peyrac's expedition would divide into two: one group, the larger, would continue as planned down the Kennebec to the sea where a ship sent by d'Urville was awaiting them, Joffrey de Peyrac and Angélique, accompanied by a few men, would travel across to the English village and, after handing the child over to her family, make their way down the Androscoggin as far as the coast where they would join up with the first group. The whole procedure should not take more than two days.

Having disposed of this matter, they did justice to Pieter Boggen's party. He had made up an old recipe passed on from one person to another wherever there were Dutchmen in the New World, all along the banks of the Hudson from New Amsterdam to Orange.

You took a large pot and poured into it two gallons of the best madeira, three gallons of water, seven pounds of sugar, some oatmeal, some mixed spice, some raisins and some sliced lemons ... The mixture was served scalding hot in a huge silver bowl placed in the centre of the table, so that each guest could plunge his silver spoon again and again in the fragrant cordial.

There is nothing better to cheer a man up and dispel gloom.

In addition to the Peyracs and their son the Baron Saint-Castine was there, Monsieur Defour, the corporal of the garrison of Saint John, and the French captain of the filibuster ship from Tortuga with his chaplain.

The Dutchman with his two English puritan assistants completed the party.

Angélique was the only woman, and her presence and that of the chaplain prevented the party from becoming too rowdy.

But Angélique was determined that they should not regret her being among them and managed to create a happy atmosphere in which each man shone, feeling himself to be the centre of attention. Great bursts of joyous laughter rose up from the trading post, mingling with the mysterious sounds of the river and the night.

When the party broke up they were all feeling very happy and very friendly. They left the Dutchman on his island and, crossing the river by moonlight, returned to their respective camps or ships.

'I shall come and see you tomorrow,' Baron Saint-Castine whispered to Peyrac. 'I have some important matters to communicate to you. But tonight we must sleep. My head is reeling. Goodnight to you all.'

And he disappeared into the forest, surrounded by a group of Indians who had suddenly appeared out of the shadows, like so many ghosts, to escort him back.

The sentries were on watch at the camp, having been given

strict orders by Peyrac to keep a close guard. For greater security the party was occupying only two huts, so that no one remained alone at night. The Count and his wife had abandoned their own private shelter, for Houssnock attracted the scum of all the forest lands, and there were redskins from everywhere, some of them baptized Indians with their gold crosses and rosary beads among their feathers. This was still very much French Acadia, French Canada, despite the presence of the Dutchman and his English assistants. These were still the woodlands, and throughout the woods of America the French ruled.

CHAPTER NINE

'WHAT A pity!' Angélique sighed ... 'Could there be anyone more charming than Baron Saint-Castine? And I do so enjoy meeting Frenchmen ...'

'Because they dance attendance on you?'

They were neither of them sleepy and Joffrey supported Angélique as she walked somewhat unsteadily along the river-bank.

He stopped and, laying his hand on her cheek, turned her face towards him.

In the golden moonlight she looked all flushed and animated and her eyes seemed to flicker, full of stars.

He smiled, indulgent and tender.

'They think you are beautiful, my love,' he whispered. 'They pay tribute to you ... I enjoy seeing them at your feet like that. I am not too jealous. They know that you are one of their race, a Frenchwoman, and this makes them proud. And they belong to our race too. Even if we are chased to the ends of the earth and separated from our own people, this fact will always remain. I enjoy meeting my brother Frenchmen too – and reading in their sincere, fearless eyes the admiration they have for you. A crazy, ungovernable race; and we belong to it too, my love. That fact will always remain!'

A willow tree cast a deep shadow beside them, and together they stepped into the darkness, leaving the brilliant light of the moon in favour of this welcome obscurity; then clasping her against him he kissed her gently on the lips. Desire, their familiar yet ever surprising desire, welled up within them, like a living creature between them, hot-blooded, burning and devouring.

But they could not tarry for dawn was about to break, and there was no privacy in the forest. They made their way back slowly, walking as in a trance enfolded in their desire, with that secret, that tide between them to quicken them, that touch of pain experienced from an impetus cut short but unwilling to die, which spelt regret and complicity in the smiles they exchanged.

Joffrey de Peyrac's hand, resting lightly against her hip, was full of promise to Angélique.

And as for him, the movement of her leg against his brought him torment and delight.

But that would have to wait.

In a few days' time in Gouldsboro, with all the charm and delight of procrastination. How slowly would those hours tick by, swollen with anticipation . . .

Once again they exchanged a few words with the men on guard.

The huts they had constructed were full of sleeping figures, but Angélique felt too wide awake to join them and chose to remain outside. She sat down alone beside the water, her arms clasped round her knees and her chin resting on them while her eyes strayed over the golden surface of the river.

Delicate wraiths of mist in evanescent streaks.

She was feeling happy and full of a vibrant, impatient energy. Everything had a savour that delighted her. Just as she enjoyed the certainty that she would make love with him, so did she find pleasure in waiting. Their day-to-day existence ordered their lovemaking; they sometimes found themselves forced to live for long days on end completely caught up in their work, far removed from pleasure, then a single look, a single tender note in the voice would set them suddenly afire, make them giddy with the urgent need to be alone.

Then she would sink into the heady darkness, would be submerged by what she in her own mind called 'my golden darkness', and would founder in her oblivion of the world and indeed of life itself.

Thus it was that their love life was so closely interwoven with the fabric of their day-to-day existence that it became at times like the subterranean murmur of a stream, an imperceptible melody, and at others like the great gusts of a storm, dominating everything and isolating them in the centre of the world, enslaving them to its laws, but at the same time, freeing them from every law.

This love life of theirs, strung out along the days, the nights, the months and the seasons, was their shared secret, the leaven of their radiant joy, something she felt constantly afire within her. It was like a gentle weight pressing on her loins, a feeling of faintness about the heart, something which filled her whole being as a child fills its mother's womb, the mystery of the spirit in the tabernacle. Love . . .

She longed to be back in Gouldsboro which, like Wapassou, was a haven to them. At Gouldsboro there was a great wooden fortress built on the edge of the sea, and the fort contained a huge room with a vast, fur-covered bed. She had slept there with him, and would sleep there again while the stormy seas sent huge clouds of spray up from the rocks and the wind howled through the sloping trees along the promontory. In the shelter of this palace, the lights in the rustic but solid houses of the Huguenots would go out one by one.

In the morning everything would be pure and sparkling; with the islands glistening like jewels in the bay. She would take a walk on the beach with a group of children following her, wander round the new port, and eat lobster with its salty, delectable tang, and savour oysters and other shellfish.

Then she would open up coffers full of wares brought over by ship, and tidy them away, she would put on new, rustling dresses and other adornments, and try out new hair styles. At Gouldsboro there was a full length mirror set in Venetian bronze, where she would see a fresh reflection of herself; what kind of image did she think would appear?

Such was her serenity that she had no fear of finding that she had altered for the worse. She would merely be different. She had acquired the face and appearance she had dreamed of in vain for so many years; the face of a happy and utterly contented woman.

Was this not miraculous? Less than a year before she had staggered on to these shores full of fear. Tense, thin and haggard, with a kind of inner tension and exhaustion, she had staggered across the pink sands of Gouldsboro and almost fallen to her knees like one about to give up the ghost. But Joffrey de Peyrac's arm had sustained her.

All the cruel battles she had had to fight throughout her youth had come to an end there.

And how far away they seemed now, those fifteen years

during which she had wandered alone, carrying the entire weight of her existence on her own shoulders. Today she felt younger than she had then, for now she was protected and loved.

A childlike joy occasionally cast its glow over her whole being and an immense confidence had replaced the suspicion – that of a frightened hunted animal – that had lurked within her. For as she had stepped on to that beach a beloved sturdy arm had encircled her. And from that moment on, it had never let her go.

'How young it makes you to be loved,' she thought, 'I used to be old. I was a hundred years old. Always on the alert, aggressive and ready to fight.'

But now, when fear came, it was no longer the same, blind, irremediable anguish she had felt when she had been struggling against the King and the overpowerful forces leagued against her.

The man in whose shadow she rested today was strong, clear-headed and prudent. He took responsibility for everything without anxiety; he was different from the others. But he knew how to reach them and make them his friends, and she was beginning to realize that the spirit of a single man worthy of the name could move mountains, for the spirit is stronger than matter.

He would triumph over his enemies, over those lurking in the darkness, those who rejected his power. So mighty was he that he would draw them to him through his astonishing wisdom and energy.

The country would find peace, the nations put their houses in order, the forests would be cleared and cities founded and filled with people. Enough of the natural beauties would always remain to give dignity to these new destinies. The New World would be forever rich and admirable, but liberated from fruitless warfare.

Half benumbed by her reverie and the headiness of this spectacular night, Angélique's thoughts clothed themselves in her unusual surroundings, draped themselves in the contained passion of nature, tuned themselves to the tension that lurked everywhere. Nothing could impair her secret jubilation.

Let the unsavoury smell of warlike feasting be wafted over the forest, and the drum beat in the distance like an anxious, impatient heart, everything was still basically simple. She was concerned with these things but they could not reach her.

Standing out in relief against the pale brilliance of the night sky, she could see towards the south-west the little three-masted filibuster rocking at anchor on the bend of the river.

On the other hand, when she looked upstream in the other direction, all was luxuriant blackness, heavy with mist and smoke, intermittently spangled with the red glow of the fires the Indians had lighted in their wigwams.

A fox yelped. A heavy but supple animal scurried through the grass beside her. It was Cantor's wolverine. For an instance she caught the glimmer of its eyes wide open in the darkness, unconsciously ferocious; they seemed to be asking some question of her.

PART TWO

The English Village

CHAPTER TEN

THE FOLLOWING morning Angélique was sitting in the small back room of the trading post, busy sewing a scarlet cotton dress for Rose-Ann, thinking that her family would like to see her prettily dressed when she arrived rather than looking like a wretched prisoner of 'these abominable French people'.

Through the open window she caught sight of a raft crossing the river. There were three horses on it which Maupertuis, the trapper who worked for Peyrac, had brought up the previous day from the coast. He was accompanied by his son and Cantor.

As soon as they reached the island, the boy ran as fast as his legs could carry him up to the trading post, which he entered in a state of high excitement.

'Father says that you are to set off straight away for Brunswick-Falls with Maupertuis. He himself is unable to accompany us but I am to go with you as interpreter. We shall link up with him again tomorrow or the next day at the latest at the mouth of the Kennebec, where our boat is already lying at anchor.'

'What a nuisance,' said Angélique, 'I have not quite finished this dress. Now I shan't have time to make the bows for the bodice. Why is your father unable to accompany us?'

'He has to meet some Etchevemin or Mic-Mac chieftain – I am not sure which, on the coast ... someone Baron Saint-Castine is very anxious to introduce to him. With the Indians you have to take your chances as they come ... They are so fickle. So Father thought it best to set off immediately and entrust us with taking the child back to her people. I have already collected your things from the camp on my way here.'

Angélique helped the little English girl to put on her pretty dress and then pinned on the lace collar and cuffs old Joshua had produced from some bale of merchandise.

Then quickly she did her hair again and buckled on the leather belt that held her pistol.

The horses were waiting outside, already saddled and held on a tight reign by Maupertuis and his son. Out of sheer habit Angélique checked harness and saddle and noted the presence of the leather bag she had prepared that morning. Then she inquired of each man how much ammunition he was carrying.

'Well, off we go then!' she decided.

'What about me, what am I to do?' asked Adhemar the soldier, who was sitting outside the door on an upturned barrel, his musket between his knees.

He had become a general laughing stock, and much fun was had at his expense. Knowing how terrified he was of Angélique, or possibly because he did not know what else to do with him, the corporal from the fort of Saint John had ordered him to serve as Madame de Peyrac's personal guard, so Adhemar, torn between his superstitious fear and the dictates of military discipline, was suffering the torments of the damned.

Maupertuis cast a pitying glance at him.

'You stay here, old chap!'

'But I can't stay here alone: the place is full of savages!'

'Well come with us then,' Maupertuis replied crossly. 'Your corporal and the others have already gone off with Monsieur de Peyrac.'

'Gone?' stammered the lad, on the brink of tears.

'Well come with us, I tell you. It's perfectly true we can't leave him here alone,' he said with an apologetic glance towards Angélique. 'And he will be an extra gun, in any case.'

They said goodbye to the Dutchman, and on reaching the opposite bank of the river plunged into the semi-darkness of the forest where a fairly clear path led off beneath the trees towards the west.

'Where are we going to?' asked Adhemar.

'To Brunswick-Falls.'

'What's that?'

'An English village.'

'But I don't want to go to any English village! They're enemies!'

'Oh shut up, you silly booby, and get on with it.'

The path was scarcely visible because of the new spring growth, but the horses managed to make their way unerringly along it with that sixth sense animals seem to possess for recognizing paths that men have frequented, in spite of the countless obstacles thrown across their way by bushes and brushwood. Spring had come in all its impudence to overlay the wild winter blackness of the forest with tangles of green shoots; but they were young and flexible and easily pushed aside. The grass was short and soft and the undergrowth full of light. They found the remains of the abandoned village which they had been told to look out for, then plunged into the woods again. Shortly after, they caught sight of the glistening waters of a lake through an avenue of aspen and birch trees; there it lay gleaming in the sun, without a ripple, as smooth as a mirror. By now it was almost noon and the silence deepened, while a kind of torpor settled over everything, filled only with the buzzing of insects.

The child was riding pillion behind Angélique, while Maupertuis and Cantor rode the other two horses. The soldier and the young trapper had little difficulty in following on foot, since in any case the horses were unable to travel faster than walking pace along the path. But they did make it possible for the woman and child to be spared the fatigue of walking.

Adhemar kept on casting nervous glances about him.

'Someone's following us, I tell you.'

They finally called a halt to satisfy him, and he strained an ear to listen.

'It's Wolverine,' said Cantor.

And the animal suddenly appeared in the undergrowth beside them, crouching as if about to spring, its vicious looking little mouth stretched in a snarl that bared its two white pointed fangs.

Cantor laughed at Adhemar's discomfiture.

'W-whatever is that creature?'

'It's a wolverine that's going to eat you alive.'

'But it's as big as a sheep!' the man wailed.

From that time on he kept turning round to see if Wolverine was following him and the mischievous creature sometimes brushed his legs to make him jump.

'If you imagine it's fun to walk with that on your heels! ...

They were all greatly amused and little Rose-Ann had never laughed so much.

The forest here was like that on the opposite bank. There were gentle valleys that sloped down to tiny streams and waterfalls, then climbed again on the other side up to stony plateaux covered in pines and stocky cedars cooled by a fragrant breeze, but which soon dropped down again into the frothy greenery of deciduous trees, almost with delight, like plunging into the sea.

After the heat of the day a breeze sprang up that made the leaves tremble and filled the undergrowth with soft murmurs.

They stopped once more to examine the map old Joshua had given them. After passing another abandoned Indian village the route became less clear but Cantor took a bearing with his compass and assured them that if they kept on in the same direction for another two or three hours they would reach their destination.

Although he did not possess Florimond's infallible sense of direction, Cantor, like his elder brother, had a keen sense of observation which prevented him from ever getting lost, and furthermore both of them had been extensively schooled in this matter by their father, who, ever since they were young boys, had made them familiar with the workings of sextant, chronometer and compass.

Angélique had implicit faith in her son, although she could not help regretting that Joffrey de Peyrac had been unable to accompany them, and, as the hours went by, she became more and more at a loss to understand the reasons for such a hasty departure.

Why was Joffrey not there? And how deserted and silent the forest was, and yet at the same time how much noise there was since the wind had risen.

'Did Monsieur de Peyrac not explain to you why he had to make this sudden unexpected journey?' she asked, turning towards the trapper. She knew him less well than the others because he had not spent the winter with them at Wapassou, but she knew that he was loyal and reliable.

'I did not see Monsieur le Comte myself,' the man replied. 'It was Clovis who brought me the message.'

'Clovis?'

A vague feeling of alarm began to grow within her. There was something strange about the whole business. Why had Joffrey not written her a note? It was not like him . . . messages passed from mouth to mouth . . . Clovis? . . . Her horse stumbled against a stone projecting slightly from the ground, and she had to concentrate all her attention on keeping it heading in the right direction.

Through the deep emerald-green tracery of the oak leaves the massive trunks could be seen, branching out into black boughs like candelabra.

It reminded her of the forest of Nieul at the time of the ambushes . . .

Plunged in her memories, she longed to get out of this deep shade.

'Are we on the right road, Cantor?'

'Yes, yes,' the young man replied with a further glance at his map and compass.

But a little farther on he dismounted and he and Pierre-Joseph, the young half-caste, carefully scrutinized the surroundings. The track disappeared into the undergrowth at this point, yet the two young men insisted that that was the way to go. The trees began to hedge them in more and more until they formed a narrow tunnel which grew darker and darker. On reaching a bend, however, the light grew brighter, marking the end of the tunnel in a patch of sunlight.

But it was at this moment that Maupertuis raised his hand and all of them, even the horses, stopped dead at the signal. Some imperceptible change had taken place, a change which indicated that the deserted forest had become not exactly peopled, but as if inhabited by some other presence.

'Indians!' Adhémar whispered, almost swooning.

'No, Englishmen,' Cantor replied.

A silhouette had risen up against the sunny halo in the gap between the branches, and a more extraordinary sight one would find it hard to imagine.

Hunch-backed, twisted, shod in enormous buckled shoes out of which a pair of skinny calves rose, dressed in a broad brimmed, incredibly high sugar-loaf hat, a little old man was standing at bay at the exit from the wood. In his two hands he clasped an old blunderbuss with a short, bell-shaped barrel stuffed full of grapeshot, a weapon that would undoubtedly have caused as much damage to the man who fired it as to his victims.

The newcomers were careful to make no move.

'Halt!' shouted the little old man in a high-pitched, penetrating voice. 'If ye be spirits, ye had best be gone, or I fire!'

'You can see that we are no spirits,' Cantor replied in English. 'Just a minute, please.'

The old man raised his antiquated gun and burrowed with one hand in his doublet from which he drew an enormous pair of tortoiseshell-rimmed spectacles, which he placed on his nose thus giving himself the appearance of an elderly owl.

'Yes! I see!' he muttered.

He drew out the end of each syllable with suspicious deliberation.

He came towards the horsemen with little mincing steps, examining Cantor from top to toe and pretending not to see Angélique.

'And who art thou, that speakest in the Yorkshire tongue, like those accursed professors in Boston? Hast thou no fear of wandering in the woods, like an honest Christian? Dost thou not know that ill betides lads and lasses that wander in the woods? They might encounter the Black Man and perform manifold abominations with him. Is it not thou that taunteth me, oh son of Belial the lustful, Prince of the Waters with whom begot thee one witches' sabbath the woman that accompanies thee? I would not be surprised! To boot, thou art too handsome to be of human kind, young man!'

'We are on our way to see Benjamin and Sarah Williams,' Cantor replied without excessive surprise, for he had encountered oddities of this kind before among the Boston Illuminati. 'We are escorting their granddaughter Rose-Ann, the daughter of John Williams.'

'Ha! Ha! To Benjamin Williams.'

The old man bent forward to examine the little girl in the red dress, screwing up his piercing eyes behind the thick lenses of his spectacles.

'Dost thou say that this child is granddaughter to Williams? Ho! Ho! What a jest! How we shall laugh!'

And he rubbed his hands together in glee as if he had suddenly been told an excellent joke. 'Ha! Ha! I can just imagine it!'

Unobtrusively, his sharp eyes had taken in all the other members of the party: the two trappers with their leather jackets fringed in the Indian style, their belts and coloured Canadian bonnets, and the French soldier behind them in his faded but still recognizable army tunic.

He replaced his gun on his hunched shoulder and stepped aside from the path.

'Well then, pass your way, Frenchmen,' he said, still chuckling to himself. 'Go along then and take old Ben's granddaughter to him. Ha! Ha! I can just imagine the look on Williams's face! Ha! Ha! What a joke! But count ye not on any ransom, for he is a close man . . .'

Angélique had more or less managed to follow the conversation. Although she had found the old man's English perfectly intelligible, she had grasped almost nothing of what he was trying to convey. Fortunately Cantor kept his serene calm.

'Are we still far from Brunswick,' he asked politely. 'We fear we may have lost our way.'

The man gave a pout and shook his head, as if to say that when people are crazy enough to go walking in the devil's own forest, they should know where they are going and manage without help.

During this conversation another figure had appeared and

crept up silently behind the old man. He was a tall Indian with a cold stare, an Abenaki from the Sokoki or Sheepscot region to judge by his sharp profile with its two prominent incisors. He carried a lance in his hand and a bow and quiver of arrows slung across his back. He listened to the conversation with a look of complete indifference.

'Could you really not tell us the way to Brunswick-Falls, worthy old man?' Cantor insisted, unable to think of any further means of persuasion.

But his request, although formulated with every possible courtesy, transformed the face of the old gnome who grimaced in anger and stormed off with a volley of abuse, in which Angélique caught, as he went by, verses from the Bible, curses, prophesies, accusations, and whole sentences of Latin and Greek, all of which conveyed that the people of Brunswick – called Newehewanik by the Indians – were all crazy, ignorant unbelievers, possessed of the devil, and that he, George Shapleigh, would never again set foot in their place.

Cantor persisted in his request with all the guilelessness of youth, and little by little the old man calmed down, growled a bit, launched a few more anathemas, then turning his back on them, set off ahead of them down the path, while his Indian, still silent and expressionless, followed at the end of the line.

'Does this mean that this crazy old coot has decided to show us the way?' Maupertuis growled.

'So it seems,' replied Cantor. 'Let's follow him! We shall soon see where he takes us.'

'Offer him a seat on one of the horses,' Angélique suggested. 'He may be tired.'

Cantor passed on his mother's suggestion, but the Englishman, without turning round, gesticulated with such vehemence that it was quite clear they had offended him and that in any case, in his eyes, horses were also naturally to be regarded as creatures of the devil.

He pranced swiftly along and, in spite of his heavy shoes it was astonishing to note that he made not the slightest sound and seemed scarcely to touch the ground.

'He is an old medicine-man,' Cantor explained, 'who claims to have combed every forest in America in search of plants and tree bark for his medicine. That alone would explain the suspicion with which his compatriots must view him. For in New England people who go off into the woods are not liked, as he has just told you himself. But, odd as he is, I think we can trust him to put us on the right road.'

'I don't want to go to these English people and I don't like walking with an unknown Indian at my heels,' Adhemar grumbled through the shadows.

Every time he turned round he caught sight of the dark, stony face and the eyes like pools of black water staring at him. A cold sweat soaked his shirt, as it had often done before during his many moments of fright. He plodded on, stumbling over tree roots.

The little man in the pointed hat bounded on ahead like a dark elf, a will-o'-the-wisp in mourning weeds, occasionally vanishing as he entered some shadow then reappearing in a shaft of reddish sunlight falling through a gap in the trees. But throughout all these twistings and turnings of the way, Angélique noticed with impatience that night was falling. The hollows of the ravines were beginning to fill with purple.

As he walked, the old man occasionally turned right round, muttering a few indistinct words, with his arms raised, and his skinny fingers spread as if pointing up at something in the air.

'I am beginning to wonder whether he is not completely insane and whether he has any idea where he is taking us,' Maupertuis said at last, ill at ease. 'These English!'

'It doesn't matter where he takes us so long as he gets us out of this forest,' Angélique replied, her patience exhausted.

Almost immediately, as if in fulfilment of her wish, they emerged on to a vast plateau covered in green grass and strewn with rocky outcrops and juniper trees. An occasional wind-beaten cedar or cluster of black fir trees stood out from the plain like sentinels. Far, far away beyond a ridge of wooded hills and valleys, the eastern sky was like mother-of-pearl, the kind of sky one sees over the sea. It was a long way off. A promise. But the wind that blew across the plateau carried a scent that was familiar, indefinable, and full of memories.

After winding its way between the rocks and bushes the path ran down into a little valley which the night had already filled until no glimmer of light remained. The far slope rose in front of them in a smooth curve whose higher black crest stood out against the pale sky. It was from there that the half forgotten smell came. The strong, homely smell of a *ploughed field*.

They could see nothing through the darkness, and could only

guess at the presence of the rich, damp earth smelling of spring, and its deep ploughed furrows.

Old Shapleigh began to mutter and snigger.

'Yes, here we are! Roger Stoughton still in his field. If he could do away with the night, and the stars, and the sleep that weighs upon his eyelids, how happy would Roger Stoughton be. He would never know a moment of rest. He would labour on, digging, scratching, breaking up the ground, for ever and ever, nor would he rest his hand from toil. His fork would turn and never cease, like the devil's own fork in the depths of hell, for ever and aye'.

'But the devil's fork is barren, whereas mine is not, you uncouth old man,' came in reply a sepulchral voice from the ploughed field. 'The devil only uses the tip of his fork on the dregs of men's souls, whereas I bring forth fruit from the earth which the Lord blesses . . .'

A dim shadow moved towards them.

'And to that end I shall never be able to devote sufficient of the days of my life,' the voice went on as if delivering a lecture, 'I am not like thee, old sorcerer, that fearest not to sully thy soul by consorting with the rude wilderness of nature. Oho! Whom dost thou bring us tonight, spirit of darkness? Whom dost thou bring us from the accursed lands?'

The peasant drew closer, then stopped, and craned his neck towards them.

'The place is rank with Frenchmen and Indians,' he growled. 'Halt! Hold your ground!'

They sensed him raise a gun to his shoulder. During the whole of this monologue, Shapleigh had replied with a volley of sniggers, as if greatly amused. The horses kept shying, upset by this voice that scolded at them out of the darkness. Cantor summoned up his very best English to greet the peasant, introduced little Rose-Ann Williams, and, without attempting to hide the fact that they were French, took care to mention his father's name: Count Peyrac of Gouldsboro.

'If you have any connexions with Boston or Casco Bay you will surely have heard of Count Peyrac of Gouldsboro. He has commissioned several ships from the New England shipyards.'

Without deigning to reply, the peasant drew closer, and circled round them, sniffing at them like a suspicious dog.

'I see thou still hast this horrid redskin creature skulking at thy heels,' he remarked, still addressing the old medicine man.

'It were better to bring a nest of serpents into a village than a single Indian!'

'If I enter the village, so will he,' the old man replied aggressively.

'And we shall all wake up dead in our beds tomorrow and scalped by those traitors, as happened to the people of Wells, who offered shelter to a wretched Indian woman one stormy night. She showed her redskin sons and grandsons how to get in, opened the gate of the fort to them and the white men were all massacred. For, thus spake the Lord: "Never shall ye forget that the land into which ye enter is a land stained by the uncleanness of the people of that land ... Ye shall not give your daughters unto their sons, nor take their daughters unto your sons, and take no thought for their prosperity, neither for their comfort, and thus shall ye grow strong ..." Whereas thou, Shapleigh, thou growest weaker with every day that thou hast truck with these Indians ...'

After this gloomy biblical language silence reigned once more, and shortly afterwards Angélique realized that this inhabitant of Brunswick-Falls had finally decided to let them pass.

In fact he even went ahead of the little cluster of people and began to climb the hill in front of them. Then as they emerged from the hollow, they found themselves once more walking through the brightness of the long drawn out spring evening. A gust of wind brought them the smell of stables, and the still distant sounds of cattle being driven home from the fields.

CHAPTER ELEVEN

THEN SUDDENLY, against a golden sky streaked with bold russet lines, loomed the shape of a big English farmhouse.

The house was isolated and a single lighted window seemed to cast a wary eye over the dark valley from which they had emerged.

As the travellers drew closer they could make out the shape of fenced enclosures. It was a sheepfold, where the shearing was carried out and cheese made. Several men and women turned round and stared at the three horses that brought the strangers.

The farther they continued down the long track the nearer

they seemed to get to the glow of the sunset.

A bend in the path revealed the entire village with its wooden houses rising one above the other up the side of a hill crowned with elms and maple trees.

They overlooked a grassy curve with a stream running through it.

Some washerwomen were coming back from the stream with their wicker baskets, laden with clothes, balanced on their heads, their blue cotton dresses flapping in the wind.

Beyond the stream, the fields rose in gentle slopes up to the forest with its serried ranks of trees.

The path became a road and, after sloping gently downwards, led up between the houses and gardens.

Lighted candles behind the window panes or parchment squares dotted the crystal-clear evening air with stars, taking the place of the daylight and giving the peaceful scene a glittering brightness as if strung with precious stones.

And yet, by some mysterious grapevine, when they came to a halt at the other end of the village before an imposing gabled house with an overhanging upper storey, almost all the inhabitants of Brunswick-Falls were gathered behind them, openmouthed and wide-eyed, a sea of blue and black clothes, astonished faces, white coifs and pointed hats.

As Angélique dismounted and gave a general greeting, the crowd shrank back in alarm with a vague murmur, but when Maupertuis stepped forward and lifted little Rose-Ann to the ground, the murmur swelled to a roar of stupefaction, indignation, and protest and muttered questions and conjectures began to pass from one to another.

'What on earth have I done?' asked Maupertuis in dismay. 'It isn't as if they had never seen a trapper before, is it? And in any case, we are at peace, or so I thought!'

The old apothecary was dancing about like a newly landed fish.

'It's here! It's here!' he kept on repeating impatiently, pointing to the door of the big house. He was full of glee.

He was the first to climb the steps of the wooden porch and push the door open with a firm hand.

'Benjamin and Sarah Williams! I bring you your granddaughter Rose-Ann from Biddeford-Sebago and the Frenchmen who have captured her,' he cried in his sharp, triumphant voice.

For a split second Angélique saw inside the room: there was a brick fireplace at the far end adorned with numerous copper and pewter utensils, and two old people, a man and a woman sitting on either side of the fire, dressed in black, as stiff and formal as portraits; they both wore identical white, starched ruffs, and the woman an imposing lace coif, and both sat very upright in high-backed, carved chairs. An enormous book lay open on the old man's knees, no doubt a Bible, and the woman was spinning flax with a distaff. Close by, at their feet, sat some children and servants dressed in blue, working spinning wheels.

It was only a fleeting vision since at the very mention of the word Frenchmen the two old people leapt to their feet, the Bible and distaff fell unheeded to the floor, and with astonishing agility they seized two guns from the chimneypiece, apparently loaded and ready to fire, and took aim at the new arrivals.

Shapleigh chortled even louder than before and rubbed his hands together, but almost at once the sight of Angélique pushing the little girl before her seemed to create such utter dismay in the old people, even more violent than that caused by the appearance of the French, that their hands began to shake and their weapons suddenly seemed too heavy for their old arms ... The gun barrels drooped slowly as if overcome by stupefaction.

'Oh God! God!' the old lady's pale lips muttered.

'Oh Lord!' cried her husband.

Angélique dropped them a curtsy, begged them to forgive her imperfect English, and told them how happy she was to be able to return the child who had been through so terrible an experience, safe and sound into the hands of her grandparents.

'She is your granddaughter, Rose-Ann,' she insisted, for it seemed to her as if they had not yet grasped the fact. 'Are you not going to kiss her?'

Still unsmiling, Benjamin and Sarah Williams looked gloomily down at the child, and together heaved a great sigh.

'Yes, yes indeed,' old Ben said at last, 'yes indeed, we can see that this is Rose-Ann and we would like to kiss her, but first, she must, she really must remove that unspeakable scarlet gown.'

CHAPTER TWELVE

'YOU MIGHT just as well have brought her along stark naked, with the devil's horns in her hair,' Cantor pointed out to his mother a little later.

Realizing what a sad miscalculation she had made, Angélique was full of self-reproach.

'Whatever would they have said if I had had time to make the golden bows for the bodice of that red dress?'

'The mind boggles,' agreed Cantor.

'You have lived in New England, you should have warned me. I could have spared my fingers, instead of making her a special dress to take her back to such dreadfully puritanical people in.'

'Please forgive me, Mother ... But they might equally well have turned out to be a less intolerant sect. Such do exist. And in any case, I thought it would be fun to see their reaction.'

'You are as bad a mischief-maker as that quaint old apothecary, whom they seem to be as chary of as the plague. I wouldn't be surprised if he was looking forward to seeing the effect Rose-Ann's red dress would have on them from the time he first set eyes on it. No doubt that was why he agreed to show us the way.'

All of them including the unfortunate Rose-Ann, had been ushered into a kind of parlour leading off the main room, no doubt to get the child, in her ridiculous and shameful get-up, out of sight of the gaping crowds as quickly as possible, along with the woman who had brought her, whose gaudy and unseemly attire only too clearly indicated the nation and corrupt religion to which she belonged – a Frenchwoman and a Papist!

What strange creatures these Puritans were; one could not help wondering whether they had a heart ... whether they had any sex. When one saw how cold their family relationships were, it was difficult to imagine that any act of love could ever have brought their families into existence. And yet Mr and Mrs Williams had numerous progeny, and there were at least two families with their children installed in the big house at Brunswick-Falls. But Angélique was at a loss to understand that no one seemed to be concerned about the fate of John and Margaret

Williams who had been taken prisoner by the Indians and carried off to Canada.

The tidings that her daughter-in-law had given birth to a child under appalling difficulties in the Indian forest lands, had left Mrs Williams cold. And her husband had launched out into a long diatribe to the effect that John and Margaret had received their just desserts for their unbiddableness.

Why had they not stayed at Biddeford-Saco, on the coast, a well-established, God-fearing colony, instead of thinking, in their pride, that they were the Lord's Anointed, chosen to found their own colony in a wilderness which was as fraught with peril for their souls as for their bodies, and, instead of having the final audacity to call this new settlement, which was the fruit of their pride and indiscipline, by the very same name, Biddeford, as the place in which they had been born? And now they were in Canada and it served them right. He, Ben Williams, had never considered that his son John had the makings of a leader.

He waved aside the details Cantor attempted to provide about the captives, saying that he had already heard all about their capture from Darwin, the husband of his daughter-in-law's sister, who was a somewhat limited young man and who was preparing to re-marry. 'But his wife is not dead,' Angélique tried to explain. 'At least she wasn't when I last saw her at Wapassou . . .'

But Benjamin Williams was not listening. As far as he was concerned everything that lay to the north of the great woods, those far off, impenetrable regions where Frenchmen, possessed of the devil, sharpened up their scalping knives in the midst of clouds of incense, might as well be regarded as part of the Next World, and, as a matter of fact, very few English men or women had ever returned from those regions.

'Now tell me honestly for once,' Angélique asked Cantor, 'is there anything about my clothes which could possibly offend them? Am I improperly dressed without realizing it?'

'You should put something across *there*,' said Cantor sententiously, pointing to the low neckline of Angélique's bodice.

They were laughing like a pair of children, watched unsmilingly by poor Rose-Ann, when the serving maids in blue dresses came in carrying a wooden tub hooped with copper bands and a large number of pitchers full of steaming hot water. A tall young man, as solemn as a parson, came to fetch Cantor, who followed him, putting on the same formal, worried expression which was so out of place on fresh young faces.

The maids, on the other hand, attractive girls, their cheeks rosy from work in the fields, seemed far less strait-laced. As soon as they were out of the watchful eye of their old master, they had a smile and a lively sparkle in their eyes as they scrutinized Angélique, whose arrival was a major event in their lives. They examined admiringly every detail of her costume, simple as it was, and followed her every gesture, which did not however prevent them from bustling hither and thither, bringing a cake of soap in a wooden bowl and handing round towels warmed in front of the fire.

Angélique dealt with Rose-Ann first of all. She was no longer surprised that the little English girl had at times seemed a trifle slow witted, when she saw what kind of background she came from. The atmosphere of La Rochelle gave only a faint idea of what it was like.

Nevertheless, when the moment came to dress her again and Angélique went to put on the dark dress that had been put out for her, the timid child rebelled. Her stay among the French, although short, had been her undoing – or at least that is how his Reverence the Pastor would have seen it. For she suddenly and passionately pushed aside the dismal dress, buried her face in Angélique's bosom and burst into tears.

'I want to keep my pretty red dress!' she cried.

And as if to emphasize where she had come by this rebelliousness, she repeated the phrase several times in French, to the great consternation of the servants. That ungodly language on the lips of a Williams, this shameless outburst of temper and wilfulness, this avowed coquettishness, all this was terribly disconcerting, and boded nothing but ill . . .

'Mistress Williams will never agree to that,' said one of the girls hesitantly.

CHAPTER THIRTEEN

OLD SARAH WILLIAMS stood very straight, very tall, very thin, regal and imposing, and gazed solemnly down at her granddaughter and at Angélique.

They had gone to fetch her to settle the dispute, and indeed no one could have better summoned up the notion of Justice and Renouncement than this tall woman, Sarah, who, seen close to, was very impressive in her dark clothes, her neck held erect by her pleated ruff.

Her eyelids were big, heavy and bluish, covering dark, slightly protruding eyes which every now and then flashed in her very pale face whose time-worn curves had a touch of majesty.

And one could never forget, looking at her thin, pale hands clasped piously, the speed with which they were still capable of grasping a gun.

Rose-Ann was still crying and Angélique stroked her hair.

'She's only a child,' she pleaded, looking at the intractable old lady. 'It is in a child's nature to like bright things, joyous things, pretty things...'

It was then that she noticed that Mrs Williams was wearing an exquisite Flanders lace bonnet, one of those very inventions of the devil, inducements to the sin of vanity, which old Ben had denounced only a short while previously.

Mrs Williams lowered her heavy eyelids and appeared to reflect. Then she gave a curt order to one of the girls, who returned carrying a folded white garment, which Angélique saw to be a cotton pinafore with a large bib.

With a gesture Mrs Williams indicated that Rose-Ann might put on the offending dress again on condition that she covered up some of its provocative splendour with the pinafore.

Then, turning towards Angélique, she gave her a conspiratorial wink, and the ghost of a sly smile flitted across her tight lips.

Having made these mutual concessions, the Williamses and their guests forgathered again at the table for the evening meal.

Maupertuis and his son had sent to say that they were being entertained by a member of the community with whom they had once had dealings in furs, on a journey they had made to Salem.

Adhemar was wandering like a lost soul along the grassy paths of the colony, followed by a crowd of curious young Puritans who from time to time would put out a timorous finger to touch the blue uniform of a soldier of the King of France, and his musket, slung from one discouraged arm.

'The forest is full of savages,' he wailed, 'I can feel them all around.'

Angélique came out to fetch him.

'But come, Adhemar, we have not met a soul all day! Come in and take some refreshment.'

'And sit among those heretics who hate the Virgin Mary? Never!'

So he remained outside the door, squashing mosquitos on his cheeks and considering the horrors lying in wait for him on all sides in this horrible country – savages, Englishmen ... He had even come to feel more secure in the presence of a certain person who was suspected of being a diabolical spirit, but who had at least the merit of being French. And what was more, she spoke to him gently and patiently, this woman they called the She-Devil, instead of being unkind to him. So he would stand guard to defend her since the King's recruiting officers had made a soldier of him and had put a musket in his hands.

Angélique had been given a bowl of warm milk with a beaten egg in it. This simple dish, with its almost forgotten savour, filled her with delight. Then there was boiled turkey with a strong mint sauce to give it some flavour, and corn on the cob. Then they were served a pie with a cover of pastry through which rose the delectable smell of stewed bilberries.

The Englishmen were startled to learn that Count Peyrac and his family had been living in Upper Kennebec, more than 400 miles from the sea. Of course, they were Frenchmen, but the exploit was still regarded as very much out of the way, especially as women and children were involved.

'Is it true that you had to eat your horses?' they kept on asking.

The young men were especially interested in this French gentleman, who was a friend and a delegate of Massachusetts Bay. What were his plans? Was it true that he was trying to make an alliance with the Indians and his French compatriots, in an attempt to put an end to the murderous raids against New England?

Old Benjamin took no part in the discussion. He had of course heard tell of Count Peyrac but preferred not to let his mind dwell on the razzle-tazzle of all the different nations who claimed nowadays to inhabit the county of Maine.

Was it not enough that there was hardly any room left along the shores of Massachusetts? He did not like to think that there were any other people on earth than the members of his little tribe.

He would have preferred to be *alone* with his people, at the dawn of time, or like Noah emerging from the Ark.

He had always fled towards the empty spaces, always tried

to imagine that they alone were able to praise their Creator, 'the well-beloved flock, the elect of God to His greater glory', but the world always caught up with him and reminded him that the Creator must needs share out his gifts among innumerable, uninteresting and ungrateful peoples.

Angélique, who saw at a glance in the Patriarch a roving leader of men – she only had to look at his long, bold, inquisitive nose above his white beard, and his intolerant eyes – asked herself why he was so angry with his son for having wanted to follow the independent example of his father, by leaving Biddeford-Saco to settle at Biddeford-Sebago. But this was one of those classic mysteries in the relationship between father and son that have existed since the world began. Human failings show through the toughest and most saintly of shells, and Angélique began to feel the first promptings of affection and sympathy towards these intransigent, upright people.

Cheered by the excellent meal, she began to sense a certain comradely warmth that bound together these people with their sombre clothes and principles.

But once these principles had been decreed and loudly proclaimed, more human feelings reasserted themselves.

Rose-Ann had kept her red dress, and Angélique, although a Frenchwoman and a Papist, had nevertheless been accorded the honours of the family table.

Cantor's presence intrigued them. This young man with the bright eyes seemed to belong neither here, nor to any other specific place.

The English accepted him unanimously on account of his excellent English and his knowledge of Boston; then, remembering that he too was French and a Papist, they drew back. Every man present, old Benjamin, his sons and sons-in-law, examined him curiously from beneath their churlish brows, questioning him, making him talk, and carefully considering each of his answers.

Towards the end of the meal the door opened and in came a huge fat-bellied man, whose appearance threw an immediate chill on the jovial, friendly atmosphere which had gradually been built up.

The two grandparents immediately put on their most rigid expressions.

It was the Reverend Thomas Patridge. The fact that nature had made him an Irishman and endowed him with a full-blooded constitution, over and above the normal difficulties that all men experience in their attempts to achieve the virtues of mildness, humility and chastity, had made it possible for him to achieve the moral rectitude which made him one of the most outstanding ministers of religion of his time only by means of a far ranging and fastidious scholarship, a constant denunciation of other men's sins, and frequent outbursts – like jets of steam forcing up the lid of a saucepan – of a righteous and devastating anger. In addition to all that, he had read Cicero, Terence, Ovid and Virgil, spoke Latin, and knew Hebrew.

He glowered at the assembled company, stopping when his eyes reached Angélique with a reaction of feigned shock as if the sight of her was worse than he could ever have imagined, glanced sadly and contemptuously at Rose-Ann who was unashamedly covering herself with bilberries, then wrapped himself about in his huge, long Genevese cape, as if to insulate himself from so much wickedness.

'I see, Ben,' he began in a sepulchral voice, 'I see that wisdom has not come to you in your old age – you have introduced Jesuits and Papists here, you have the temerity to welcome at your table the living image of the woman who precipitated the dread fall of the human race, Eve, flaunting her irresponsibility and her seductive wiles! You dare to welcome into the bosom of your God-fearing family a child who can bring you nothing but shame and confusion. And, last but not least, you dare to welcome him who met with the Black Man in the forest and signed with his own blood the infamous book held out to him by Satan himself, from whence he derives his impunity to travel the Pagan paths, but which should bar him for ever more from crossing the threshold of any pious home . . .'

'Art thou speaking of me, Pastor?' old Shapleigh interrupted, raising his nose from his bowl.

'Yes, you, you fool!' the pastor thundered. 'You who without care for your soul have dared to dabble in magic to satisfy your shameful curiosity.

'I, whom the Lord has granted the spiritual insight that can read deep into the secret of men's consciences, it is not difficult for me to see that diabolical spark glistening in your eyes . . .'

'And I, Pastor, I read in the bloodshot eye – and although the blood is not infernal it is nonetheless thick and a danger to thy health, I can read that one day thou willst find thyself struck down by some violent outburst of temper if thou takest not care . . .'

And the old 'medicine-man' stood up and walked over to the

outraged minister with a knowing expression on his face, forcing the man to bend forward so that he could examine the whites of his eyes.

'I would not urge thee to be bled,' he said. 'There would be no end to the task. But I have in my bag a few herbs that I sought out thanks to my shameful curiosity, which, if thou followest my treatment, will enable thee to rave and rant as often as thou feelest the need without risk to thy health.

'Get thee to bed, Pastor. I will attend thee, and in order to keep the demons away I will burn some coriander and fennel seeds.'

That was the end of the pastor's outbursts for that particular evening.

CHAPTER FOURTEEN

THE ROUGH-HEWN beams smelt of honey, and a few bunches of dried flowers had been hung up in the nooks and corners between them.

Angélique wakened for the first time that night. The shriek of a nightjar filled the star-spangled darkness. Its two note cry incessantly repeated was like the creaking of a spinning wheel, now close, now dying away. She got up and, leaning her two hands on the edge of the window, peered out into the forest. She knew that the people of New England have said that the cry of the nightjar, with its two monotonous notes, says: 'Weep! Weep! poor William!' ever since an early settler called William discovered the massacre of his wife and children. He had thought he heard the nightjar's cry during the previous night, but it had been Indians hiding in the undergrowth signalling to one another as they closed in on the white man's cabin.

Then suddenly the cry ceased; a shadow crossed the night sky – two wide pointed wings, a long, rounded tail, a soft, silent flight broken by sudden darts this way and that and a glimpse of a single, luminous red eye. The nightjar was on the hunt.

A multitude of crickets, grasshoppers and frogs filled the night with their noisy chirping and croaking, while from the forest came the scent of wild animals, the fragrance of wild strawberries and thyme, the stale smell of cow-byre and mud.

Angélique got back into the tall oak bed. Its twirly-whirly

bedposts supported a frilled canopy but the chintz curtains remained undrawn on this hot June night.

The linen sheets, woven by Sarah Williams with her own hands, had the same fresh smell of flowers as the room.

A wooden trestle bed had been pulled out from under the big bed and a mattress laid on it. Rose-Ann was sleeping in it for this last night.

Angélique fell asleep again almost immediately.

When she opened her eyes again, the sky was greyish-green above the dark, harmonious line of elms on the hillside, and the song of the hermit-thrush, sweet and solemn, had replaced the plaintive cry of the nightjar. The smell of garden flowers and lilac bushes against the shingle-board walls was driving out the emanations of the night and the forest.

Marrows and pumpkins, growing in the grass at the foot of the houses in the shelter of their own coiling leaves, shone as if painted in the heavy morning dew.

The smell of lilac in the gardens had a wonderful freshness in the dew-drenched air.

Once again Angélique rested her elbows on the edge of the little window. One by one the quaint shapes of the wooden houses began to emerge from the morning mists, their hipped roofs showing their broken and irregular surfaces, and an occasional angle sloping almost down to the ground. With their gable ends, their overhanging upper storeys, their huge, solid brick chimneys rising straight up through the centre of the roof ridge, they were very like miniature Elizabethan manor houses. Most of them had been built in white pine which took on a silvery glow in the growing light.

Some of the barns were built of rough-hewn logs, thatched with straw, but the general effect of the village was one of prosperity and neatness.

Candles began to glow behind the little diamond-shaped leaded panes of the unshuttered windows. The whole impression was one of cosy comfort born of care and attention lavished on the details of life, and of the value placed on time, which must never be wasted. Life in these isolated valley communities seemed to be made up of these minute but essential details. Colourful gardens must be planted, less for the delight of the eye and the heart than because they must be stocked with a wealth of medicinal, edible and aromatic plants.

Angélique, surprised and captivated by it all, found herself wondering what kind of people these Englishmen were, who had grown accustomed to count on none but themselves, whose first thought on waking was of prayer. How different they were from the people she was accustomed to live with. Driven to the shores of America by their passionate and unshakeable resolve to pray after their own fashion, and by the necessity of finding a piece of land where they could do so, they had brought with them a God in their own image who forbade playgoing, music, cards and scarlet dresses, in fact anything that was not Work or Worship.

The integrity of productive work well done was the fountainhead of their exaltation and pleasure in life. Their sense of perfection was their joy and the tranquility of their home life was their substitute for sensuality.

But their theology, having eliminated the saints and the angels, left them with nothing but demons, which they saw on every hand. They knew the full hierarchied order of them from the little genii with pointed nails that pierced their sacks of grain, right up to the dread principalities and powers of darkness with their cabalistic names.

And yet the beauty of the land to which the Lord had led them pleaded on the side of the angels.

Torn thus between gentleness and violence, between the lilac and the thorn, between ambition and renunciation, they felt justified only to live with a constant preoccupation about their last end.

Even so their minds did not dwell sufficiently on that fact, or such at least was the view of the Reverend Patridge, urged by him with much vehemence in his sermon on every Sunday.

As she leaned out of her window, Angélique was surprised to see the day bleak with no accompanying sign of activity in the village. No one left his house, apart from a few women going to fetch water from the river, which they did in a leisurely manner.

It was in fact Sunday. Sunday! For the Catholics too, as she was reminded by the snivelling of Adhemar beneath her window.

'Today is the Feast of Saint Anthony of Padua, Madame.'

'May he help you to find your head again and the courage you have lost!' Angélique replied, referring to the fact that Saint Anthony is reputed to help people find lost items of property.

But Adhemar did not think this funny.

'It's an important feast day in Canada, Madame. And here I am, instead of taking part in a fine procession in a good, holy French town, here I am, at the back of beyond, surrounded by the very heretics who crucified Our Lord. I shall be punished, for sure! Something is going to happen, I feel it . . .'

'Hold your peace,' whispered Angélique, 'and put away your rosary beads. The Protestants don't like such things.'

But Adhemar went on clutching convulsively at his rosary, muttering prayers begging for the protection of Our Lady and the Saints, and followed everywhere he went by a throng of little Puritans, never breathing a word, their shoes shining even brighter today, wide-eyed beneath their round hats or black bonnets.

The fact that it was Sunday, which was something the French had stupidly not foreseen, quite upset their plans to depart.

Everything came to a halt. It was out of the question to busy oneself for a journey – the whole village would have been scandalized.

Old Shapleigh, as he strode through the village with his pack and his blunderbuss on his shoulder, accompanied by his Indian and evidently heading for the forest, was followed by scowls and black looks, murmurs and even some threatening gestures. But he showed not the slightest concern, and went off sniggering and sardonic as always. Angélique envied him his independence of mind.

The old man had inspired her with the same admiration she had once felt for the remarkable Savary. His concern had been *science* and he had long since set at nought the prejudices of his coreligionists that in any way interfered with the pursuit of his dominating interest. When, as he walked through the forest, he began to dance about waving his pale, tapering fingers, it was because he had noticed some flowers and buds among the leaves, which he was pointing out to himself, naming them with their Latin names and noting the place where they grew.

Had not Angélique behaved just like this when she went looking for simples in the woods around Wapassou?

Old Shapleigh and she had recognized in each other a kindred spirit, and she was sad to see him set off and vanish with his Indian into the shady ravine that led to the Androscoggin river.

A bell began to ring on the hillside, and the faithful set off in the direction of the meeting house, a fortified building that stood above the village among the elms. The meeting house served not only as their church, but as the centre of their civic affairs as well.

Built of planks, it was indistinguishable from the other houses except for a small pointed belfry and the fact that it was square in shape. It served also as a fortress and, in the event of an Indian raid, the villagers could shelter there; two culverins were housed in the upper storey and their black muzzles, visible through the loopholes, framed the bell tower, a symbol of peace and prayer.

Here, after the manner of the New England Fathers, the people of Brunswick-Falls came to hold their assemblies, praise the Lord, read the Bible, attend to the business of the colony, admonish and be admonished, condemn their neighbour and be condemned, God having his part to play in all these tasks.

Angélique felt some hesitation in following this austere company, for a remnant of her former Catholic education made her feel a certain embarrassment at the idea of entering a heretic church. It was a mortal sin, an incalculable danger to the soul of the faithful. A reflex with its roots in her impressionable childhood years.

'Shall I put on my dress?' little Rose-Ann asked.

As she walked up towards the church with the child, Angélique could see that the inhabitants of Brunswick-Falls seemed to have relaxed their strict rules about clothes in honour of the Lord.

Even if there were no other red dresses like the one she had made for Rose-Ann, there were pink, white, and blue ones to be seen among the little girls. There were lace bonnets, satin ribbons, broad-brimmed hats with tall black coifs, adorned with silver buckles or feathers, which the women wore over their bonnets with their narrow, embroidered turned-back edges. Lace bonnets were an English fashion, but a very becoming and practical one, and Angélique herself often wore one on her wanderings in America.

There was a quiet elegance about them in harmony with the discreet pale wooden houses, surrounded with lilac bushes, and the softness of the flax-blue sky.

It was a lovely Sunday in Newehewanik – the land of the spring.

As Angélique passed, the villages smiled kindly at her and nodded their heads, and seeing her making towards the church, they followed close behind, pleased that she was to be their guest that morning.

Cantor joined his mother.

'I feel that we must not refer to our departure, it would not be fitting,' Angélique told him. 'But your father's ship is waiting for us at the mouth of the Kennebec, this evening, or tomorrow at the latest . . .

'I think we could take our leave after the service. Today the animals have remained in the fields with a single shepherd to look after them. The calves were allowed to suckle from their mothers, so as to make it unnecessary to do any milking. It's a day of rest for everyone. But I saw Maupertuis a little while ago, leading our horses down to the river. He said he was going to let them graze there while he and his son kept an eye on them, and that he would bring them back towards noon. Then we can set off, even though it will mean camping in the forest tonight.'

On arriving at the open square before the meeting house they found a platform with a kind of wooden stand on it pierced by three holes, the middle one bigger than the other two. That was the hole for the head, Cantor explained, whereas the other two merely held a man's wrists. This was the famous pillory in which miscreants were held on public view. The barbarous contraption had a notice board beside it on which were written the name of the occupant and the reason for his punishment.

The penal equipment of the little Puritan colony consisted of this pillory and a whipping-post.

Fortunately, this morning the pillory was empty, although the Reverend Patridge intimated in his sermon that in all probability it would shortly be occupied.

Seated among the faithful, who remained motionless as wax figures, Angélique learned that the fashionable costumes that she had noticed that morning were not the result of any lawful desire to honour the Lord's Day, but rather of a kind of madness which seemed suddenly to have assailed the minister's unruly flock. Some brainstorm from abroad ... One had not to look far to see from whence it came since it originated in a semi-oriental religion whose corruption down the centuries had only narrowly failed – under the crook of leaders vowed to the service of the devil – had only just failed to draw the entire human race to its doom. There followed a catalogue of historical figures in which the Popes Clement and Alexander rubbed shoulders with Astaroth, Asmodeus and Belial. Angélique understood enough English to make out that the ranting pastor was referring to the present Pope as anti-Christ in one breath and Beelzebub in the next, and thought he was laying it on rather thick.

It all reminded her of her youth, and the squabbles she and the other children used to have with the Huguenot peasant boys, and of the heretic farms in Poitou, which were pointed out with reprobation, their people living apart from the Catholic communities, with their solitary tombs beside a cypress tree.

Thomas Patridge reminded them that the attributes of graciousness were fleeting.

He thundered against hair worn too long, either by the men or the women. Too much brushing, immodest curls. These things were damnable, idolatrous.

'Berthos! Berthos!' he shouted.

One wondered which demon he was invoking now, but it was only the sexton he was calling to order, instructing him to go and wake up some impudent man who had fallen asleep in spite of the shouting.

Berthos, a gnome with a pudding-basin haircut, sprang up and made for the sleeper with his long switch that sported a doe's foot and a feather, and hit him violently on the head with it. The feather fulfilled the same purpose with the ladies, but somewhat more delicately, for this he would twiddle beneath their noses if an overlengthy sermon made them feel drowsy.

'Miserable sinners! Miserable sinners!' the minister went on in his lugubrious tones, 'You remind me in your obliviousness of the men of Laish who, according to the Bible, took no thought for their safety and their defence while their enemies the children of Dan were whetting their knives and preparing to slay them. But they went on laughing, and dancing, thinking that they had no enemies in all the world, for they refused to see what was going on, and took no precautions against it.'

'I'm sorry, but I protest,' old Benjamin Williams interrupted, sitting bolt upright, 'pray do not suggest that I have no care for my people's safety! I have just sent a message to the Massachusetts Government to ask their Honours to be good enough to send us eight or ten strong, watchful men to protect us during the harvest period . . .'

'It is too late!' bellowed the minister, furious at this interruption. 'When the soul is not sanctified, all man's precautions are set at nought. Amen, amen I say unto you: by harvest time you will be no more. Even by the morrow, perhaps, yea even before the night, how many of you may not already be dead! The Indians are all about us in the forest, ready to attack! I can see them. I can hear them sharpening up their scalping knives, yes, I can see scarlet blood glistening on their hands, your blood . . . and yours,' he shouted, suddenly pointing towards some of the congregation, who grew pale. By now everyone was terror-stricken.

Next to Angélique sat a frail little old lady, called Elizabeth

Pidgeon, whose job it was to instruct the girls of the village; she was shaking with fear from head to toe.

'For scarlet is not the colour of joy,' Thomas Patridge declaimed in a lugubrious voice, staring hard at Angélique, 'It is the colour of calamity and you have brought it among us, senseless people that you are! Soon you will hear the voice of the Almighty ring out from the heavens above saying: "Thou has preferred the pleasures of this world to the joys of looking on My face. Wherefore get thee gone, get thee forever out of my sight!" And you will plunge down into the darkness of Hell, there to dwell forever in the bottomless, black abyss, forever ... forever, and ever and ever!'

Everyone was shuddering. They came out hesitantly on to the sun-drenched square, pursued by the echo of that implacable, sepulchral voice.

'For ever! ... For ever, and ever, and ever!'

CHAPTER FIFTEEN

'WE'LL NEVER hear the end of that red dress,' Angélique grumbled.

The serenity of the Sunday meal accompanied by readings from the Bible could not entirely dispel the uncomfortable feeling left by the pastor's sermon. After lunch Angélique spent some time in the kitchen garden, examining the various herbs and crushing sprigs between her fingers to identify them by their smell. The sultry air was full of the busy hum of bees. She suddenly felt an intense desire to see Joffrey again. The world seemed empty and his presence in her in this English village struck her as odd, intolerable, like wondering in a dream what one is doing in a certain place and realizing that something strange is going on, something inexplicable.

'Whatever is Maupertuis thinking of?' she called across to Cantor. 'Just look! the sun is going down, and still he has not come back from the forest with the horses!'

'I'll go and see,' Cantor shouted back, and immediately set off at a brisk walk towards the opposite end of the village.

She watched him make his way towards the trees that formed a green screen all round the village. She was about to call him back, to shout: 'No, Cantor, don't go! Cantor, my son, don't go into the forest.' But he had already vanished round a bend in the path which led to the sheepfold and the farthest house in the village before the forest. So she went back into Benjamin's house, climbed the stairs, closed her leather bag in haste, picked up her pistols, threw her cloak over her shoulders, put on her hat, and went down again. Some of the serving maids were sitting beside the windows, doing nothing, dreaming or praying. Not wishing to disturb their meditation, she passed them by and went on out into the grassy village street, with little Rose-Ann running behind her in her red dress.

'Oh, don't go away, dear lady,' the child murmured in her clumsy French as she caught up with Angélique.

'My darling, I *must* leave now,' Angélique replied without slowing her step. 'I am very late already. I do not know how you spend your Sunday here, but I should already have reached the coast where there is a ship waiting for me. It is so late already that we shall not get there before dawn . . .'

With touching affection and solicitude, the little English girl tried to take her bag from her and carry it, and together they climbed the hill and followed the bend in the path before coming in sight of the last houses in the village, the smallest and poorest, built of logs and roofed with grasses and bark, then, in the distance the last house of all, the big sheep farm. Before reaching it they still had to pass a barn in which maize was stored, where the Frenchmen had spent the night and where Adhemar must now have sought refuge to sleep off his fears. Then there was the cottage of the school teacher, Miss Pidgeon, surrounded by a tangle of flowers, and standing alone at some distance from the solid sheepfold with its gable end and its wind-vane – a handsome building set in the midst of well-fenced pasture lands. Beyond came the ravine up from which they had climbed the previous night, with a few ploughed fields running down the slope, then the domain of trees, rushing waters and steep rock faces – the forest.

In Miss Pidgeon's garden, suddenly appeared the stately figure of Mrs Williams in the midst of the hollyhocks, from which her nimble fingers were busy plucking the spent flowers. She beckoned imperiously to Angélique, who put down her bag and walked towards the old lady to bid her goodbye.

'Just look at these hollyhocks,' said Mrs Williams. 'Do they have to suffer just because it's the Lord's day? I have been taken to task once again by our pastor, but I silenced him. We have had our fill for today . . .'

She pointed her index finger, which was covered with a leather glove, towards the little house behind her.

'He's in there now, haranguing Elizabeth about her latter end, the poor creature!'

And her nimble hands resumed their task, while her sharp eyes beneath their heavy eyelids darted a quick glance at Angélique, and the corners of her severe lips lifted in the ghost of a smile.

'Perhaps they will put me in the pillory,' she said. 'And they will write on the board, "For excessive fondness for holly-hocks"!'

Angélique looked at her, a little taken aback, with a trace of a smile on her lips too. Ever since the previous day, when she had first found herself face to face with this forbidding old lady, the latter had seemed to take a certain pleasure in suddenly reveal-ing certain unexpected sides of her character. Angélique no longer knew what to make of her, and now wondered whether Mrs Williams was making fun of her, joking, trying to provoke her, or whether she, Angélique, had failed to understand the English words. The idea crossed her mind that the worthy Puritan lady might conceivably have a slight partiality to some strong liquor, gin perhaps or rum, which might at times put her in a facetious mood, but she quickly dismissed this thought as incon-gruous, monstrous. No, it was something else, a kind of tipsiness it well might be, but unconscious, stemming from some very pure source.

Then, standing in front of this stately woman, who stood solid and severe like a rock, a good head taller than herself, yet who would suddenly burst forth into lighthearted independence, Angélique felt the same sense of unreality that she had experi-enced earlier on, a feeling of doubt as to whether she was really there, a sensation that everything about her was fluid, and that earth was slipping from under her feet. A feeling that she was about to wake up but could not . . .

But it was nothing. Nature stood still, heavy with the scent of flowers and the hum of bees.

Sarah Williams came out from among the hollyhocks, let-ting her fingers glide lovingly across their stems, with their tight clumps of green, pink and pure white.

'Now they are happy,' she murmured.

She pushed open the gate and advanced towards Angélique, removing her glove as she did so and placing it in a large pocket hanging from her belt that contained several small gardening tools. As she did so her eyes never left the face of the stranger who the day before had brought her back her little grand-daughter.

'Did you ever meet King Louis XIV in France?' she asked. 'Did you ever speak to him? Yes, I feel sure you did. You still have the glow of the Sun. Ah! you Frenchwomen, how graceful you are! Walk a bit, will you,' she asked with a gesture to in-dicate Angélique should move away from her, 'walk over there for me ...'

The strange smile at the corners of her mouth grew more marked, as if some inner gaiety were about to burst forth.

'I too am becoming very much of a child. I love things that are bright, graceful and fresh ...'

Angélique walked a few steps as the old woman had asked her, then turned round. Her expression was quizzical but yet, although she was quite unaware of the fact, had something childlike about it. Old Sarah Williams fascinated her. Standing there in the middle of the path – the single path that did duty as footpath, street and road, leading right through the village from the forest to the meeting house up on the hill – in the shade of the great elms, the greenish tint from whose leaves made her waxen cheeks look even more sallow than usual, the tall English-woman with one hand on her hip held herself so erect, her neck was so long and elegant above her little starched ruff, that any queen might have envied her her bearing. Her slender waist, drawn in by tight stays, merged below into fuller curves emphasized by a farthingale, a king of padded roll of black velvet worn like a belt around the hips. Such had been the fashion at the beginning of the century, and Angélique had seen her mother and her aunts dressed in this way. But her black mantle, gath-ered up over a dark purple underskirt, was worn shorter than in those days, and, as she held it in a little against her waist with one hand, Mrs Williams showed no concern at revealing that she wore riding boots, likewise black but daintily made, which must have been much more comfortable for moving about the wet fields and paths.

'How beautiful she must have been,' thought Angélique. Per-haps she would be like her one day ... She could see herself wearing boots like those, and striding briskly over her domain. People would stand slightly in awe of her, and she would be full of self confidence, free, her heart bursting with joy at the mere sight of a meadow full of flowers or a small child taking its first steps. She would in all probability be less stiff, less severe. But was Mrs Williams really so severe? ... She was coming towards her now, and her face with its heavy, somewhat drooping but harmonious lines, was lit up by the emerald glow from the undergrowth and bore an expression of unforgettable contentment. She stopped beside Angélique, and her expression suddenly changed.

'Can you not smell the smell of red men?' she asked puckering her dark brows and resuming her haughty, forbidding expression once more.

There was horror and repulsion in her voice.

'Can you not smell it?'

'No, truly, I can't,' Angélique replied.

But she shuddered in spite of herself. And yet it seemed to her that she had never known the air so full of perfume as on this hillside where the fragrance of honeysuckle and creeper mingled with garden smells dominated by the scent of lilac and honey.

'I smell that smell often, too often,' said Sarah Williams, shaking her head as if in self reproach. 'I can always smell it, it pervades my whole life. It haunts me. And yet it is a long time since Benjamin and I have had to use our gun to defend our home against those red serpents.'

'When I was a child ... and later again when we lived in that cabin near Wells ...'

She broke off, with a shake of her head, unwilling to dwell on memories of fear and fighting, all so similar.

'There, there was the sea ... As a last resort you could escape that way. But here, there is no sea ...'

They walked on a few steps more.

'Is it not beautiful here?' she inquired, her voice losing its sense of urgency.

Little Rose-Ann was kneeling in the grass picking coral-shaded columbines.

'Newehewanik,' the old woman murmured.

'Land of Spring,' said Angélique.

'You know that, do you?' the Englishwoman asked, glancing swiftly at Angélique.

Once again her intensely black eyes beneath their veined lids stared fixedly at Angélique the stranger, the Frenchwoman, as if trying to read in her, to guess at some answer, some explanation.

'So you love America, do you?' she said. 'And yet you are so young ...'

'I am not as young as all that,' Angélique protested. 'My elder son is seventeen and . . .'

Old Sarah interrupted her with a burst of laughter, the first time Angélique had seen her laugh, a thin, spontaneous laugh, almost like a little girl, that showed her long, slightly horsy but perfect, healthy teeth.

'Oh yes, you are young,' she repeated. 'You have not lived, my dear!'

'Oh no?'

Angélique was almost angry. It was true that Mrs Williams must have been some twenty-five years older than Angélique, and thus entitled to show a certain condescension, but Angélique considered that her own life had been neither so short nor so lacking in interest that she could be said to have seen nothing of it . . .

'Your life is just beginning!' Mrs Williams affirmed in a voice that brooked no reply. 'It has only just started!'

'Really?'

'How charming you sound when you say that? Ah, you Frenchwomen, how lucky you are! You are like a flame beginning to sparkle and grow, full of self confidence, in a dark world that holds no terrors for you! Only now are you beginning to live; can you not feel it? When one is a very young woman, one has to bear the burden of building one's life, of proving oneself.

A crushing burden! And one is all alone . . . Once one ceases to be a child, is there anyone more solitary than a young woman? . . . But when you reach forty or fifty, then you can begin to live! One has done with proving oneself; that is all over. One becomes as free as a child again, one finds oneself . . . I think I never was so happy as the day when I realized that my youth had gone, had gone at last,' she sighed. 'Suddenly my soul grew light, my heart warmer and more responsive, and my eyes were opened on the world. God himself seemed to have grown friendly. I was still alone, but I had grown used to that. I bought two of the prettiest lace coifs I could find from a pedlar who came to the village, and neither the wrath of the pastor nor Ben's reproof have managed to prevent me from wearing them ever since.'

She laughed again, a mischievous laugh, and touched Angélique's cheek as she would have that of a child. Angélique had forgotten that she must be off! The sun seemed to be standing still in the sky, lying like a huge full-blown flower, still bright

86

yellow, on a bed of tiny, white, downy clouds just above the horizon.

She was listening to Mrs Williams, who took her by the arm as they walked slowly together towards the village. Most of the houses were still half hidden by the turn in the path and the slope of the ground, by a crystalline mist which seemed to be rising from them, fed by the stream that ran along below the houses.

'You love this land, don't you, Madame?' Mrs Williams went on. 'That is a sign of breeding. It is so beautiful. I have not got to know it as much as I would have liked, but you, you will get to know it better than I. When I was young, I hated the wretched, dangerous life we led on these shores. I wanted to go to London, about which we were told by sailors and our elders. I left there when I was six, and I still remember its jostling spires, and its narrow lanes crowded with creaking coaches. As a girl I used to dream of escaping, of going back to the old world, and the fear of damnation was the only thing that stopped me doing so. No,' she said as if replying to some remark Angélique had made, 'no, I was not pretty in my youth. I am beautiful *now*, because I have reached my fulfilment. But when I was young I was too thin, too tall, dull, pale, really unattractive. I have always been grateful to Ben for agreeing to marry me in exchange for a plot of ground and a fishing sloop he wanted from my father. The value of his own lands with their little creek became enhanced because they were next to ours. It was a wonderful opportunity for him. He was bound to marry me, and he didn't hesitate.'

She winked an eye at Angélique.

'And he never regretted it either, as far as I know.'

She laughed softly.

'But in those days I would not even have brought a glimmer to the eyes of the pirates who used to come ashore near by to trade the rum and cloth they had plundered in the Caribbean for some of our fresh food. They were gentlemen of fortune, often Frenchmen. I can still see their tanned buccaneer's faces, and their clothes that looked so outlandish next to our dark dresses with their white collars. They would never have dreamed of harming us for we were as poor as Job. They were delighted to encounter white men along this wild stretch of coastland, and to eat the fruit and vegetables we grew. There they were, a godless and lawless lot, and we with our exaggerated piety, and yet there was kinship between us, we were all marooned on the edge of the earth.

'Now there are far too many people along the coast and far too many ships of ill repute in the bay. So we chose to get away, to live in the frontier lands . . .

'I surprise you, my child, with these tales, these admissions . . . but you must remember your God is less terrifying than ours. When we grow old, either we become mad, or spiteful, or we become witches, or else we just do as we please. Then everything grows calm, and nothing really matters any more!'

She shook her coif once more in a gesture of defiance, then of approbation and serenity.

Yesterday evening she had been so stiff, so implacably distant, and yet today she had shown such delicacy, almost humility!

Once again it crossed Angélique's mind that the worthy Puritan lady might have some hidden weakness for an equally well hidden flask of plum-brandy or gin; but she immediately dismissed this doubt, for her heart was moved by the sudden confidences the old lady had made as if in a dream.

She was later to relive this touching scene and understand its significance . . .

Fate pausing in its inexorable march, but its course already set, was prompting a woman who was approaching her final hour to spontaneous, almost thoughtless gestures – stirrings, one might say, of the soul, the expression of an ardent heart, a heart that had ever been warm and loving beneath the rigid exterior imposed by her uncompromising religious beliefs.

Old Sarah turned towards Angélique and, taking her face between her two long, white hands, she lifted it towards her, looking down at it with motherly intensity.

'May this land of America shower blessings upon you, my dear child,' she said softly and with great solemnity, 'and I beg you . . . I beg you, save it from destruction!' Her hands slipped away and she examined them as if she herself had been quite overcome by her own gesture and words.

She stiffened, and her face grew as cold as marble once more while her piercing black eyes fixed themselves on the vast expanse of sky that lay like a huge inverted shell over the valley.

'What is happening?' she murmured. She stopped to listen, then set off once more. They walked several paces in silence, then Mrs Williams halted again, and suddenly grasped Angélique's wrists so hard that she made her jump.

'Listen!' said the Englishwoman, her voice sounded quite different: clear, precise, and icy cold.

Then they heard a confused, distant sound coming to them through the evening air.

An unidentifiable, inarticulate sound like the roaring of the sea, or of the wind, above which rang out a distant, feeble, high pitched shriek:

'Abenakis! Abenakis!'

Hastily, Sarah Williams drew Angélique away towards the bend in the road that hid the rest of the village from their sight. It looked calm, deserted and asleep.

But the roaring sound was growing louder, thousands of hooting voices above which could still be heard the desperate cry of a handful of villagers who had begun to run like terror-stricken rats between the houses.

'The Abenakis! The Abenakis!'

Angélique looked back towards the fields, and a terrifying spectacle met her eyes. It was what she had feared, what she had sensed, what she had been unwilling to believe! An army of half-naked Indians, brandishing tomahawks and cutlasses, was pouring out of the forest; like so many ants driven from their nest, in a matter of a few seconds the Indians had completely covered the fields in the valley, and were spreading out in a dark, moving tide, a thick, red flood, a tidal wave that broke across the countryside, with its death cry going before it:

'You-ou-ou-ou! You-ou-ou-ou!'

The tide of Indians reached the stream, swept over it, reached the near side, began to climb up the hill and came to the first of the houses.

A woman in a blue dress ran up the slope towards them, staggering as if drunk, her mouth a black hole in her blanched face as she shouted at them.

'The Abenakis!'

An unseen something struck her between the shoulders; she gave a kind of hiccup and fell face down on the ground.

'Benjamin!' Sarah Williams cried. 'Benjamin! He is all alone up there in the house.'

'Stop!'

Angélique tried to hold the woman back but she broke away and ran straight ahead towards the house, fearing her aged husband might be taken by surprise, as he dozed over his Bible.

Sarah had got only a hundred yards when Angélique saw an Indian leap from the undergrowth, catch up with her in a few lithe strides, and strike the old woman down with a single blow from his tomahawk. Then, bending over her, he seized her coif and her hair and, with a flick of his wrist, scalped her. Angélique shuddered as she turned to make her escape.

'Run!' she shouted to Rose-Ann pointing towards the sheepfold: 'Over there near the forest, run quick!'

She herself ran as fast as her legs would carry her. As she reached Miss Pidgeon's garden, she stopped to pick up the bag she had left there, flung open the gate and dashed into the house where the Reverend Patridge and the old maid were still deep in their discussion on the last end of man.

'The savages! ... They are coming! ...'

She was so breathless, she could no longer find the right English words, and tried in vain to explain.

'The savages!' she repeated in French. 'The Abenakis ... they are coming ... take refuge in the sheep farm ...'

It had already occurred to her that this solid looking farm, apparently fortified, could well sustain a siege and make feasible some kind of defence.

In a crisis, spontaneity as well as experience and habit count. Angélique saw the corpulent Thomas Patridge leap to his feet, pick up little Miss Pidgeon in his arms like a doll, bound across the garden and race without further ado towards the suggested place of shelter.

Angélique was about to follow them, but changed her mind and, hiding behind the house door, she loaded her two pistols, kept one of them in her hand, then went outside again.

Fortunately this particular part of the village was still deserted. The woman who had fallen at the bend of the road after climbing the hill still lay motionless, with an arrow between her shoulder blades.

This area, hidden from the other houses by the slope and the bend in the road, had not yet claimed the attention of the Indians, apart from the one who had scalped Mistress Williams and who had then gone off in another direction.

The noise coming from the other parts was deafening and horrible, but here all was still silent, a kind of agonized, febrile waiting. Even the birds were silent.

Still running, Angélique managed to reach the barn where the maize was stored.

There was Adhemar asleep!

'Get up! The Indians are here! Run! Run to the sheep farm! Take your musket with you!'

As he fled in terror, she seized Maupertuis's guns and powder horns which were hanging from a hook.

She was trying feverishly to load the gun, scraping her fingers as she did so, when something suddenly came tumbling down behind her and she saw an Abenaki Indian, who had entered the barn by the roof and was now slithering down a huge pile of maize. She swung round, still clutching the musket by the barrel, and struck the redskin across the temple with the butt. He fell to the ground and she made her escape.

The shady path was still deserted as she began to run down it. Then she heard someone running behind her, and, glancing over her shoulder, saw that it was an Indian – whether it was the one she had stunned or another, she knew not – who was gaining on her fast and holding his hatchet erect.

His feet made almost no sound on the grass, and Angélique could not stop to take aim. Her only hope of escape was to run as fast as she could and she felt as if her feet were no longer touching the ground.

At last she reached the courtyard of the sheep farm and leapt behind a farm wagon. The Indian's hatchet rang against the wood and the sharp metal wedge buried itself in the wagon. Doing her utmost to control her breathing, Angélique took aim and fired at the redskin at point-blank range. He fell across the gateway, his two hands clutching his powder-blackened breast.

A few strides more and she had reached the threshold of the house where the door was opened to her even before she had time to knock. They closed it again immediately and barred it with two solid oak battens.

CHAPTER SIXTEEN

IN ADDITION to the parson and Miss Pidgeon, the French soldier Adhemar and little Rose-Ann, the other occupants of the farmhouse were Samuel Corwin, the owner, and his household – his wife and three children, two young hands employed by him and a servant girl – old Jos Carter, a neighbour, and a couple by the name of Stoughton together with their baby, who had also been visiting the Corwins at the time of the attack.

There was no weeping or wailing; American farmers had perforce become inured to battle and bloodshed. The womenfolk were already busy swabbing out the barrels of the guns taken down from over the hearth.

Samuel Corwin had positioned his gun in one of the many loopholes with which the house was provided, as was usual in New England houses, especially those built in the early days. Through another hole, the occupants were keeping watch on what was going on outside, and they had seen the Countess of Peyrac strike down the Indian pursuing her.

They threw her a swift, grim glance as she came in: she had brought more guns, she was like the others, efficient and diligent. The minister had thrown his frock-coat over a bench and stood in his shirt sleeves preparing powder charges, his lips drawn back over his strong, prominent teeth. He was waiting for a gun to be made available to him, so Angélique handed him Maupertuis's musket and herself took Adhemar's, as he was trembling like a leaf.

One of the children began to cry and someone spoke softly to it to silence it.

In the vicinity of the house all was quiet. All that could be heard was a distant roaring noise like the sound of the sea, which from time to time rose to a crescendo as the massacre proceeded.

Then there came a series of dull booms, and Angélique remembered the small cannons in the fortified church. One could only hope that some of the villagers had managed to take refuge within its walls.

'The Lord will protect His own,' the pastor muttered, 'for they are even as His army.'

At once someone gesticulated furiously to him to keep quiet.

A small band of Indians were running along the path, torch in hand. They seemed to have come from the direction of the ravine and did not stop.

A child began to cry again, whereon Angélique suddenly had an idea: she went over to one of the huge empty cauldrons used for cheese making, and suggested to Rose-Ann and three of the smallest children that they might like to hide inside it. It would be like being in a nest, she said, and they must not move.

She half closed the lid. In their hiding place the children would be less liable to panic and run less risk of being knocked over by the combatants.

Then she returned to her observation post.

There were some redskins standing by the fence; they had noticed the body of one of their fellows sprawled across the path.

There were four of them talking and glancing towards the house. In the red glow of the sunset, their faces, daubed with war paint, were a terrifying sight, and Angélique, crowded into this confined space with the white men, all of whose lives were at peril, felt the dread of the redskins growing upon her, and her flesh began to creep.

The Indians pushed open the gate and advanced across the yard, crouching slightly like wild animals, full of mystery and terror.

'Fire!' ordered Corwin quietly.

A volley of shots rang out, and when the smoke had dispersed they saw three of the Abenakis writhing in their death throes on the ground, while the fourth was making good his escape.

Then there came a general onslaught, savages coming up from out of the ravine behind the house in a great tide that soon seemed to rise around them on all sides. The brown bodies grew more and more numerous, and their whoops mingled with the detonations of the guns.

The besieged party went on firing automatically, handing the discharged guns back to the women and catching up a loaded weapon, while brushes were drawn quickly through the burning hot barrels, and feverish hands tipped up the powder flasks, snapped the flintlocks into position to the accompaniment of sharp clicks that punctuated the thunder of the gunfire, and the howling and shrieking outside. Smoke stung their parched throats, and the sweat running down their faces had a bitter taste at the corners of their open lips through which their breath came in hoarse gasps.

Angélique dropped her musket. No more ammunition! She picked up her pistols, loaded them, filled her pockets with small-calibre bullets, stuffed as many as she could into her mouth to have them as handy as possible, then tied her powder horn and box of Turkish primer to her belt so as not to waste a single movement with them either.

There was a rending sound in the roof and an Indian slithered to the floor at the far end of the room, landing beside Pastor Patridge, who struck him down with his gun butt. But a second redskin was hard on the heels of the first and brought down his tomahawk on the Reverend Thomas's far from fragile skull. His knees gave beneath him and the redskin, seizing him by the hair, had just begun to run his knife across his forehead in a broad incision when he received the charge of Angélique's pistol full in the chest.

As the Indians continued to pour in through the roof, the English backed away towards the great chimney breast, where Angélique tipped the heavy wooden table on its side and pushed it across one corner of the room so as to constitute a rampart, behind which they all took refuge. She was to ask herself later where she had found the strength to do it. The frenzy of battle lent her superhuman power, intensified by a literal fury at the thought that she had allowed herself to be trapped so stupidly in this village of foreign settlers, in which she might well lose her life.

From their point of refuge, the settlers continued to fire in two directions: towards the far end of the room where the attackers kept leaping in from the roof, and towards the door, which was beginning to give way beneath the blows of Indian hatchets.

It was sheer slaughter and thanks to this deadly crossfire the whites with desperation and firearms on their side almost won the day. But their ammunition was running out, and Corwin, struck just below the shoulder blade by a hatchet, collapsed with a cry.

With a snake-like wriggle, one of the Indians slithered between the wall and the side of the table and, seizing a woman by her skirt, pulled her towards him. She fought back like one possessed and dropped the powder horn she was holding.

Over the top of the table old Carter was stunning anyone who came within striking distance of his gun butt. But as he raised his arms to bring down the weapon yet again, the blade of a hunting knife was slid treacherously between his ribs. He staggered and doubled up, like a straw-filled puppet with dangling arms.

Then suddenly, like a circus acrobat performing a trick, someone at the back of the room leapt into the air, passed right over the heads of the rest, legs spread wide like a dancer, and landed among the Englishmen, behind them in fact, on the other side of the table.

It was the Sagamore Piksarett, chief of the Patsuiketts and the most renowned warrior of Acadia.

Angélique heard his mocking voice behind her, and a hand seized her violently by the nape of the neck.

'You are my prisoner,' said the Patsuikett in triumphal tones.

Angélique dropped her now useless pistols and seized him with both hands by his long tresses tied with fox feet.

Because she knew him, because his weasly face with its wicked eyes was familiar to her, she no longer felt any fear and even ceased to consider him and his horde of Indians as enemies. They were Abenakis, and she knew their tongue and was familiar with their strange, primitive thought processes. She turned her head sharply to one side and spat out the two bullets she still had in her mouth.

'Was it to capture me that you took this village?' she shouted at the Indian, still clinging to his hair. 'It was Black Robe that ordered you to, wasn't it?'

And her green eyes pierced him with such a devastating glance that he stood transfixed. It was not the first time that Sagamore Piksarett and the white woman from the Upper Kennebec had met.

She had been marked out as his enemy! But what woman had ever dared to grasp him thus by his ceremonial tresses and look him so boldly in the face while death hung over her head. Once she had stood between him and the Iroquois with the same look on her face. She knew no fear.

'You are my prisoner,' he repeated fiercely.

'I accept that I am your prisoner, but you shall not kill me nor hand me over to Black Robe, because I am a Frenchwoman, and because I gave you my cloak in which to wrap the bones of your ancestors.'*

All about them the shouting and the throes of battle continued and reached their paroxysm. The fighting was now hand to hand. But the end soon came, and the shouts of rage, horror and defiance gradually died down, giving place to a panting silence through which the groans of the wounded soon began to make themselves heard.

Carter had been scalped, but the other Europeans were alive, for the Abenakis were above all interested in the ransom they could secure by their capture. The Reverend Patridge, after struggling free from the mountain of bodies beneath which he had been buried, stood swaying on his feet between two braves, his face covered in blood.

An agonized cry rent the air: 'Help me, Madame, or I am a dead man!'

It was Adhemar, who had been pulled out from under some piece of furniture.

* See *The Countess Angélique.*

'Don't kill him!' cried Angélique. 'Can't you see that he's a French soldier?'

It was certainly not obvious.

Angélique was quite beside herself, obsessed with the idea that she must escape from this trap into which she had so foolishly blundered. The tragic absurdity of the situation made her extremely angry and heightened her defensive reflexes.

For the past few moments one single thought had come to dominate all others in her mind. *She knew these Indians.* And this was how she would escape the trap that had been set for her. They were wild beasts, but wild beasts could be tamed. In the desert of the Maghreb, Colin Paturel had talked to the lions and won them to his will ... She began to realize that Piksarett's war party were separate from the other Indians and had attacked from the opposite direction, and that the battle around the farm had no connexion with the rest of the fighting.

Piksarett hesitated. Some of the things Angélique had said puzzled him. 'I am a Frenchwoman!' He had been taught to fight the English. Moreover, he would never forget the magnificent cloak which she had given him for his ancestors.

'Have you been baptized?' he asked.

'Of course I have,' she cried in exasperation, crossing herself several times and calling on the Virgin Mary.

Through the shattered door Angélique thought she glimpsed the familiar figure of a Canadian trapper. She rushed forward, recognized him and called desperately to him.

'Monsieur de L'Aubignière!'

It was Three-Fingers from Trois Rivières. Hearing her shout, he turned and came back towards her. When it came to fighting, he scorned the white man's weapons. In his hands he held a polished wooden tomahawk and a small Indian hatchet whose razor-sharp blade was red with blood. His blue eyes shone in his powder-blackened, bloodstained face, and there was more blood on his deerskin clothing and on a row of scalps slung from his multicoloured belt.

How could she ever make contact with this man? How could she ever circumvent him? He was an incorruptible knight, a warrior of God, his mind possessed, like those of Maudreuil, de Loménie, and Arreboust, with his dream of vengeance, salvation and paradise ...

But he did recognize her.

'Madame de Peyrac!' he exclaimed. 'What are you doing

here among these damned heretics? Woe betide you!'

He entered the devastated house which the Abenakis, having gathered together their prisoners, were looting.

She seized him too by the collar of his jerkin.

'Black Robe,' she cried, 'I am sure I saw Black Robe across the prairie with his standard ... It was Father d'Orgeval who led you into battle, wasn't it? He knew he would find me in this village!'

She was stating facts rather than asking questions, and he stared dumbfounded at her, with open mouth.

He tried to find a reply, an excuse:

'You killed Pont-Briand,' he replied at last, 'and you and your husband are turning Acadia upside down with your alliances. We had to lay our hands on you ...'

So that was it.

Joffrey! Joffrey!

They were going to kidnap and carry off as a prisoner the wife of the formidable gentleman from Wapassou who had already made his mastery felt in the land of Acadia.

They would take her to Quebec, and put pressure on Joffrey through her. She would never see him again.

'Maupertuis?' she asked breathlessly.

'We have taken both him and his son and put them under arrest. They are both Canadians of New France, and on a day like this, they should be among their brothers.'

'Did they take part in the attack with you?'

'No. Their case will be tried in Quebec. They have served the enemies of New France ...'

How could she win him over? He was fanatical, uncompromising, credulous, cunning, greedy, unstable, believed in miracles, saints, in the cause of God and the King of France, and the supremacy of the Jesuits. A second Michael the Archangel. He was not interested in her. He had his orders. And he had to redeem himself in the eyes of his all-powerful superiors.

'Do you think that after this Count Peyrac, my husband, is going to help you sell your beaver skins in New England,' she shouted at him through her teeth. 'Don't forget that he has advanced you a thousand pounds and has promised you double that if you make a profit ...'

'Hush!' he said growing pale and looking about him.

'Get me out of this, or I shall shout the truth about you from the house tops of Quebec.'

'Let us not quarrel,' he whispered, 'we can still sort things out. We are some distance from the rest of the village. I have not seen you . . .'

Then, turning towards Piksarett, he went on:

'Let this woman go, Sagamore! She is not an English woman and her capture would bring us bad luck.'

Piksarett stretched out his red, oily hand and laid it on Angélique's shoulder.

'She is my prisoner,' he repeated in tones that brooked no reply.

'So be it,' said Angélique feverishly, 'I am your prisoner, I do not gainsay that. You can follow me wherever you like, I shall not object. But you shall not take me to Quebec . . . What would you do with me there? They would not want to buy me from you since I have already been baptized. So take me to Gouldsboro, where my husband will pay you handsomely, any ransom you care to ask.'

It was a spine-chilling game of poker. These wild beasts must be tamed, perplexed, persuaded. But she knew them. The most absurd arguments sprang to her mind, but it was precisely these that worked on these furtive, devious minds. It was out of the question to deny Piksarett's rights over her, for he would have immediately struck her down with a blow of his tomahawk just to assert them, but she knew him to be free, capricious, and absolutely independent of his Canadian allies; inasmuch as he was now deprived of the glory of having obtained another soul for his dear French friends' paradise, since she was already baptized, he had begun to hesitate, and to doubt the importance of his capture. She must win him over before any other Frenchman, who knew what was to be gained by Madame de Peyrac's capture – perhaps even the dreaded Jesuit himself – appeared round the bend in the road. Since de L'Aubignière, by good fortune, was an accomplice . . .

Burning brands began to fall on their heads as they spoke, for Piksarett's Abenakis, poking about with their torches in their search for plunder, had set the farmhouse on fire.

'Come along! Come along.' Angélique urged the people, pushing them outside. She helped up some of the English who were either wounded or stunned, then added: 'Good heavens, the children!'

She ran back into the house, raised the lid of the cauldron and lifted the children out one by one, dumb with fright. The revelation of this incongruous hiding place caused general hilarity among the Indians, who doubled up with mirth, slapping their thighs and pointing at the spectacle.

The heat was becoming unbearable; a beam crackled and half collapsed in a shower of sparks.

Everyone ran out into the yard, clambering over dead bodies and debris.

The sight of the trees so close, and of the shady forest ravine, spurred Angélique's desire to flee. Every second counted.

'Let me go down to the sea, Sagamore,' she said to Piksarett, 'or your ancestors will be angry with you for showing me so little consideration. They know that my personal spirits do not deserve to be treated lightly. You would be making a grave mistake were you to take me to Quebec. On the other hand, you will have no cause to regret coming with me.'

The tall Abenaki's tormented expression reflected the conflict of his mind, but Angélique gave him no time to disentangle his thoughts.

'Make sure that we are not followed. Report that I was not in the village,' she said to Three-Fingers, who was also confused by the speed of events and Angélique's authoritative tone. 'We shall show you our gratitude. Do you know where my son Cantor is? Did you capture him?'

'I swear to you by the Blessed Sacrament that we never set eyes on him.'

'Off we go then,' she said. 'I am going. Come on! Come on!'

'Hold a minute!' exclaimed Piksarett, seeing that she was gathering together the English survivors from the farm. 'These people belong to my braves . . .'

'Well, let them come too. But only the masters of the captives.'

Three lumbering feathered giants leapt forward shouting, but a sharp word from Piksarett stopped them in their tracks.

Angélique paused only to pick up one of the children, to drag one of the women with her and give a shove to the huge figure of Thomas Patridge who staggered off, blinded with his own blood.

'Adhemar come here! Hold this boy's hand and don't let him go, whatever you do. Bear up, Miss Pidgeon!'

She scrambled down the slope, turning her back on the ravaged, burning village, dragging them off to freedom as so often before, in La Rochelle, in Poitou, and even earlier, back in the dark days of her childhood, fleeing, ever fleeing with a flock of outcasts she had snatched from the jaws of death.

That evening the soul of old Sarah walked with her as she plunged ever deeper into the forest and was swallowed up in the silence of the dark trees with the English survivors from Brunswick-Falls.

With them came Piksarett and the three Indians who considered the English people as their chattels. They loped along behind them keeping a certain distance back. There was no attempt to catch them up.

Angélique knew this, she sensed it, and as they all got farther from the doomed village, she began to fear the Indians less, realizing that they had lost much of their warlike, hysterical tension.

The English were mystified by Angélique's conduct, and kept glancing back and complaining that the savages were pursuing them.

'You have nothing to fear,' Angélique replied. 'There are only four of them now instead of a hundred. And I am with you. They will not harm you any more. I know them. Fear nothing. All you have to do is keep on walking.'

Piksarett's thoughts were now as clear to her as if she had formed them herself with a savage's brain.

He was childish and loved anything original, novel, unusual. He was superstitious too and Angélique's personal spirits both intrigued and frightened him.

Full of curiosity, he followed close behind her, holding his impatient braves back with a word, fascinated to know what was going to happen now, and what was the nature of those cunning, fleeting, indomitable spirits he had seen dancing in the green flashes of the white woman's eyes.

Farther on the calm waters of the Androscoggin river shone through the branches below them. Some canoes had been drawn up on the bank; they climbed into them and began to glide downstream towards the sea.

CHAPTER SEVENTEEN

IT WAS NIGHT ... At the foot of the waterfall, in the darkness lit fitfully by the fireflies, in the warm darkness filled with the croaking of frogs and the smell of burning, the Europeans snatched a brief rest. Huddled one against the other close to the birch-bark canoes, shivering in spite of the warmth, some prayed while others moaned softly.

There they awaited the dawn.

Among those whom Angélique had brought from the burning farm were farmer Stoughton, his wife and baby, and the entire Corwin family. Corwin's two farmhands and his servant girl had also managed to follow.

Rose-Ann huddled close to Angélique, while Adhemar sat on her other side, and would gladly have done the same; as it was he stayed as close to her as he possibly could.

'They are up there,' he whispered. 'From the moment I first set foot in this land of savages, I just knew I would lose my scalp one day!'

Frail little Miss Pidgeon had not suffered a scratch and it was she who had led the Reverend Patridge, who, for the time being had become little better than a body with no head, for not only had he been blinded with blood but he was barely conscious and managed to remain on his feet only by sheer force of habit and because such big-framed men are incapable of falling to the ground unless actually dead. As soon as she had been able to do so, the kindly teacher had washed his face for him and bound her shawl around his forehead. Then finally, when they reached the boats, Angélique had managed to open her bag in which she kept a sachet of yellow powder, an iron salt that Joffrey had given her, which had the property of favouring the clotting of blood, and by this means she had succeeded in stopping the bleeding.

Although half scalped, the pastor would no doubt only be left with an ugly scar across his forehead, which admittedly would do nothing to make his looks any less disconcerting than they had been.

He was sleeping heavily and the grating sound of his laboured breathing filled the intervals of silence. Beneath the bandaging, the whole of one side of his face was swollen and had gone blue. It was just as well that it was dark, for nature had not favoured him in the first place and now he looked absolutely hideous.

A little girl was standing rigidly erect, and crying, her face showing white in the darkness.

'You must sleep, Mary, try to sleep,' Angélique said softly in English, 'you must try to sleep.'

'I can't,' the little girl wailed. 'The savages are watching me.'

All four of them were sitting up above the waterfall, four

Abenakis, one of them the mighty Piksarett, and they sat looking down into the darkness in which their wretched prisoners were huddled together.

In the glow of the small campfire one could make out their copper-coloured faces and flashing snake-like eyes.

They had continued to follow the whites, watching them with considerable fascination and curiosity, but they had made no attempt to attack them. They were perfectly calm now and were smoking and talking together. What was going to happen? What would these unknown spirits that lived in the white woman from Wapassou think of next? What action would her personal spirits dictate? Glances were exchanged across the leaping waters of the fall.

Angélique did her best to reassure her protégées.

'They will do us no further harm. We must get them down to the coast and there my husband, Count Peyrac, will know exactly how to treat them, how to flatter them, and will offer them handsome gifts in exchange for our lives and our freedom.'

They stared at her, dumbstruck, sensing in their cold, exaggeratedly puritanical minds that she too was of a different species from them, a little frightening, even a little repugnant to them. This excessively beautiful white woman, who was able to converse with the Indians in their own language, seemed to have the capacity of getting inside their cruel, dark pagan minds in order to tame and subjugate them the more effectively.

They were aware of what she was, and both feared and despised her, somewhat as they did old Shapleigh, while realizing at the same time that they owed her their lives, and certainly their liberty.

It was because of her indecent familiarity with these savages, because of the easy way she spoke to them, because of the vehement harangues in that hated pagan tongue that tripped so lightly off those beautiful lips, that they had seen the mood of the Indians change, had seen their own lives spared and had been able to make their escape through the woods, far from the site of the massacre, under the very eyes of the Indians.

They were conscious of this miracle and of the necessity for remaining under her protection, reassured by the very sound of her voice, and they did their best to excuse her strange ways, by reminding themselves that after all she was French ...

Sometime in the middle of the night Angélique climbed up to where the savages sat above the waterfall to ask them quite straightforwardly whether they had a piece of bear fat or some seal oil that she could use to cover the burns of little nine-year-old Sammy Corwin, for they were causing him a great deal of pain.

The Indians bustled about and soon produced a moose bladder containing some precious seal oil, which had an unpleasant smell but was pure and wholesome.

'Do not forget, oh woman, that that boy belongs to me,' one of the braves said to her. 'But take good care of him, for to-morrow I shall take him with me back to my tribe.'

'That boy belongs to his father and mother,' Angélique replied. 'We shall buy him from you.'

'But I laid my hand on him in battle ... and I want a white child in my wigwam.'

'I shall not let you take him away,' Angélique replied with unshakeable calm.

Then she added to appease the man's anger:

'I shall give you many other things, so that you shall not lack your share of the booty ... tomorrow we will hold council.'

Apart from this incident, the night passed uneventfully. They heard no more of the massacre. As they were making their escape they had glimpsed, at a bend in the river, a distant red glow, as Brunswick-Falls, the frontier village, burnt to the ground.

They crouched there, their minds blank, seeking refuge in the darkness.

As the grey dawn began to creep up the sky, something came slithering down the slope, weaving through the grass and brushwood as it came, and there stood Wolverine, baring his teeth in what on this occasion looked like a welcoming grin. Cantor followed hard on his tracks, carrying a sleeping English child in his arms, a little boy of three with his thumb in his mouth.

'I found him standing beside his mother who had been scalped,' he explained. 'The woman kept on saying to him: "Don't be frightened, I promise they won't hurt you." When she saw me pick him up she closed her eyes at last and died.'

'That's Rebecca Turner's son,' said Jane Stoughton. 'Poor child! His father was killed last year.'

They fell silent as the four Indians moved towards them. They showed no sign of aggression. Isolated as they were from the rest of the war party, and perplexed by the attitude of these strange prisoners upon whom they seemed unable to impose their right of possession, their mood had changed.

The man who had claimed the Corwin boy walked towards Cantor and held out his hands towards the sleeping child.

'Give him to me,' he said. 'Give him to me. It has always been my desire to have a white child in my wigwam, and your mother will never allow me to take the child I captured at Newehewanik. Give me this child, for he has neither father nor mother nor family nor village. What would you do with him? I shall take him away and bring him up as a hunter and a warrior, and I shall make him happy. Children lead a happy life in our wigwams.'

His expression was entreating, almost pitiable.

Piksarett had had to convince the man during the night, not without a certain slyness, that Angélique would never allow him to take possession of his young captive, little Samuel, and that were he to defy her in this, she would change him into a moose for the rest of his life.

Torn between his fear of so sad a fate and the desire to vindicate his rights, he reckoned that an acceptable solution could be arrived at if he were prepared to take the little orphan Cantor had saved.

Angélique cast an anxious, questioning glance at her son.

'What do you think, Cantor?'

For her part, she really did not know which was the right decision to take. It broke her heart to think of this little white boy being carried off into the depths of the forest; on the other hand, a certain sense of fairness, and prudence as well, inclined her to agree to the humble request of the Abenaki brave. She had hoodwinked them, had put them off sufficiently often since the previous day, and if she were to dispute too much with them over their spoils, they might suddenly lose patience with her.

'What do you think, Cantor?'

'Well,' the young man began with a shrug, 'we know that white children are not unhappy among the Indians. Perhaps it would be better to let this one go as he has not any family anyway, than all have our skulls split.'

The voice of wisdom had spoken through his lips.

Angélique remembered the wails of despair of the little Canadian boy, de L'Aubignière's nephew, when, on the occasion of an exchange, they had sought to remove him from his Iroquois foster parents.[*]

* See *The Countess Angélique*.

White children were not unhappy among the Indians.

She turned questioningly towards the English. Mistress Corwin sat clutching her son passionately to her, realizing that his fate hung in the balance, while the others made it obvious that in the present circumstances the fate of the little Turner boy was a matter of relative indifference to them. Had the Reverend Patridge been fully conscious, he might well have protested in the name of the child's eternal salvation, but he was still in a dazed condition.

It was better that the orphan boy should go rather than the Corwins' boy should be snatched from them, as the whole family had, by good fortune, been saved.

'Give the boy to him,' Angélique said softly to Cantor.

Realizing that he had prevailed, the redskin cut a few capers and made a great show of gratitude.

Then he held out his great hands and gently picked up the child who looked fearlessly up into the gaudily painted face that loomed over him.

Delighted at having obtained what he had set his heart on, a white child for his wigwam, the brave took his leave of them, and, after exchanging a few words with his companions went off, lovingly clasping the heretic child against his beartooth necklace and his crucifix, feeling that he had saved him from the barbarities of his own people and that he would teach him the true way of life of the True Men.

Cantor related how, after leaving them to search for Maupertuis and the horses, he had noticed some suspicious-looking shapes moving between the trees.

Pursued by some of the braves, he had only succeeded in shaking them off by leading them a considerable distance in the direction of the plateau.

Returning a long way round, he had heard the sound of the battle, and had begun to approach the village with the utmost care, as he had no intention of allowing himself to be used as a hostage by falling into the hands of the Canadians.

Thus it was that he had witnessed the departure of the English captives northwards, and, not seeing his mother among them, had deduced that she had managed to make her escape.

'Did it not occur to you that I might have had my throat cut or been scalped?'

'Oh, no!' Cantor replied, as if the thought had never crossed his head.

He had wandered round the burning ruins of Brunswick

village and had encountered Three-Fingers from Trois Rivières, from whom he had learned that Madame de Peyrac was safe and heading in the direction of the Bay of Sagadahoc, with a handful of survivors.

The incident with the child seemed to have proved that for the present anyway the Indians were allowing Angélique a certain latitude when it came to making decisions that concerned them all. However odd the situation might be only a few hours after their assault on the English village, it was perfectly consistent with the fickle mentality of the redskins.

Through sheer force of personality Angélique had taken them off in a different direction from that intended, and they had almost begun to forget why they had been fighting the previous day, what they were doing here with her and a handful of stupid Englishmen, and were now concerned only to know how this adventure on which she had launched them would turn out.

Piksarett nevertheless saw fit to recall certain essential principles.

'Don't forget that you are my prisoner,' he broke in, pointing his finger at the nape of Angélique's neck.

'I know, I know, I have already told you that I accept that. Am I in any way preventing you from staying close to me? Ask your companions if they think I look like a prisoner trying to escape?'

Perplexed by the subtlety of her argument in which he sensed there was something fishy but also comical, Piksarett leaned his head on one side in order to think better and his slanting eyes sparkled with delight while his two companions noisily made known their opinions to him.

'In Gouldsboro you will even be able to sell me back to my own husband,' Angélique explained. 'He is a very wealthy man and I am sure that he will not hesitate to deal generously with you. At least, I hope not,' she went on, letting her face fall suddenly, to the great amusement of the three Indians.

At the idea that Angélique's husband might be obliged to buy back his own wife their mirth knew no bounds.

There certainly was much entertainment to be had from following the white woman from the Upper Kennebec and the English people she had taken in tow.

It was a well-known fact that no animal exceeded the Yenngli (the English) in clumsiness, and these particular Yenngli made even more clumsy than usual through fear and their wounds, floundered along, sprawling on the ground at almost every step, and capsized canoes on the slightest provocation.

'Oh! These Yenngli! They will make us die of laughter,' the Indians kept on saying, going into contortions of mirth. Then, to make clear that they were the masters, they would suddenly add:

'Get along with you! Go on! Walk, you English! You have killed our missionaries, burned our huts, jeered at our beliefs. Unless you are baptized by the Black Robes, you are nothing to us, not even palefaces, although their pagan ancestors were gods!'

Kept on the move by all this chatter, the wretched party reached the Bay of Segadahoc two days later at the meeting point of the mouths of the Androscoggin and the Kennebec.

The mist blotted out the horizon of the estuary but, mingling with the sea fog from the shore, they could still smell a suspicious whiff of fire.

Angélique climbed briskly up a small hill. There was not a sail in sight. She could see no trace of a ship on the grey horizon.

Angélique knew instinctively that the bay was deserted. No vessel was lying out there at anchor keeping a lookout for signs of a human presence on the shore, before coming in to take them on board.

There was no sign of the *Rochelais*, a small yacht flying a red pennant, with Le Gall waiting to welcome her on board, or even Joffrey!

No familiar presence. No one at the agreed rendezvous.

A thin drizzle had begun to fall, and Angélique leaned against the trunk of a pine tree. The whole place smelled of death, of the wilderness. On her left, she saw a billowing mushroom cloud of black smoke rising into the sky; it came from the direction of Sheepscot, an English settlement she had been told lay at the mouth of the Androscoggin, where she had intended to leave the survivors of Brunswick village before going on board the *Rochelais*.

But it now looked as if Sheepscot too had been burned down and no longer existed.

An overwhelming feeling of distress swept over Angélique and she felt her strength ebbing away. She turned round and saw that Piksarett was observing her. She must not show him that she was frightened. But she could not go on.

'They are not there,' she told him, almost despairingly.

'Whom were you expecting?'

Then she explained that her husband, the lord of Wapassou and Gouldsboro, should have been there with a ship to meet them. He would have taken them all to Gouldsboro, where he, Piksarett, would have been given the most beautiful beads on the earth, and would have drunk the very best firewater in the world ...

The redskin shook his head sadly and seemed genuinely to share her disappointment and anxiety. He looked around him uneasily.

Meanwhile Cantor and the English were climbing the hill more slowly, followed by the other two Indians.

They sat down wearily under the pine trees to shelter from the rain, and Angélique explained the situation to them. The three Indians began an excited discussion.

'They say that the Sheepscot Indians are their worst enemies,' Angélique explained to the English people. 'They come from the north, they are Wonolancets.'

She was not surprised, knowing that Indians were perpetually at war among themselves, which meant that if they strayed only a short distance from home, they could find themselves in enemy territory where they risked their lives unless they were in large numbers and armed.

'It makes no difference,' said Stoughton gloomily, 'whether they are Sheepscot or Wonolancets, it is all the same to us. They can scalp us just the same. Why have we bothered to come as far as this? We shall all be dead soon.'

The silent coastline seemed to conceal a hidden menace. From behind every curtain of trees, every promontory, they expected to see Indians rush out with raised tomahawks, and now Piksarett and his men seemed just as ill at ease as their prisoners.

Angélique made an effort to get on top of her fear.

'No! No! This time, I am not going to give way,' she said, clenching her fists, not quite sure whom it was she was defying.

First of all, she decided, they must leave this stretch of the coast, where the Indian war was bursting into open flames again and attempt at all costs to reach Gouldsboro. There might be other villages farther along and other boats available.

Gouldsboro! Joffrey de Peyrac's territory. Their own domain! Their refuge. But Gouldsboro was so far away!

There was not a single sail in the estuary.

A few hours earlier, not yet twenty-four hours back, old

Sarah Williams had taken Angélique's face in her hands and had said to her: 'America! America! You must save it!'

This had been her last message, a trifle wild, perhaps, for death had already been there, lurking in the bushes, about to strike her down. Was it the same kind of anxiety that Angélique felt now as the desolate evening closed in on them with the scent of seaweed, mist, and slaughter?

'Hi!' said Piksarett, laying a hand upon her shoulder.

And he pointed to two human shapes climbing up the slope from the shore.

She had a moment of hope but then saw, from his pointed hat, that it was the old medicine-man John Shapleigh and his Indian.

They all ran to meet him to see if he had any news, and he told them that he had just come from the beach, and that over yonder the Indians had burned everything. A ship? Had there been a ship? No.

Those inhabitants who had escaped scalping or being taken prisoner had taken refuge among the islands in their boats.

Seeing the despair of the unfortunate refugees from Brunswick-Falls, finally, not without great hesitation and many grimaces, and also because Angélique sought his advice, he suggested that he might lead them to a hut he owned about ten miles away on Casco Bay, where they could rest and be cared for.

In spite of the discomfort of spending a misty night in the open, most of them, including Angélique herself, felt hesitant to leave the agreed meeting place. The ship from Gouldsboro might have been delayed, and might well turn up in a few hours' time, or at dawn on the following morning.

The matter was settled by the sudden appearance of a group of about ten Sheepscot Indians at the edge of the wood.

As if by magic, Piksarett and his braves melted from sight. Angélique wondered whether she had exchanged one Indian escort for another less amenable, but fortunately Shapleigh and his companion were on good terms with the newcomers. Old Shapleigh, a medicine-man accepted as on a par with their best jugglers, was greatly respected in the region where he had been practising for over thirty years. His influence with the Indians enabled him to extend his protection to Angélique and her companions, and the Sheepscot Indians were even so obliging as to suggest that they might watch out for the possible arrival of any ships at this point of the coast. They carefully noted the description of the *Rochelais* and promised, should they see it, to direct it on to Maquoit Point where old Shapleigh had his cabin.

CHAPTER EIGHTEEN

JOFFREY DE PEYRAC gave a start of surprise.

'What? What did you say?'

He had just been informed that Madame de Peyrac had set off without him for the village of Brunswick-Falls with her son to take the little English girl back to her family.

This piece of information had been given him quite casually by Jacques Vignot, who had joined the Count on Cape Small, near Popham, where he had gone some two days earlier with Baron Saint-Castine.

Packing cases containing wares for barter, that had been held up for lack of ships to transport them, had just arrived from Houssnock, escorted by the carpenter and one soldier.

'But which day was it that Madame La Comtesse took this strange decision?'

'Just a few hours after your own departure, Sir, the very same day . . .'

'Did she not receive my message telling her that I might be away for several days and asking her to wait patiently for me at the Dutchman's trading post?'

The two men did not know. What a reckless thing to have done! thought Peyrac. With all these rumours of war about. The Dutchman's post was by way of being a fortified encampment, where she would have run no risk. But to set off into the interior of the country, almost unescorted . . .

'With whom did they go?'

'With the two Maupertuis.'

'What an extraordinary idea! She must have been crazy!' he exclaimed in anger.

He swore at Angélique inwardly, finding it hard to overcome a profound sense of anxiety about her that had suddenly swept over him.

She must be crazy, she must indeed! It was inconceivable. She had behaved completely irresponsibly! When he saw her again, he would have some pretty hard things to say to her, for he must make her understand that in spite of their privileged position the region would not be safe for a long time to come, especially to the west of the Kennebec.

He began to calculate. Three days had elapsed since he himself had set off towards the coast and Angélique, apparently at the same moment, had set off for the frontier town ... But where could she possibly be now?

It was raining, and mist hung over the bay, loud with the murmur of the rising tides as its swift-flowing currents swept around the half-submerged islands.

It was on account of these equioxial tides that many of the Europeans and Indians who should have come to the rendezvous by way of the sea, had been delayed.

The great Tarratine chief Mateconando wanted everybody to be present, so while they waited they had begun their preliminary discussions. On the Sunday, Baron Saint-Castine's chaplain, a Recollect Friar with a thick beard and a face even more tanned than that of a pirate, had said Mass.

Then at last on the Tuesday, that same morning, the entire population of what was known more precisely, amid the myriad convolutions of the coastline, as the lesser gulf of Maine, had met together in one spot. The last of the packing cases of presents had just arrived and the ceremony was about to begin.

It was then that Peyrac heard of Angélique's escapade.

Where would she be by now? Had she gone back to Houssnock? Or had she, in accordance with the plan they had previously discussed, travelled down the Androscoggin, one of the branches of the Kennebec estuary, to Merry Meeting Bay where Corentin Le Gall was to wait for them with the *Rochelais*?

In his uncertainty, he decided to send for his equerry Yann le Couennec.

He instructed him first to take a good meal, then to check the condition of his weapons and his shoes and to prepare himself to set off post haste.

Then he sat down and scribbled a brief note while one of the Spanish soldiers of his guard deferentially held his inkhorn for him.

When Yann presented himself ready to set off, he handed him the note but added his own special instructions.

If Yann found Madame de Peyrac at the Dutchman's trading post, they should all pack up and join him here. If, on the other hand, she had not yet returned from Brunswick-Falls, he, Yann, should set off there himself, and should find Madame de Peyrac at all costs, wherever she was, and bring her back to Gouldsboro by the quickest route.

With these strict instructions, the man set off. Peyrac was obliged to make a considerable effort to put out of his mind his acute anxiety about Angélique, and to concentrate his full attention on the meeting which was about to take place; for, at the summons of Baron Saint-Castine, all these little people had come from far off, often at no small danger, just to meet him.

In addition to the Indians from all the principal tribes of the area, a few scattered white men, ignoring their differences of nationality or the antagonisms of their countries of origin, had decided to come together and hold council around the French nobleman from Gouldsboro.

There were English traders from Pemaquid, from Croton, from Oyster River, Wiscasset, Thomaston, Woolwich, Saint George, Nevagan, in all about twenty Englishmen who traded in small, scattered outposts along the fiords of Muscongus Bay, the Damariscotta river and the mouth of the Kennebec. And their neighbouring enemies had also come, with whom, when they were not actually killing one another, they would exchange household goods and milk from a few rare cows: Frenchmen from Acadia, settlers and fishermen, a Dumaresque or a Galatin from Swans Island, where they bred sheep, grew flowers and potatoes side by side with the direct descendants of Adam Winthrop from Boston, Dutchmen sent over by Campden and even an elderly, hoary Scot from Monhegan Island, the proud Island of the Sea with its granite cliffs, the most isolated of the whole bay – he was a MacGregor who had come over with his three sons and whose tartan plaids floated across there in the gusty wind at the far end of the headland.

The State of Massachusetts had expressly recommended that the English and the Dutch should get in touch with Count Peyrac if one day they were to find that they needed protection in their far-flung outposts along this wild coast of Maine, infested as it was with Frenchmen and bloodthirsty Indians, an area people must be a bit mad to venture into.

The Acadians in their turn followed the lead of Baron Saint-Castine.

The Scots did exactly as they fancied.

In brief, there were all sorts there.

Once again, as he thought of Angélique, Peyrac cursed

women, whose caprices, often charming but more often than not ill-timed, brought nothing but trouble and complications to men's undertakings.

Then, pulling himself together, he went to meet his guests, surrounded by his Spanish guards in their steel breastplates and morions.

Baron Saint-Castine accompanied him, and the great chief Mateconando came towards him in his most magnificent robe of doeskin embroidered with shells and porcupine quills. His long oily hair, greased with seal oil, was surmounted by a flat, round hat of black satin with a narrow brim, decorated with a white ostrich feather that must have been at least a hundred years old.

One of his ancestors had been given this feather by Verrazano himself, the Florentine explorer, in the service of the French King Francis I. When he had passed this way with his one-hundred-and-fifty-ton ship, he had been one of the first to name this land Arcadie on account of the beauty of its trees. The name, in a slightly altered form, had subsequently been retained.

Fixed to this sixteenth-century nobleman's hat, the lily-white ostrich feather, showing only traces of yellow, bore witness to the care with which the Indians, dirty and careless in their habits as they generally were, had preserved this relic.

The greatest of all chieftains wore it only on the most solemn occasions.

Joffrey de Peyrac gave the Tarratine chief a damascene sword of gold and silver, some decorated cases of razors, scissors and knives, and then strings of shiny blue glass beads each about six feet long, in exchange for which the Indian presented him with some mother-of-pearl shells and a handful of amethysts, a symbolic gesture of friendship.

'I know you have no greed for furs, and seek only for our alliance.'

'You see,' Saint-Castine had explained to Peyrac, 'I want my Indians to stop fighting, otherwise in a few decades they will have been wiped out.'

The great Tarratine chieftain laid an affectionate hand on Baron Saint-Castine and looked at him with admiration.

Saint-Castine was a man of average height, perhaps even on the short side, but was incredibly strong, agile, hardy, quick-witted, and sensitive, and he had won the devotion of all the coastal tribes.

'I shall make him my son-in-law,' Mateconando confided in Peyrac, 'and later on he will succeed me as chief of the Etchemins and the Mic-Macs.'

CHAPTER NINETEEN

'ANGÉLIQUE ...! Pray heaven nothing has happened to her! I should have taken her with me. Saint-Castine caught me unprepared. I ought never to leave her on her own, by day or by night, not for a moment ... My precious, my crazy love ... She has been independent for too long. As soon as she is left alone, she feels the need to be free again ... I must make her understand the dangers that surround us. I shall have to be stern this time ... But now I must put aside these worries ... I must concentrate my mind ... I must not disappoint all these people who have come to meet me. I realize what young Saint-Castine is asking me in their name. What a remarkable lad! He sees things as they are, but he knows his limits ... What is he asking of me? To perform a task which is surely impracticable ... to follow a path beset with pitfalls ...'

Such were Count Peyrac's thoughts as he sat on the thick grass in front of the bark hut that had been erected for him.

Once all the ceremonial, the feasting and smoking were over, he had left the others, saying that he wished to be alone for a few hours, and had sat smoking, staring out at the headland on which an occasional larger wave sent up a white plume of foam.

The ocean battered the tree-clad shore, sending clouds of spray among the fir trees, the cedars, the oaks and the giant copper beeches, and occasionally, when the wind changed, there came blowing from the undergrowth a sweet smell of hyacinth and wild strawberries.

Joffrey de Peyrac beckoned to Juan Fernandez, the tall hidalgo who commanded his guard, and asked him to fetch the French baron, feeling that he would prefer to chat with the enthusiastic Gascon on his favourite topic rather than remain alone; for the thought of Angélique kept on coming back to his mind with a nagging sense of apprehension which prevented him from arriving at any useful conclusion.

Baron Saint-Castine joined him with alacrity and sat down beside him. In accordance with the traditions of the country he drew out his pipe from the folds of his cloak and began to smoke too. Then he started to talk, but the conversation was almost entirely a monologue, presenting his whole world, with its dreams, its projects and its perils . . .

The rain had stopped, but the mist still hung about and the camp fires seemed to tremble through it like huge red orchids in full bloom, stretching out along the coast, and each light was doubled by a halo.

As dusk fell the roar of the sea grew deeper, mingling with the cry of birds flocking up the estuary. They were Jaeger gulls, with long brown wings like those of swallows, and predatory beaks.

'There must have been a storm at sea,' the baron said as his eyes followed their flight. 'Those little pirates only seek shelter on land when the sea is too stormy for them to settle on it.'

He took a deep breath and, smelling the fragrance from the forest, heaved a deep sigh. Summer was drawing near, and in those parts summer meant trouble of the very worst kind.

'This is the time of year when the cod-fishing boats of all nations invade our shores,' he said, 'along with buccaneers from Santo Domingo. A plague upon the thieves! They run less risk by holding up our poor ships bringing provisions over from France to our settlements in Acadia than they do by attacking the Spaniards. And God only knows there are few enough of these ships, and yet they still have to be seized under our very noses. A filthy breed, these Jamaican filibusters!'

'Gold Beard?'

'I have not encountered him yet.'

'I think I heard talk of him when I was in the Caribbean,' Peyrac went on, puckering his brow in an effort to remember. 'On my last trip out there. The gentlemen of fortune spoke of him as a good sailor, and a leader of men . . . He would have done better to remain in the West Indies.'

'Rumour has it that he is a French pirate who has recently acquired letters of marque in France from some rich society founded for the purpose of fighting French Huguenots wherever encountered. That would explain his attack upon your people at Gouldsboro, and it also sounds like the sort of thing our administration in Paris would do. The last time I was over there

I saw that advancement depended more and more on religious zeal, which is making our task in Acadia particularly complicated ...'

'Do you mean that people ought to remember that the original founders were Protestants?'

'And that the most Catholic Champlain was originally only cartographer to Pierre de Guast, Lord of Monts, a notorious Huguenot.'

They exchanged smiles, delighted to feel that they understood one another as readily in all matters.

'That was a long time ago,' said Saint-Castine.

'And it's growing longer and longer ... I am interested in what you have to tell me, Baron, and am beginning to understand why this particular pirate should be so set on attacking Gouldsboro in spite of its well hidden position. If this is some holy mission of his, how did he hear about Gouldsboro?'

'News travels fast. In these parts there are not more than three Frenchmen in every hundred leagues, but at least one of them will be a spy for the King ... and the Jesuits.'

'Be careful, my boy.'

'You laugh? But it doesn't make me laugh. I want to live in peace here with my Etchemins and my Mic-Macs. Those people from Paris and the privateers in their pay have no right to come to these parts. They don't belong to the Bay.'

'The Bay? Give me the Basques any day, who hunt whales, or the fishermen from Saint-Malo who make our coasts stink with their dried cod. They at least have a right to be in Acadia. They were coming here 500 years ago ... But their brandy and their orgies with the Indian girls ... What a disaster! ... On the whole I think I even prefer the ships that come up from Boston, for at least we can barter with them for hardware and cloth. But there are too many of them, far too many of their ships.'

He made a sweeping gesture that encompassed the whole horizon.

'Hundreds of them ... hundreds of English ships, everywhere, everywhere. Well armed, well equipped. And there's Salem down there, their great drying centre, and their pitch, their tar, their turpentine, their raw hides, and their whalebone and seal and whale-oil – 80 to 100,000 hundredweight of oil a year they make – it stinks, but it pays. And I'm expected to hold on to French Acadia ... to keep it for the King with my four cannons, my wooden fortress that measures sixty feet by twenty, and to compete with the English on the fishing grounds with my fifteen longboats . . .'

'But you are not as poor as all that,' said Peyrac. 'They say that you are doing very well in the fur trade.'

'Oh yes, I am already well off myself, that I grant. But that is my business, and the reason why I want to be rich is to help my Indians, to make them more stable, to help them to prosper. The Etchemins make up the largest block of my tribes but I also have Mic-Macs of the Tarrantine tribe. They are Souriquois of Canada, the same as those that inhabit Casco Bay, related to the Mohicans. I can speak all their dialects, five or six – Etchemins, Wawenoks, Penobscots, Kanibas, Tarrantines, they're my men, the best of all the Abenakis. And it's on their account that I want to be rich, in order to care for them, to civilize them and protect them . . . Yes, protect them, crazy, splendid fighters that they are!'

He puffed away for a while at his pipe, then once more stretched his arm out towards the foam-fringed darkness, towards the west.

'Now, out there, in Casco Bay, I own an island which I wrested from the English not long ago. And not just to get rid of them, but because there was a legend attached to the island. It lies near the mouth of the Presumpscot near Portland, towards the south of Casco Bay, and from time immemorial has been regarded by the Mohicans, the Souriquois and the Etchemins as the site of an ancient paradise, for they have a saying which goes: "If you have once slept on that island, you will never be the same man again." But it had been in the hands of English farmers for several generations, and the Indians were unhappy not to be able to meet there to hold their ancestral feasts, when the heat of August makes the inland area intolerable. So I took it and handed it over to the Indians.

'What joy! What delight! What celebrations we had! But if peace is not maintained, what is the point of all these efforts?'

'Do you think that peace is in danger?'

'Not only do I think so, I am certain of it. And that is why I was in such a hurry for you to meet Mateconando. Yes, since the Treaty of Breda things have been going more or less all right. But the peace is about to be broken. Father d'Orgeval, that paladin of the days of yore, has mobilized the Abenakis of the north and west who are men of the forest and almost as formidable as the Iroquois. And as for the great Piksarett, their chief, the most devout Christian ever produced by a missionary,

who can be expected to cope with him? He is terrible! ...
Monsieur de Peyrac, war is imminent.

'Father d'Orgeval wants war and he has prepared well for it.
I am sure that he came here with orders and directives from
the King of France himself, to rekindle the conflict against the
English. This would suit our sovereign, it appears, and one must
admit that this Jesuit is the most formidable politician who has
yet set foot in these lands. I know that he has sent one of
his priests, Father Maraicher de Vernon, on a secret mission to
New England, right down to Maryland, to seek some pretext to
break the truce, and no doubt Father d'Orgeval is only awaiting his return before unleashing his offensive. A short while
ago I received a visit from Father de Guérande who had come
to ask me to join their crusade with my friendly tribes, I dodged
giving a straight answer. I know I am a French nobleman, an
officer, and a fighting man, but ...'

He suddenly closed his eyes as if in pain.

'I can't bear to see any more of it.'

'Of what?'

'The holocaust, the slaughter, the endless massacre of my
brothers, the unforgivable extinction of their race.'

When Saint-Castine spoke of his brothers Peyrac knew that
he was referring to the Indians.

'You see, it is so easy to involve them in war: they are so
quickly roused and so easy to deceive. You know as I do, sir,
that the strongest of all passions among the redskins is an implacable hatred of their enemies and above all of their friends'
enemies – that is their code of honour. It is not in their nature
to live peaceably, but I have seen too many die already of those
I loved, and to what end?

'You can understand what I can tell no one else ... We are
too far from the sun here. You understand what I mean?
We cannot, from this distance, do anything to enlighten the
King. We are forgotten, we are alone. The Administration only
remembers us when the time comes to collect its dividends on
fur trading or to ask us to send troops against the English on
behalf of the Jesuits and their holy wars. But it is not true that
we belong to France. No one belongs to anyone out here in
Acadia. All these islands, these peninsulas, all these hidden
coves are inhabited by free men. Whether French, English
Dutch, Scandinavian, fishermen or traders, we are all in the
same boat – furs and cod, barter and coastal trade. We are the
people of Frenchman Bay, the people of the Atlantic coast ...

we share the same interests, and the same needs. We ought to come together under your aegis!'

'Why mine?'

'Because there is only you,' Saint-Castine replied with ardour. 'You alone are strong, invulnerable, you are with everyone and yet remain detached. How shall I put it? We know you are friendly with the English, and yet I am certain that, were you to go to Quebec, you would have all the fine people there eating out of your hand. And even ... You see, we Canadians are no doubt brave and shrewd, but we lack something that you possess – political judgement. Face to face with a man like Father d'Orgeval we count for little. You alone can stand up to him.'

'The Jesuits are a very powerful order, the most powerful of all, in fact,' Peyrac replied in tones devoid of emotion.

'But ... so are you!'

Joffrey de Peyrac turned his head to look at his companion. His thin, youthful face was dominated by his flashing eyes ringed with blue that gave him a slightly effeminate look, which possibly explained why he was thought to look like an Indian; for there is sometimes something sexually ambiguous in the lines of their beardless faces. In his case, it was the refinement of an ancient unconquerable race, made up of a mixture of Iberians and Moors, and, perhaps of remote Asiatic ancestors. The same kind of mixed blood flowed in Peyrac's veins too, and he owed his height, unusual in a Gascon, to his mother's English ancestry.

Baron Saint-Castine looked anxiously at the older man.

'We are ready to rally beneath your standard, Monsieur de Peyrac ...'

Peyrac went on looking at him, summing him up as if he did not hear what he said. So a whole nation was looking to him, finding its expression in this young voice with the musical lilt of the accent of Guyenne, their native province.

'Believe me, believe me,' the voice repeated, 'if the fighting continues and constantly flares up anew, it will be the destruction of us all.'

'And the first to go down will be the most vulnerable, our Indians, our friends, our brothers, our relatives ... yes, our relatives, for every man here in Acadia has a father-in-law, brothers-in-law, sisters-in-law, or cousins out there in the forest. We are tied to them by the ties of the blood of the Indian women we have loved and married. And I myself am soon to marry Matilda, my little Indian princess. What a treasure the child is, Monsieur ...

'But they will all die unless we protect them from their own warlike impulses. For one day the English will grow tired of being endlessly slaughtered. The English along our coasts certainly don't like war, and they are slow to be excited. The one thing they hate is sin, and it will take many more scalps slung from the belts of the Abenakis before they are persuaded to take up arms. But then, God protect us! They are slow to move but when once they make up their minds to it they fight as they till the ground ... heavily, methodically, without passion or hatred, let me tell you, but as if it were a duty, a religious duty. They will sweep clean the land the Lord has given them. They will exterminate my Etchemins and my Souriquois to the last man, just as they exterminated the Pequots forty years ago and the Narrangasetts not long since ... to the last man, I tell you, to the very last man!'

He was almost shouting.

'Naturally I have tried to explain all this to the people in Quebec, but I've had enough of that! They say that the English are cowards and that we must hurl them into the sea, and sweep the American coastline clear of all its heretical, protestant vermin ... This may be true. The English are cowards, but they are a tenacious people and thirty times as numerous as we Canadians; fear can make them terrible, treacherous and cunning ... I know these Englishmen, I have had plenty to do with them, I have scalped enough of them in battle. No, no one can reproach me for having been a bad French officer, I have more than a hundred English scalps drying on the walls of my fortress at Pentagouet, scalps that I collected, together with my Indians, in fights with the settlements along the Bay. Two years ago we almost reached Boston; if only our King had sent us just one warship, we could have conquered that. But he does absolutely nothing to help "his" French Acadia ...'

He stopped, quite out of breath.

Then he continued, pleading touchingly:

'You will help, won't you, Monsieur? You will help me to save my Indians?'

Count Peyrac had leaned his head on his hand, hiding his eyes.

It seemed to him that never had he wished so acutely for Angélique's presence beside him.

If only she were here! If only he could feel her close to him. A gentle, merciful feminine presence, silent, deeply silent as she knew so well how to be on occasion, in a subtle mysterious way that was hers and hers alone.

How understanding was her silence! How compassionate, and shrewd too. The very presence of his wife seemed to atone for every crime and every horror that had been mentioned.

He raised his head, looking destiny straight in the eye.

'All right!' he said. 'I will help you.'

CHAPTER TWENTY

THE FOG HUNG so thickly over the estuary that the piercing cries of the gulls were muffled, and came to them through the swirling mists like the uneasy wailing of souls in torment.

On his way back to Houssnock, Joffrey de Peyrac was about to part company with Saint-Castine, when they caught sight of a ship sailing ghost-like up the Kennebec. Driven indolently along by a sluggish wind, the vessel passed close to them with a silky whispering sound. She was a small trader or privateer of about 120 to 150 tons and her mainmast, from which flew an orange-coloured pennant, was scarcely taller than the pointed tops of the ancient oaks that lined the river bank. She slid past and disappeared like a dream, but a little later, through the mist, they heard the noise of an anchor chain being paid out. The ship was heaving to, and someone made his way towards them along the roughly marked path beside the water. It was a sailor wearing a red-and-white striped jersey and a belt with a cutlass.

'Would one of you gentlemen be Monsieur de Peyrac?'

'I am.'

The sailor pushed his woollen cap back a little in a cursory gesture of greeting.

'A message for you from the vessel we spoke to in the bay off Seguin Island just before we entered the Dresden current.

'If we happened to meet you, they said, it was a yacht called the *Rochelais*. Madame de Peyrac was on board and sent a message that she was joining your Lordship at Gouldsboro.'

'Ah good,' Peyrac exclaimed, greatly relieved. 'When did this happen?'

'Yesterday, just before sundown.'

It was now Wednesday. So, he told himself, Angélique must

have successfully completed her rash expedition to Brunswick-Falls. The *Rochelais*, which had been cruising in those waters, must have taken her on board, and no doubt there were special reasons connected with cargo or winds that had obliged the captain, Corentin Le Gall, to set off again.

Reassured about the fate of his wife and son, the Count was no longer worried about his own possible delay. He would find some other means to make his way swiftly to his lands at Gouldsboro. Not for a moment did he suspect the man they had met of lying, for such deceit is a rare thing among seafaring men.

'Come back via Pentagouet with me,' Baron Saint-Castine suggested. 'The land route is probably still muddy and cluttered with branches snapped off by the thaw, but it will still be quicker than going by sea, if your choice is between waiting for a good ship or making do with the boats you left at Houssnock, which would certainly take their time.'

'A good idea,' Peyrac agreed. 'Hi there, you!'

He called out to the sailor, whose outline was beginning to disappear into the mist.

'Here's something for you,' Peyrac said, handing him a fistful of pearls.

The sailor gave a start and stared open mouthed at Peyrac.

'Pink pearls, 'lambis' pearls. From the Caribbean . . .'

'Yes. I expect you will find a use for them. They don't come most people's way.'

The man seemed embarrassed by the magnificence of the gift.

'Thank you, my lord,' he stammered at last. Then he gave several quick little bows and, still looking at Peyrac, suddenly began to look frightened, and took his leave of them as if taking flight.

And this was why, when Angélique reached the coast at Sabadahoc, she had found the bay deserted.

CHAPTER TWENTY-ONE

GEORGE SHAPLEIGH's home on Maquoit Bay was nothing more than a decrepit log-and-bark cabin, battered by the wind and standing on the tip of a promontory with leaning cedar trees.

The fence enclosing the property scarcely merited the name

of palisade, but Angélique and her English companions had taken nearly a day to cover the three leagues that separated the Androscoggin river from this long narrow peninsula, and the proffered shelter was welcome.

A fat old Indian woman who lived there and was perhaps the mother of the Indian accompanying the old medicine man gave them some pumpkin mash to eat, followed by clams, large shell-fish with delicious, pinkish flesh, of a similar variety to those found in Brittany. The hut also contained large quantities of herbal remedies – powders, herbs and balms, in boxes made of bark – which enabled Angélique to set about the task of treating the sick and wounded.

Although the woods had been spangled with the silvery flowers of the trientala, the star-flower, growing thick amid the tender grass, and in spite of the gentle cooing of doves and wood pigeons, the march had tried them sorely. The poor English had to be sustained and encouraged, for they were worn out, jaded, wounded and terrified. While they feared an encounter with evil spirits as they crossed the marshlands Angélique was far more anxious about the possibility of suddenly running into more shrieking painted savages with raised hatchets.

Twenty corpses stretched out in a flower-strewn valley, their skulls covered in blood, left to the circling birds of prey, would not mean much in that spring when almost 3,000 warriors set out to attack the New England settlements, devastated more than fifty of them and massacred several hundred settlers ...

Fields of iridescent flowers, downy dogwood, coral-red columbines twisting on their slender stems in the shade of the monumental oaks, for centuries to come the banks of the lovely Androscoggin river would tell their terrible tale.

Here they had reached the sea, and beyond the headland lay Casco Bay with its innumerable islands.

The sea crept in everywhere, in among the rocks and the trees, and they could smell the tang of salt and seaweed in the brisk wind while the barking of seals along the beaches mingled with the deep roar of the surf.

Around the log hut was a small field planted with maize, pumpkins and beans, and at the edge of the cliff, beneath a clump of stocky willow trees some beehives were beginning to come to life.

For two days they waited for sight of a sail. Then a Sheep-scot Indian, a friend of Shapleigh's, who came by, said that no paleface ship had been sighted in the direction of Sabadahoc.

What was the *Rochelais* doing? Where was Joffrey? Angél-ique was beginning to grow impatient, and in her mind's eye she began to envisage a horde of Abenakis to the east of the Kennebec, swarming down towards Gouldsboro.

What if Baron Saint-Castine had lured Joffrey de Peyrac into a trap? No, that was impossible. Joffrey would have suspected something ... But had not her own instinct failed her and found her strangely off guard? Had she not made fun of poor Adhemar when he had cried out in despair 'They are preparing their war cauldrons! Who are they going to kill?'

Adhemar seemed to have completely taken leave of his senses. He mumbled prayers over his rosary beads and stared about him with a lost look. And once again, he was right. On this solitary headland in this remote region, they were as isolated and as abandoned as if they had been on a desert island, yet their isolation did not entirely protect them from prowling savages who took a fancy to their scalps.

At any other time, the able-bodied among them might well have attempted to make their way on foot to some other settlement along the English coast of Maine, which was dotted with small villages, and there find a ship. But at that time, most of these wooden hamlets were in flames, and to head west would have been tantamount to walking straight towards the redskin knives. It was better to keep clear, to let themselves be for-gotten, wretched pale-skinned creatures stranded on this horrible, cruel coast of a wild, unruly continent. At least they had a roof over their heads, medicines for the sick, vegetables, shellfish and sea foods to feed their hunger, and a semblance of a fence to give them the illusion of safety. But their total lack of weapons worried Angélique; for, apart from old Shapleigh's blunderbuss with its limited supply of ammunition, all they had was Adhemar's musket with neither gunpowder nor bullets, a few cutlasses and their personal knives.

The sun had come out again, and Angélique entrusted Cantor with the task of watching the horizon for any sail which might be seen playing hide-and-seek among the islands, and which might possibly come close enough to them for them to be able to send some signal. But every ship they saw seemed to be head-ing in some other direction. With their white or brown sails billowing out over the brilliant blue waters, these vessels, totally unresponsive to any sound or gesture they might make, seemed from this great distance to behave in a human way and to show a degree of indifference that made their hearts ache.

In spite of his fear of the local tribes, Piksarett of the Abenakis had continued to keep his prisoners, as he still considered them, under intermittent surveillance. In fact he seemed rather to be looking after them, for during their trek down to the coast he had even put in an appearance to carry an exhausted child.

Then, when they were in the hut, he came and set down before them a calabash full of some wild root plants much appreciated by the English, who called them potatoes. Baked in hot ashes they were extremely tasty, less sugary than sweet potatoes or artichokes. He also brought them sweet smelling lichens and a huge salmon, which he grilled himself on a stick.

When the three savages appeared, with the giant Indian in the lead, the poor Brunswick-Falls folk started back hastily, for the Patsuiketts' belts were hung with drying scalps recently acquired from their relatives and friends. After exchanging a few words, Piksarett and his acolytes went off into the woods, but often when Angélique went outside to scan the horizon, she would see Piksarett and his two red companions on the other side of the fiord, perched in the treetops, watching something or other in the bay. They would wave to her and shout jokes, of which she only caught a mere scrap of phrases, but which she sensed were intended to be friendly.

One had to get used to the free and easy ways of the savages, and their rapidly changing moods, which had both a dangerous and a reassuring side, and one had to try to live with them as one might with wild animals, which can be tamed only by the ascendancy and force of character of the tamer. For the time being she had nothing to fear from them.

But should she once appear to falter, then indeed she would have everything to fear.

Piksarett had introduced her to his two braves, whose names were very easy to remember – Tenouienant, which means he-who-is-knowledgeable, he-who-is-skilled-in-business, and Ouaouenouroue, that is to say, he-who-is-as-cunning-as-a-dog-in-hunting.

On the whole she preferred to call them by their baptismal names, which they had told her with considerable pride – Michael and Jerome. These names, with their mild, pious associations, could scarcely have been more incongruous, applied to these men with painted faces – red encircling the left eye, symbol of the first wound, white around the other for clairvoyance, a dreadful black line across the forehead to frighten the enemy, a blue chin, the finger of Great Spirit, and so on – surmounted and encircled by a wild bush of hair mingled with feathers, furs, rosary beads and medals.

Their bare chests tattooed and painted, their leather loincloths flapping in the wind, often barefooted, smeared with grease, hung about with weapons, they would come towards her when she called them.

'Michael! Jerome!'

And she held in her laughter, suddenly touched at the sight of them.

Their language had a dreadfully difficult accent, which it was almost impossible to pick up, almost an English accent! It was precisely on account of his rather ridiculous title, Piksarett, chief of the Patsuiketts, that she had never managed to take him quite seriously. But, as he explained, even that was not the full story. Originally, on account of his happy nature he had been called Piouerlet, that is to say, he-who-understands-jokes, but his warlike exploits had caused his name to evolve towards Pikasou'rett, in other words, the terrible one, which the French pronounced Piksarett to make things easier.

So Piksarett it was!

Ever since the day when she had stood between him and the wounded Iroquois and had given him, in exchange for his enemy's life, her dawn-coloured cloak, the adventure of their strange friendship had begun, an alliance that supplied material for the gossip of the day, that startled, scandalized, disturbed and infuriated.

Angélique did not yet know the part that Piksarett would play in her life over the next few weeks, but she felt no fear of him.

He sometimes assumed a thoughtful expression and seemed to be replying to some unspoken question.

'Yes,' he would state, 'we had decided to deal with the Englishmen, but then the Frenchmen came back, and how could I disappoint those who had baptized me?'

Then, running his hand over his necklace of medallions and crosses, he went on:

'Baptism has been a good thing for us Wonolancets, whereas it was bad for the Hurons: they nearly all either died of smallpox or were massacred by the Iroquois. But we, we are Wonolancets, and that is different!'

Old Shapleigh talked a great deal to Angélique too. He had discovered how much she knew about plants, was only too happy to teach her more and argued with her when she did not share his particular beliefs. After examining the medicines she carried in her travelling bag, he reproached her for using belladonna, the devil's herb, because it had grown in the garden of Hecate.

On the other hand he was particularly fond of southernwood, 'a magnificent herb under the influence of Mercury and worthy of higher esteem than it receives'.

For the planets and their powers were also enclosed in these boxes, and he claimed that a piece of copper, a sprig of vervain and a dove were all 'Venusian'.

And about the blessed thistle he would say:

'That is a herb of Mars, who, under the sign of Aries, cures venereal diseases, out of antipathy for Venus who causes them. I sell a lot of it to seafaring men. They come and ask me for it under the pretext that they have plague on board, but I know what that means . . .'

And then, suddenly becoming genuinely scientific once more, he would give a Latin name to almost every herb he knew, and among all his wizard spells at the bottom of an old chest, she found a copy of the *Herbatum virtutibus* of Aemilius Maces, and one of the remarkable *Regimen sanitatis salerno* – veritable treasures!

Two days passed thus. They were like shipwrecked people, uncertain what fate held in store for them.

Towards the south-west, when the air was clear, they could just make out the curving line of the coast, from which puffs of grey rose, slowly merging with the hazy atmosphere that hung over the bay, pink and blue and milky white, like fine porcelain . . .

The grey patches marked the location of fires kindled by Indian torches . . .

Freeport, Yarmouth, all the neighbouring villages were in flames; Portland itself was threatened.

All that was far away, too far for them to descry the masses of people fleeing for their lives across the bay. Tall sails appeared and disappeared, like so many white wings mingled with those of the endlessly wheeling seagulls, cormorants and petrels.

There were so many birds that in spite of the dazzling June light, a sudden twilight would descend as thousands of wings swept in great waves across the sky, attracted this way and that by schools of cod, herring, tunny and mackerel, that had come to spawn in the waters of the great Massachusetts Bay which lies like a cornucopia open at one end to the Atlantic Ocean and closed at the other by the prosperous and terrible French Bay,* famous for its monstrous tides.

During their third day on Maquoit Point, Cantor said to his mother:

'If by tomorrow no ship or boat has cast anchor in this accursed place, I shall set off on foot, and follow the coast eastwards. If I can keep out of sight of the Indians and find a canoe here and there in which to cross channels and deltas, I should eventually reach Gouldsboro. By going alone, I shall attract less attention than if we travelled as a party.'

'Won't it take you days and days to complete an expedition of this kind?'

'I can walk as fast as any Indian.'

So she agreed to his plan, although she felt more apprehensive about his parting from them. She found comfort in the vigour of his youth, which had adapted itself to meet the unexpected contingencies of American life.

Something had to be done; they could not wait on indefinitely for some problematic help to turn up.

That evening, she continued to keep watch, aided by the brightness of the evening sky.

Screeching birds came to rest upon the waters in the estuaries of the many rivers. The soft, impalpable mist began to clear. Casco Bay was sinking to rest in dazzling serenity. The sea, flecked with gold, held up its islands like jewels, refulgent with many tinted gleams – burnt topaz, sulphur blue, jet black. There were 365 of them, so it was said, as many as there were days in the year.

The brightness faded again. The gold lost its lustre. The sea turned chill and wan, and little by little the land and its meandering shores melted into impenetrable darkness. The smell of the bay rose towards them, borne on the harsh wind. The entire landscape seemed to be made of brass and bronze.

Over towards the east, at Harpswell Point, just after the sun had disapeared, Angélique glimpsed. It looked as if made of gold as it was caught in the last rays of the setting sun. And then almost immediately she found she could see it no more.

'Did it have a giant shinbone on its prow?' cried the old medicine-man. 'I wager it was furling its sails, before returning to port. I know it. That was the ghost ship that appears at Harpswell Point whenever some calamity is about to befall him – or

* The present Bay of Fundy.

her – who sees it. And the port for which it is bound is – Death.'

'It was certainly not furling its sails,' rejoined Angélique crossly.

And young Cantor, seeing that she was upset by the old wizard's words, gave her a knowing wink by way of reassurance.

PART THREE

The Pirate Ship

CHAPTER TWENTY-TWO

The following morning very early, Angélique, being unable to sleep, went down among the rocks laid bare by low tide to gather shells. On a nearby beach the colony of seals, apparently in a state of high excitement, were giving vent to piercing cries that echoed round the coves.

Angélique went across to have a look at them, for normally they were peaceable animals. Clumsy and ungainly on land, their dark, glistening bodies looked delightfully supple when seen in the sparkling waters at sunset.

That morning, as she drew near, she discovered the cause of their unrest. Two or three of the seals lay dead, already shrouded by clouds of wheeling, screeching sea birds. They had been brutally bludgeoned to death, and their fellows, the giant bulls, lords of the beach, were trying angrily to drive off the greedy, feathered assailants.

As Angélique took in the scene she gave a start of fear, for the massacre was the work of human hands. MEN MUST HAVE BEEN HERE . . .

And they were not Indians, for the latter hunted seals only during the month of January, in other words in the winter season.

Angélique gazed around the creek. A ship, probably the one which Shapleigh had called a ghost ship, must have moored there during the night in the misty darkness.

She climbed back up the slope.

The sun had not yet appeared, for it was hidden behind a bank of cloud on the horizon, but the sky was a pristine blue, pure and calm.

Then a tang came to her through the fresh air, the tang of burning grasses, different from that of the smoke rising from the small stone chimney on the hut. Swift and light-footed, gliding instinctively behind the bushes and pinetrees, she made her way along the edge of the promontory that overhung the fiord.

The smell of smoke, the smoke of green wood and damp grass, was growing stronger.

Peering out from among the trees, Angélique caught sight

of the tip of a mast with a sail furled round it. A ship lay at anchor there, hidden by one of the many curves and bends in the long stretch of water that made its way inland. And the smoke rose up, lazily spreading out below where she stood, accompanied by a murmur of voices. Angélique lay down on the ground and crept forward to the edge of the cliff, but was unable to see those who had set up camp below her on the narrow strip of pebbles edged with seaweed. Only their voices appeared closer and she caught snatches of French and Portuguese spoken in rough, coarse tones.

On the other hand, she could now see the whole of the ship which was, in fact, a mere sloop.

Back at the hut, she called the children inside. Now that they had recovered from the weariness of the march, they had begun to play with a little horsehair ball.

'There are men camped down at the creek,' she told Cantor. 'They have a boat which would take at least eight or ten of us, but I am not sure they would be generous enough to give us passage.'

She felt little faith in men who were capable of the needless slaughter of innocent animals which they did not even bother to pick up.

Cantor in his turn set off to take a look at the place Angélique pointed out to him and returned saying that he had seen 'them', that there were five or six of them, no more, and that they belonged to the piratical rag, tag and bobtail that haunted the North American coastline during the summer in search of booty, no doubt less valuable but correspondingly less hard to acquire than that of the Spanish vessels.

'We need that boat,' Angélique insisted, 'if only to fetch help.'

She addressed her words mainly to Cantor and to Stoughton – the only other able-bodied man in any state to help her reach a decision.

The pastor was only half conscious, suffering as he was from a high fever. Corwin was injured, and in great pain, and required all his powers of concentration to keep from swearing in the presence of the pastor. The two farmhands, burly, taciturn men, were prepared to tackle anything requiring muscle but were useless when it came to offering advice. Old Shapleigh was dissociating himself from his guests, saying that he must leave them that evening or the following day to go off into the forest, as it would soon be the night when wild vervain must be picked.

And as for Adhemar, he had no sense of responsibility.

Only Stoughton remained, a farmer, who, though lacking in imagination, was courageous, and Cantor, son of a nobleman, whose short life had already been rich in experience. In her son, Angélique placed her trust in the wisdom of early adolescence, a period of development which combines instinctive prudence, a sense of one's own powers and the boldness of manly courage.

Cantor undertook to capture the sloop under the buccaneers' very eyes, and to sail it round to the other side of the promontory, where the rest of the company would embark.

At this point in the discussion Angélique stood up and went across to open the door, realizing immediately what it was that had attracted her attention outside.

The cry of a nightjar could be heard, repeated over and over again, a deep throated, insistent cry.

Piksarett was calling her.

She ran to the edge of the headland and there, on the opposite shore, at the top of a black oak, she caught sight of the Indian who, half hidden amidst the leafy boughs, was making frantic gestures in her direction, pointing to something just below where she stood.

She looked down towards the shore and her blood ran cold, for there were men, clambering up towards her, pulling themselves up by tufts of juniper and the stunted pines that grew in the fissures of the cliff face.

Beyond any doubt, they were the pirates from the sloop, and when one of them, realizing that they had been detected, raised his villainous countenance and looked up at her, she saw that he held a knife between his teeth.

They too must have discovered that they had neighbours on this lonely shore, and, inveterate pillagers that they were, they were on their way to take them by surprise.

But seeing that their surprise attack had been discovered, they cursed abominably and began to scramble more rapidly up the cliff.

Angélique's eyes lighted on the beehives beside her. Before running away, she seized one of them, and just as the filibusters reached the edge of the plateau, she hurled the hive and its buzzing contents at them.

The object struck them full in the face and they immediately began to yell and scream in the most terrifying way. She did not wait to watch them trying to beat off the black cloud of infuriated bees.

As she ran, she drew out her well-sharpened knife – a wise precaution, for the bandits had split up into two groups.

A sniggering, clown-like figure sprang up between her and John Shapleigh's dwelling. He was dressed in tawdry finery and wore a three-cornered hat with scarlet ostrich feathers. He was brandishing a cudgel.

He must either have been tipsy or have thought that from a woman he had nothing to fear, for he made a rush at her, and, as she ducked to one side to avoid his stick as it whistled through the air, he tripped and literally impaled himself on the sharp blade she had held out in front of her as her only means of defence.

The man gave a hoarse cry and for a brief moment she smelt on her face the foul breath of a rum drinker with rotten teeth. His hands ceased to clutch her, and he almost pulled her over as he fell. Chilled with horror, she thrust him aside and saw him collapse at her feet, his hands clutching at his belly, while his rheumy eyes wore an expression of utter astonishment.

Angélique was prudent enough to take no further interest in the man's fate. She raced back to Shapleigh's hut and fastened the gate of the shaky palisade.

CHAPTER TWENTY-THREE

'HE'S LOSING his guts!'

The lugubrious cry rang through the clear air of the June evening and echoed over Casco Bay.

'He's losing his guts!'

Out there behind the bushes man was calling to man, and the besieged English and French heard the cry from their carefully barricaded hut.

The day so disastrously begun was drawing to a close with the contestants more or less equally matched. Angélique and the English on one side, admittedly with few weapons, but very much on their guard behind the shelter of their log walls, and the pirates on the other, ferocious and aggressive, but terribly stung and saddled in addition with a wounded man whose guts were spilling out of him.

Unfortunately for Angélique and her companions the pirates had taken refuge by a stream close to the house in order to bathe their swollen bee-stung faces and limbs.

From this vantage point, they could prevent anyone from leaving the hut, and alternately shouted abuse and moaned. They were hidden from sight but their presence could be sensed behind a screen of trees, from which direction came the sound of their lamentations.

When the night had fallen, their wails, sighs and cries of pain filled the air at regular intervals, and what with the baying of the seals down on the beach, the noise was enough to set one's hair on end.

Soon moonlight flooded the scene; the sea turned to silver and the whole flotilla of inky black islands seemed to be about to set sail for some distant white horizon.

Towards the middle of the night, Angélique climbed on a stool and lifted a tile off the roof so that she could look outside and obtain a general view of the situation.

'Listen to me down there, you sailors!' she called in French, in a loud, clear voice.

She saw the shadowy figures of the pirates move.

'Now listen to me; we can come to terms. I have medicines here to ease your suffering. I can dress the wounds of the injured man ...

'Come forward to within two fathoms of the house and throw down your arms. We do not seek your death, we only want to save our own lives and to borrow your boat. In exchange for this, your injuries will be attended to.'

At first silence was their only reply, but it was shortly followed by the muffled sound of whispering that mingled with the gusty wind.

'We shall attend to your wounds,' Angélique repeated. 'Otherwise you will die. Bee stings are certain death, and if your wounded friend receives no attention, that will be the end of him.'

'You're telling us! The end of him ... He's losing his guts, he's had it,' a thick voice muttered out of the darkness.

'It won't do him any good, that's certain. Now be sensible. Throw down your arms, as I said, and I will take care of you.'

Coming to them through the night, her gentle womanly voice seemed reassuring, as if it came from heaven itself.

But the pirates did not give in at once. They held out till dawn.

'Hi there, woman!' someone shouted, 'we are coming.'

There was a clang of steel from behind the bushes and a heavy figure staggered out, laden with an array of cutlasses, knives, boarding swords, an axe, and a small pistol.

All of which he laid down a few paces from the palisade.

Angélique, covered by old Shapleigh's blunderbusses and by Cantor holding the musket, walked towards the man. He was almost blinded by the swelling from the bee stings that covered his entire face, while the skin of his neck, his shoulders, his arms and his hands was puffy and tight.

Shapleigh pushed his tall puritan hat back on his head and circled round the man sniggering and sniffing merrily.

'I see . . . I see! The pumpkin seems to be just ripe!'

'Have mercy on me!' the man begged.

His shirt, darkened with old bloodstains, and his short cotton breeches that left his hairy knees uncovered, were the typical get-up of an authentic buccaneer.

His belt, from which hung sheaths for knives of every conceivable size, at present empty, but very numerous, indicated beyond any shadow of doubt that he was one of those men who hunted, killed, and cut up wild pig and wild oxen on the islands of the Caribbean, then, after curing their flesh, sold it to revictual passing ships. They were ocean butchers, in fact, one could even call them traders, no worse than the rest, but driven to piracy and war by the conquering Spaniards who would tolerate no presence other than their own in the American archipelagos.

His companions behind the clump of trees were in still worse shape than he. A puny, sickly-looking ship's boy looked as if he was about to die, the Portuguese with the olive skin looked very much like a cabbage and the last man, a rather swarthy fellow, looked like a gourd. As for the man who had been wounded . . .

Angélique lifted the filthy rag that had been thrown over him, and a gasp of horror and alarm went up from the bystanders. Angélique herself had to fight back the wave of nausea that swept over her.

The gaping wound was at least fifteen inches long, through which protruded a considerable length of extruded intestine, that had the appearance of a writhing nest of serpents, twisting and squirming spasmodically, a nightmare vision of the entrails of a man with his belly split open!

Everybody stood motionless, glued to the ground, except

Piksarett, who had suddenly appeared and was examining the horrible sight with amused curiosity.

Almost immediately Angélique sensed that it was an outside chance, and the wounded man, who had not fainted but on the contrary seemed clear headed and vaguely mocking in his manner was watching her every move from bright eyes beneath his bushy eyebrows. In spite of his waxen hue and his drawn features, Angélique could see none of the signs of death on his ugly, drunken face. It seemed extraordinary, but the man looked determined to live. The stab had not perforated the gut, otherwise he would undoubtedly have died shortly afterwards.

It was he who spoke first, in a muffled voice, as he attempted to suppress a grimace:

'Yes, my lady! For a dirty trick that one takes a bit of beating, eh? Real Gippo stuff, I calls it, and I know what I'm talking about. Now you will have to sew it all up for me again.'

He must have been mulling it over during his long night of agony, and had gradually convinced himself that it might be possible. A funny little chap, not lacking in intelligence, although he was undoubtedly a prime scoundrel. He was the leader or captain of the rascally five. It did not take more than a glance at him and his companions to see what kind of men they were. The scum of the sea! Angélique looked first at the man's face, which reflected a diabolical vitality, then at the monstrous hernia with its putrid smell around which blowflies had already begun to buzz.

'All right,' she decided, 'we'll see what we can do.'

CHAPTER TWENTY-FOUR

'I'VE SEEN worse,' she kept on telling herself as she hastily laid out a few instruments from her bag on a piece of board in the hut.

That was not absolutely correct, although she had been obliged during the winter at Wapassou, to carry out what amounted to regular operations of increasing diversity and complexity. The extraordinary skill of her slender, nimble fingers, that seemed to possess a life of their own, the sure, instinctive movements of her healing hands, had encouraged her to perform experiments which in that country and at that time could only be called bold.

For example, when spring came she had nursed an Indian chief whose back had been gashed by the horn of a moose, and had made her first attempt to join the two edges of the wound with a few stitches. The wound had healed with astonishing rapidity.

Her reputation had spread, and at Houssnock a horde of redskins had descended on her, asking for treatment from the paleface lady of the Silver Lake.

She had chosen the finest needles available from the stock they used for trading, and Monsieur Jonas, with the skilled fingers of a watchmaker, had given them a slightly curved shape, which Angélique considered preferable for this kind of delicate work. She congratulated herself on having saved her precious travelling bag from all the recent disasters. It was wonderful. She found in it all kinds of things that she needed – a sachet containing a handful of crushed acacia pods, a powder rich in medicinal tannin which she kept to make poultices that might prevent poisonous humours from spreading through the body once the wound was closed. There was not enough of it, and she showed the acacia powder to Piksarett who, after examining it and sniffing at it, gave an understanding smile and dashed off towards the forest.

'You see to the ship with one of the Englishmen,' Angélique ordered Cantor. 'Make sure that it is ready to sail with part of our company. Keep on your guard and stay well armed, although these poor brutes don't look to me as if they could do much harm for the moment.'

Elizabeth Pidgeon timidly offered to help Angélique, but Angélique thought it better to send her to attend to the unfortunate victims of the bees. With the Reverend Patridge's head to dress as well, the old maid had plenty to do, and, bearing in mind the new situation, she chose from among the pirates' weapons the sword with the least jagged edge, and, tucking it bravely into her belt, trotted off to the hut where Shapleigh was beginning to dispense his remedies to the accompaniment of a great display of mirth.

Beneath the tree beside the wounded man, Angélique took a flat stone, brushed it clean, and laid out on it her needle case, her tweezers, reed clips and birch funnel, a flask of very strong brandy, a pair of scissors, and some lint, which she kept clean and white in an oil-cloth bag.

There was no need to move the man, for the stream ran hard by, and she rekindled a little fire, and placed a small earthenware pot on it with a little water in the bottom, to which she added the acacia pod powder.

Piksarett returned with handfuls of green pods, Angélique took one of them, bit into it, and pulled a wry face as she spat out the green, astringent sap. Although it had an extremely unpleasant taste, it had still not acquired the full flavour of mature tannin, which had a metallic, inky taste and possessed the invaluable property of closing wounds, helping them to heal, preventing them from going dangerously septic and finally, by its tonic and vivifying power, preventing the suppuration that made all wounds, even healthy ones, take so long to heal. These green pods would be less efficacious.

'We shall have to make do with these.'

She was about to put them on to boil when Piksarett stopped her.

'Let Maktera do it,' he said. And he pointed to the old Indian woman, Shapleigh's servant or companion. She seemed to know the properties of the plant and, crouching down beside the fire, began to chew the pods, before spreading them out on large leaves to serve as poultices. Angélique did not interfere, for she knew – the old sorcerer from Beaver Camp near Wapassou had taught her – that prepared in this way the remedy would be most effective.

Then she returned to her patient, whose eyes, still wide open, shone with both hope and fear as he saw her kneel beside him, her face framed by the gold of her hair bearing an expression of such concentrated resolution that the old buccaneer felt himself grow weak, and his villainous countenance assumed an almost pathetic look.

'Easy now, my beauty,' he whispered, and his voice seemed to have grown weaker. 'Before you start, we'd better have a chat, you and me. If you manage to patch me up, and I find myself on an even keel again, you aren't a-going to take all our arms away from us and make us hand over our old tub, are you? They're all that swine Gold Beard allowed us to try to keep body and soul together with in this damned wilderness. You wouldn't want to be even worse than him, now would you?'

'Gold Beard,' said Angélique, pricking up her ears. 'Are you members of his crew?'

'We were ... That son-of-a-bitch put us ashore here without

even enough powder to protect ourselves against wild animals, savages and people like you lot along the coast; all wreckers, every man-jack of you . . .'

'Stop talking now,' said Angélique, preserving a calm front, 'you are too talkative for a man at death's door. We'll talk about all this later.'

The man had worn himself out, and his waxen skin seemed to have shrunk back into the hollows of the bones of his face, giving it the appearance of a death mask, with a red circle round his protruding eyes.

But it was precisely his red-ringed eyelids that indicated his ultimate capacity to survive. 'He will live,' she thought, and her lips tightened. She would think about Gold Beard later.

'It is too early to lay down conditions, sirrah,' she continued aloud. 'We shall do whatever we choose with your weapons and your boat, and you will be lucky if you live.'

'In any case . . . it'll take days . . . to patch . . . the old tub . . . up,' the man whispered, unwilling to give in.

'And you too, it will take days to patch you up, you block-head. And now, my lad, save what strength you have, and keep quiet.'

And she laid her hand on the slack flesh of his brow that was sticky with sweat.

She deliberated whether to give him a calming potion, based on the very belladonna that Shapleigh did not like. Nothing was going to be strong enough to overcome the dreadful pain of the operation.

'A good strong toddy,' the man moaned, 'give me a good strong toddy, burning hot, with half a lemon in it, let me have a last toddy . . .'

'Not a bad idea,' Angélique remarked, 'It will help him to get over the shock. This filibuster is so completely steeped in rum that it may be his salvation . . . Hi, you rascal there,' she called to one of the buccaneers who was still able to walk and who had made his way towards them, 'you wouldn't have a pint of rum by you, would you?'

The man nodded as far as his painful swellings allowed him, and, accompanied by one of the Englishmen, made his way down to the camp on the shore and returned with a black glass flask with a long neck, half full of the best West Indian rum, if the smell that filled the air when Angélique uncorked the bottle was anything to go by.

'Here you are,' she said. 'Drink that, my lad, as much as you can, until the sky begins to spin round you like a top.'

Because she was suddenly talking to him in this familiar way he realized that things had become very serious.

'It's going to hurt,' he moaned, then added with a desperate glance:

'Is there anyone to hear my confession in this god forsaken hole?'

'I can,' Piksarett replied, falling to his knees. 'I am chief catechist to Black Robe and chief of all the Abenaki tribe. The Lord has chosen me to administer the sacraments of baptism and absolution.'

'Jesus Christ, a savage, that takes the biscuit or I must be barmy!' the wounded man exclaimed, and lost consciousness, either from shock or from exertion.

'It's better this way,' said Angélique.

'I'll clean the wound,' she thought, 'with warm water and some essence of belladonna.'

She picked up a small piece of bark shaped like a funnel which enabled her to direct the thin stream of water from the calabash held by Piksarett on to the wound, as she leaned over the gaping hole.

At the very first touch, light as it was, the wounded man shuddered and tried to sit up, but Stoughton's strong hands held him back.

Angélique laid the tall buccaneer across his comrade's thighs, while Shapleigh's Indians held his ankles. Finding the position uncomfortable, the wounded man half regained consciousness and begged them to lift his head so that he could swallow a few more swigs of rum, then, in a state of semi-consciousness, he allowed them to tie his wrists to two stakes driven into the ground. Angélique rolled some lint into a ball, placed it between his teeth, and supported the nape of his neck on a bundle of straw, while she checked that he could breathe easily through his nose.

The old English doctor was kneeling on his other side; he had doffed his big hat and the wind stirred his curly, white locks. Without needing to be told what she wanted, he seized the reed clips and placed the first of them in position preparatory to drawing the edges of the wound together. It was almost impossible to join them completely in this way, but Angélique, in one abrupt, resolute movement, drove her needle into the flesh which, in spite of its flabby appearance, was extremely tough and resistant, and held the skin together with her fingers while with an imperceptible flick of the wrist that required uncommon strength and dexterity, she drew the waxed thread through and tied it in a knot. She worked swiftly and rhythmically, never hesitating, leaning over the man, completely still save for the inexorable movement of her two deft hands. Old John followed her movements, helping her with clips or with his fingers when the thrust of the tortured flesh forced the clips apart.

The wretched martyr lay prostrate but his whole body was continually shaken by troublesome twitching movements, and from time to time a terrible cry broke through the gag, a cry that sounded as if it would be his last. Then the coiling mass of guts, slimy and incessantly moving, would project again, threatening to burst out, and she would have to push them back inside as if smothering some animal. The loops, white and purple in colour, kept on oozing out through the slightest gap, forming innumerable hernias, and Angélique was in constant fear lest one of these should burst or become perforated, which she realized would be fatal. But the gut held good, and finally the last knot was tied.

The man looked as if he were dead.

Angélique took the tannin poultices handed to her by the Indian woman, covered the whole of his belly with them, and bound him up tightly with the strips of cloth she had laid under his back before beginning the operation.

Bound up tight like this, all old Blockhead had to do was to get used to his intestines being in their proper place again, and it was to be hoped that they would make up their minds to stay put.

Angélique stood up, her back nearly broken. She had been working for over an hour.

She went and washed her hands in the stream, then came back and tidied her things away.

She could hear the sound of a mallet coming from the creek. The boat would be ready to sail well before its wretched captain.

Angélique de Peyrac lifted the wounded man's eyelids and listened to his heart. He was still alive. Then, as she looked at him from the tip of his filthy feet covered with corns, to his unkempt shock of hair, she felt a pang of sympathy for this miserable outcast of society whose wretched life she had saved.

CHAPTER TWENTY-FIVE

THERE WAS not room for everyone, especially not the sick and wounded, on board the pirate sloop after it had been rendered seaworthy again. Choosing who should remain and who should leave inevitably involved conflicts of conscience, and once again Angélique was obliged to give a lead.

It was obvious that Cantor, who was a skilled sailor, should captain the boat as far as Gouldsboro. Stoughton and Corwin, who had grown up beside the sea, would man the ship and it seemed right that their entire families should go with them. Their hired hands did not want to be parted from them; they would die of fear, they said, without their masters, and would not know what to do with themselves. These people alone were enough to fill the boat, and there was no question of taking on board those who were sick enough to need to lie down. From the outset Angélique had realized that she would have to stay behind with them, and never had her sense of responsibility cost her so dear. But how could she leave these dying people to their fate; the hulking parson Patridge no more than the bee-stung pirates and the surgical case, who was beginning miraculously to heal. Cantor protested vehemently, appalled at the idea of leaving his mother behind in such wretched and dangerous company.

'But you do realize, don't you,' she told him, 'that we cannot take any of these sick people on board. They would interfere with the sailing of the ship, would require care that we were unable to give them on board, and might well die at sea.'

'Well, let them stay here with old Shapleigh to look after them.'

'Shapleigh has told me that he must go off to the forest one of these nights, and that he cannot put off his journey because of the moon. I think that above all he does not want to remain alone with these dregs of the Caribbean . . .'

'And what about you, wouldn't you be exposing yourself to great danger in their company?'

'I can look after myself. And in any case, they are all as sick as dogs.'

'Not all of them. One of them is much stronger already, and I don't like the look of him.'

'Well then, here is the answer. You take him on board, and Corwin and Stoughton can keep an eye on him until you can put him ashore on some island in Casco Bay. Then make as fast as you can for Gouldsboro. With a good wind, I might even see you back here in the *Rochelais* in less than a week. Nothing very dreadful could happen to me in that time . . .'

She was trying to convince herself, and Cantor finally agreed that there was no other solution possible.

The sooner they set sail, the sooner the whole family would be reunited, safe and sound inside the walls of Gouldsboro, which they thought of as a haven of peace and the end of all their worries. At Gouldsboro there were arms, money, men, and ships . . .

Now only eight of them remained on the promotory overlooking Maquoit Bay.

It was two days since the pirate sloop, all sails set, and expertly steered by Canto, had glided out of the creek and, bowing like a seagull before the wind, disappeared behind the farthest islands.

It had borne away with it the Corwin and Stoughton families together with their servants, little Rose-Ann and the least unwell of the pirates, whom they would get rid of on one of the islands at the earliest opportunity. He had spoken at great length in his lingo to his companions before setting off, but a close watch would be kept on him.

Little Sammy Corwin, his burns still not properly healed, had stayed behind, as had the Reverend Thomas, who was too weak to travel, and Miss Pidgeon, who had elected to remain with her pastor. As for Adhemar, he had at first wanted to go, but his fear of the sea and of the English had eventually prevailed and, all things considered, he had thought it preferable to remain with Angélique, having come to the conclusion that, whether for diabolical reasons or not, she must possess some kind of protective power. So Angélique set him the task of fetching wood, water and shellfish, and of fanning the sick men, who were tormented by mosquitos. In fact the sloop would have been quite unable to accommodate anyone else, and it had taken all Wolverine's wild impudence, swimming out frantically like a fat otter in the wake of the boat, to force Cantor to find room for him on board.

Angélique felt herself bound to the fretful carcass of her surgical case, who seemed bent on remaining alive and whose name was Aristide Beaumarchand, or so one of his friends had told her. (The name meant handsome merchant, which Angélique considered highly inappropriate. Blockhead or Slitbelly were names that suited him better.)

That morning the Reverend Patridge opened his eyes, remarked on the fact that it was Sunday, and asked for his Bible so that he could prepare his sermon. They thought he was delirious with fever, and tried to calm him, but he ranted and raved and was so insistent about it being Sunday, the Lord's Day, that there was no choice but to accept that Sunday it was.

A whole week had gone by since the attack on the English village.

Angélique still entertained the hope that some of Joffrey de Peyrac's ships were cruising in the mouth of the Kennebec. Cantor had undertaken to find one. But, he said, if he could not, he could be in Gouldsboro in under two days and would send help from there. A good, big, solid ship, protected by heavy cannon, a ship in which they would be able to rest as they crossed the open sea and return home quite free of anxiety.

How wonderful!

But two days had already elapsed without any sign of a sail on the horizon.

Elizabeth Pidgeon was reading to the pastor from the Bible in a quavering voice, while two of the sick buccaneers listened with suspicious, arrogant expressions. They had to be nursed, but no one was in a hurry to see them get better. The third, the tallest and strongest, spent his time between Slitbelly's bedside and that of his other two comrades lying in the hut, holding long confabulations in some more or less inaudible lingua franca. He was looking better. He was a huge, heavy fellow of unprepossessing appearance.

'Keep an eye on him,' Angélique told Adhemar. 'Otherwise he may manage to retrieve one of his knives and stick it in our backs.'

The man showed genuine solicitude for the surgical case.

'He's my brother,' he said.

'He doesn't look like you,' Angélique commented, comparing the giant standing before her with the puny form lying under the covers.

'We are brothers of the Barbary Coast. We have exchanged blood and shared our spoils for nearly fifteen years.'

And he added with a grin made the more hideous by the puffiness of his bee-stung face:

'Pr'aps that's why I've decided not to cut your throat ... because you saved Aristide's life ...'

She had to sit up with the latter at night. She had fixed up a piece of canvas over him, as a protection, less against the sun, which the tree shaded him from, than from the dew that fell nightly, and from sudden occasional showers, or even from flying spray which the wind blew in their direction at high tide.

She watched over him, determined, attentive, astonished to see the doomed man beginning to recover, and so fascinated by the possibility of success, that there were times when she almost began to like poor Aristide.

The very evening of the operation he had opened his eyes, called for tobacco, and asked for a toddy 'with a whole lemon on it ... which I want you to peel for me, Hyacinth.'

Although he did not get his toddy and lemon, which she replaced with a well-strained fish broth, he nevertheless progressed by leaps and bounds.

And on that famous Sunday, when pastor Thomas showed signs of improvement, she said to the man:

'Now I am going to help you to sit up.'

'To sit up, do you want to kill me?'

'No, but we must keep your blood moving to stop it thickening. And I forbid you to speak to me so familiarly, now that you are out of danger.'

'Good gracious! What a woman!'

'Come and give me a hand, Barbary butcher.'

Together they took hold of the man under the arms, heaved him up and supported him in a sitting position. He was deathly pale and covered in sweat.

'Brandy! Brandy!'

'Adhemar, bring me the flagon.'

When he had taken a drink, he seemed better; she propped him up against a pile of sacks covered with pelts and gazed at him with an air of satisfaction.

He wiped his damp brow. Angélique had shaved off his vermin-infested beard and now he looked as harmless as any little grocer, hen-pecked by his wife and pestered by his creditors.

'I'm no match for Gold Beard any more,' he wailed. 'And that's a fact ...'

She helped him to lie down again, and later, when he had had a rest, she said:

'Tell me about Gold Beard, and about this talk I hear among your friends of my being born from Satan's thigh.'

'Oh, it's nothing to do with me,' he said defensively.

'Do you know who I am?'

'Not very well, but Gold Beard does. You are the French woman from Gouldsboro who people do say is a witch and in cahoots with a magician who makes gold out of shells.'

'Why not out of rum while you're at it?' Angélique retaliated, keeping a straight face. 'That would just suit you, wouldn't it?'

'Well, that's how the gossip goes among the sailors we met in Frenchman Bay. Sailors must trust one another, you know.'

'Sailors? You are more like pirates than sailors. In any case sailors don't use your lingo.'

'You can talk for the two of us if you like,' Slitbelly replied with an air of injured dignity, 'but you can't say that of Gold Beard. Now there's a gentleman for you, believe you me! And what's more, he's the best sailor on the surface of the globe. And you can believe me when I say so, because apart from that, you saw how he treated us, that son-of-a-bitch, casting us adrift, abandoning us like maroons, virtually without supplies or arms in this savage-infested hole. He told us we dishonoured his ship.'

The Portuguese pirate, now somewhat less huffy, happened to be near by and agreed with the invalid:

'Yes, I have known Gold Beard even longer than you, chief, since we were in Goa and the West Indies. I quarrelled with him over this Gouldsboro business, but I shall always be sorry I did.'

Angélique kept on running her fingers through her hair, for the wind was blowing it over her eyes and she had to keep pushing it back.

She tried to gather her thoughts together, but the deafening wind distracted her and she found it impossible to think straight.

'Do you mean to say that you knew who I was and that *I was here*, when Gold Beard put you down in the creek?'

'No, that we didn't know,' Beaumarchand replied. 'That was luck, that was. Luck that tips the wink to likely lads such as us when we find ourselves in a mess. It's not the first time that luck has got us out of a spot of bother by the skin of our teeth, and that's a fact, ain't it Hyancinth?'

'But how did you know I was here?' she insisted impatiently.

'Well, it's like this here, you see. When we realized there were people up on the cliff we climbed up and listened, and then we cottoned on that it was you, the Frenchwoman from

Gouldsboro, the Countess of Peyrac, and that you were with a crowd of English. Then, we thought our luck was in, see?'

'What do you mean, your luck?'

'Well, what Gold Beard had said, o'course – that he had orders respecting Count and Countess Peyrac, and that he had to be killed and she must be captured . . .'

'Is that all? Orders from whom?'

Angélique's heart was thudding in her breast. Her drunken patient had this to be said for him, that he was as garrulous as a magpie and forever swigging at the bottle, with the result that he chatted on without rhyme or reason.

CHAPTER TWENTY-SIX

A TWIST of the lips indicated that he did not know the answer to that question.

'It was since he went to Paris before his last campaign in the Caribbean. To get his papers signed by the minister. You went with him, didn't you, Lopez?'

The Portuguese sailor nodded.

'And who was it that had to be killed?' Angélique insisted.

'The man you're with, the Count, the man who makes gold out of shells.'

'You had to kill him! And was that why you tried to take me prisoner . . . ?'

'Gawd a'mighty! Put yourself in our place. And now that you have slit me open and sewn me up again, I know you *must* be a witch, and that's a fact.'

And he gave her a wink – although whether it was meant to be a sly or a nasty one she could not tell – accompanied by a sardonic, noiseless chuckle.

'Then why did your captain put you ashore here?' she asked.

'We fell out about the sharing out of the spoil; but that is no woman's business, even if she is a witch,' Aristide replied haughtily.

'More likely because you were out of place in his crew, if he's the gentleman you say he is,' Angélique rejoined.

It had not taken a second glance at the five pirates to see that they were scum – the kind of men Joffrey de Peyrac had had to hang from the masthead during his last voyage.

Stung to the quick, the man took refuge in a dignified silence.

'What was your Gold Beard going to do in Gouldsboro?' Angélique persisted.

The wounded man could not keep up his huffish silence for long.

'Come off it, don't be daft! Seize his lands of course!'

Angélique stared back in astonishment.

'No need to open your peepers like a couple of plates with whiskers, my beauty. I already told you that Mister Gold Beard is a privateer who has all the right credentials from the minister, his company in Paris, and even from the Government of Tortuga. And, what is more' – the wounded man held up his finger portentously – 'and, what is more, he obtained and bought as a concession from the King of France, all the land that lies between the tip of the Blue Mountains and Gouldsboro Bay.'

'Now I understand!' Angélique exclaimed.

'It is an idea he's always had in his head, Gold Beard, 'spite of him being a sailor. He always wanted to settle with some of his companions on some piece of land somewhere and grow French wheat. That was how we came to fall out with him, me and Lopez. You see, I have a mind to knock about the world until I end up feeding the sharks, and I was the one in the right of it. Gold Beard, clever as he is and for all the King's backing, he found out just where his big ideas of colonization got him. Red hot cannon balls below the waterline, that's what them Gouldsboro folk gave him. Hard as nails they are. Our poor *Heart of Mary* ...'

'What's that?'

'The name of our ship.'

Angélique made the mental note that the more villainous the intentions of pirates the more anxious they seemed to choose a pious name for their ship, no doubt in the hope of obtaining protection, or forgiveness from the powers above.

'Did your master really not know that those coastal lands were already owned by someone and that there were settlers living there?'

'We were told that there were women there. White women, not Indian. So you see, damn me, that was just the job. We were going to grab the land and start off with a wife apiece. What you call a real colony! But there was nothing doing! Red hot cannon balls, like I said, and when we tried to set foot on shore the beggars hacked us to bits. The ship was beginning to list, and caught on fire, and all we could do was to beat it for the islands like a lot of cowards. So much for my precious Gold Beard and his silly visions of grandeur, his charter under his arm and his plan to plough the land – and the women – so much for all that . . .'

He gave a raucous laugh that terminated in a fit of coughing.

'You mustn't cough,' said Angélique severely.

She made sure that his wound had not been stretched.

A dreadful, low scoundrel, this man Aristide, but if he was telling the truth, she had received some most valuable information.

She trembled at the thought that had not the Huguenots in Gouldsboro sprung so valiantly to their defence, her women friends from La Rochelle might well have fallen into the hands of these wretches.

'No, Gold Beard is not what you think,' the sick man went on, his voice weaker but still determined, as if he had followed her thoughts. 'He has the regular credentials, the King's support as a privateer sailing under the fleur-de-lis, and princes to lend him money, he has it all, I tell you. He treated me rough, but on board his ship, we had nothing to complain about. He's a gentleman, I tell you, that Gold Beard. And as for our daily ration of brandy, we got that every day just like on the King's ships. We were quite something, I tell you . . . You wouldn't have a bit of cheese, would you, m'lady?'

'Cheese? Are you mad! Go to sleep!' Angélique replied. And she pulled his covers up to his chin, tucked him in and wiped his weak mouth.

'Poor old Bockhead! You aren't worth the rope to hang you with.'

And in spite of the coldness of these shores, the barking seals, and the dark banks of fir trees standing black along the edge of the beaches, as she looked at him she thought of the pirates she had encountered in the Mediterranean with its motley population of adventurers of all races, and she felt the old fascination and fear . . .

Back in Brunswick-Falls, Mrs Williams had told her that in the old days even the toughest of these gentlemen of adventure who used to cast anchor off the poor villages of the New England settlers would never have harmed anyone, but those days were gone. Better living standards and increased wealth along the American coastline now attracted the looters.

The whole coastline needed to be cleaned up, policed, and an end put to the anarchy that everywhere prevailed. And she saw in her mind's eye the tall silhouette of Joffrey, trusty and reliable, as if involved with everything that was life and action. He appeared to her as the male principle of a new world.

Oh, my love! They had said that he must be killed . . .

He would not allow himself to be killed.

But what with the rekindled Indian war that was sending terrified populations scurrying across the bays and island, that had reopened the issue of alliances with distant kingdoms, the task looked like being a complex one, and any predatory vessels would be sure to find their fill of spoils. By what tangle of chance or design had she herself been driven here, whereas only a few days earlier she had left Fort Wapassou thinking she would make her way unimpeded to their lands at Gouldsboro?

'Lopez,' she said, breaking off her reverie, 'you were in Paris with this Gold Beard when he went to have his papers signed, and no doubt to obtain money to fit out his ship. Which lord was his patron? Who were the owners or his partners? Can you tell me any of their names?'

But the Portuguese shook his head.

'No . . . I was only there as his valet. Sometimes other valets would bring messages. There was also . . .'

He appeared to be thinking.

'I don't know his name. But if ever you meet a tall ship's captain with a port wine stain there, a purple mark' – he lifted his hand to his brow – 'watch out, your enemies are not far off. One good turn deserves another – after all, witch or no, you did save my mate . . .'

CHAPTER TWENTY-SEVEN

AND NOW evening was falling once more over Casco Bay, trailing a long orange glow out towards the west where the land slopes down in a long curve, plunging suddenly to the south in a vast caressing sweep round a land of myriad inlets and islands that fill the vast blue circle of sea, into which, drawn along by the northern currents, come swimming the blue and silver shoals of fish.

These are the breeding grounds of fish from all over the world, the junction of the great warm and cold ocean currents teeming with their vast reserves of plankton that attract the fish, offering a never-ending supply for fishermen the world over since the dawn of time.

Men from Saint-Malo used to come here in their sloops many centuries before Christopher Columbus discovered the West Indies.

During the spring months, the sea was alive with white sails, like the full-blown petals of giant water lilies.

The darker it got, the more clearly could Angélique pick out the glow of fires shining through the dark expanse, far away and flickering like stars.

'He don't drink,' Aristide muttered beside her ... 'What do you think of a sailor who don't drink?'

'Who are you talking about, my lad?'

'That dratted Gold Beard ... He don't drink except when he has a woman. And that's not often. Almost as if he didn't like women ... nor drinking. Yet he's a terrible man. When we captured Portobello he made the monks from the monastery of San Antonio walk in front of his men as a shield, and the Spaniards in the garrison were in tears as they fired on them.'

Angélique shuddered.

'The man must be a fiend.'

'No, not as much as you might think. Prayers are always said on board his ship, and anyone unruly gets sent up into the split-sail crow's-nest to say the rosary twenty times.'

Angélique, ill at ease, imagined she saw the bloodthirsty pirate's golden beard floating in the darkness. The mere thought that such a man's ship had lain at anchor for a whole night at the foot of the promontory when he had come to disembark his mutineers, made her flesh creep.

'He'll be back, you'll see,' the wounded man moaned.

Angélique was shaken by a second shudder and the howling of the wind in the cedars had a sinister sound to her ears as a sudden flash of summer lightning lit up the horizon.

'Go to sleep, my friend.'

She drew the folds of her cloak about her, for she intended to sit with him until the middle of the night, after which the other buccaneer, his blood brother, would take over. He was huddled up before the fire too, a giant of a man, his head sunk between his shoulders, and she could hear him scratching at his unkempt beard to relieve the itching of his tormented skin.

As she sat thinking of a thousand different things with her

head turned towards the stars, she did not notice that he was staring at her with glistening eyes. Now that he was beginning to recover, he found himself experiencing strange sensations when he looked at this woman. Motionless as a statue in her black cloak, her face emerging from above it like a patch of moonlight, there was always one golden curl that kept straying across her cheek until she brushed it back with her hand. This single movement conjured up the full richness of her hidden beauty in all its vigorous curves, which he so admired.

'Now me, I'm not like Gold Beard,' he said softly. 'I like women.'

And he cleared his throat.

'Don't you occasionally allow yourself a bit of fun, m'lady?'

She turned her head slowly towards the huge fellow.

'With people of your kind? No, my boy.'

'What is it about people of my kind that you don't like?'

'A face like a pumpkin far too ugly for anyone to kiss it.'

'It ain't necessary to kiss if you don't care for that,' came his conciliatory reply. 'There are other things we could do.'

'You stay right where you are,' she rapped out, seeing him about to move towards her. 'I've slit open many a man for less than that. As for you, I wouldn't bother to sew you up again, either.'

'You're a hard nut, aren't you,' he growled, frenziedly scratching at himself again. 'It's a good opportunity I'm offering you. We are all alone, we have plenty of time. Hyacinth is my name ... Hyacinth Boulanger. Do you really not feel like it?'

'No I don't, if you don't mind. Prudence dictates, Hyacinth,' she went on somewhat flippantly, so as not to antagonize him. 'Sailors marooned on beaches are not always in the pink of health. Just by looking at you I'd be prepared to wager that you're rotten with pox to the very marrow of your bones.'

'No I'm not, that's not true, I swear it,' the pirate exclaimed in outraged tones. 'The reason why I look the way I do is on account of your damned beehives that you hurled at our heads.'

Then Aristide growled:

'Stop fighting over my head as if I were already a stiff.'

Silence fell once more.

Angélique told herself that there was nothing to get agitated about. She had seen worse. But in the state of latent anxiety she was in, the desire this sinister individual felt for her in the middle of this lugubrious night along this weather-beaten, deserted coastline filled her with a sense of uneasiness and almost unbearable horror. Her nerves were so on edge that she felt an almost irresistible longing to run away as far as her legs would carry her. But she forced herself to sit still and to appear indifferent so that the man would not guess that she was afraid. Then she chose the first suitable opportunity to get up, told the buccaneer to keep an eye on the fire and on his blood brother, and walked back to the cabin.

Miss Pidgeon, leaning over the glowing embers, looked like some tiny witch busy preparing her potions.

Angélique bent down over the boy Sammy, touched his warm brow, felt his bandages, then after smiling at the old maid, went outside again and sat down behind the hut beside the Indian woman Maktara.

The half moon was just emerging from the clouds. It was a night when no one could sleep. The rapid chirping of the crickets was like a high-pitched, syncopated accompaniment to the mingled music of the wind and the sea.

The old medicine man appeared, wrapped in his flowing cloak which covered everything between his collar and the brim of his hat except the big round lenses of his spectacles across which the moonlight suddenly darted in two pointed shafts of light. His Indian followed him like a shadow, likewise enveloped in his red blanket, holding the blunderbuss cradled in his arms.

'This time,' said Shapleigh, 'I really am off to pick the wild vervain, the sacred herb, the sorcerer's weed; Juno's tear, a drop of Mercury's blood, the joy of simples. It must be picked near the rising of Sirius, when neither the sun nor the moon are above the horizon to witness the act, and hard by the night when the signs are in conjunction. I can wait no more . . . I have left you two charges of gunpowder for your musket and something to drug your patients with to render them less dangerous . . . Keep a sharp eye open for the ruffians!'

She replied softly in English: 'Thank you, Mr Shapleigh.'

He took a few steps, then turned round to listen to the soft, strange voice that had murmured in the night: 'Thank you, Mr Shapleigh.'

He looked at her. By the light of the moon Angélique's green eyes were almost unbearably brilliant.

His toothless mouth stretched in a sardonic grin.

'Are you off to the Witches' Sabbath?' he asked. 'Will you ride your broomstick tonight? It's tonight or never for a woman like you. With this moon you will meet the devil with the goose's legs ... Do you not have the wand painted with the Sabbath Salve? You know the recipe? A hundred ounces of lard or human fat, five of hashish, half a handful of flowers of hemp, the same of poppy flowers, a pinch of hellebore root, and some crushed sunflower seed...'

As he spoke in English she did not grasp the meaning of what he was saying, but he repeated the formula in Latin, and she gave a start of fear.

The old Indian woman, broad and heavy, accompanied Shapleigh along the peninsula as far as the edge of the forest, then made her slow solemn way back. Angélique asked herself what part this Maktara played in the life of the mad old Englishman, for Indian women only very rarely became servants. Had she been his squaw? That would help to explain the way his compatriots had ostracized him, for they considered all contact with the redskins degrading.

Angélique was later to hear the story of this strange couple who lived on the extreme point of Maquoit Bay, the tale of a young Indian girl, the last survivor of the exterminated tribe of the Pequots who, forty years earlier, had been sold as a slave in the market square of Boston. She had been bought on behalf of his masters by a young English apprentice, recently arrived from England with his apothecary's diploma in his pocket. Holding her by a rope he had set off dragging the girl behind him, and it was then, as he looked at her slender doe-like body, and her eyes as black as shaded pools of water, that he had found himself in the grip of that obscure passion for good and for madness that haunts every son of Shakespeare.

So, instead of returning home he had walked straight off into the forest. This was how the two of them had become outcasts together.

CHAPTER TWENTY-EIGHT

OVER THE BROWN shining plain of the rocks laid bare by the tide, a man came leaping through the remaining pools of water.

As he drew closer, Angélique recognized Yann le Couennec, the Breton from Wapassou, her husband's equerry.

She ran to meet him, wild with joy, and threw her arms about him.

157

'Yann, my dear Yann! How pleased I am to see you! Monsieur le Comte . . . where is he?'

'I am on my own,' the young Breton replied.

Then, seeing the disappointment on Angélique's face, he went on:

'When Monsieur le Comte heard that you had set off for the English village, he gave me orders to find you, at all costs. I have been following your tracks for a week now, from Houssnock to Brunswick-Falls, then all down the Androscoggin.'

He drew a letter from his jacket.

'Monsieur le Comte asked me to give you this.'

She grasped the note eagerly, delighted to have something of his in her hands, but resisted the temptation to kiss the note before breaking the seal.

She hoped it would contain some proposal from Joffrey for a meeting somewhere along the coast, or would announce his arrival in spite of all signs to the contrary. But it only contained a few rather abrupt lines: 'If this message reaches you at Brunswick-Falls, return with Yann to Pieter Boggen's trading post. If you are already back at Houssnock, wait patiently for me there. But try, please try, to do nothing reckless or impulsive.'

The tone of the letter – it was almost as if there were some repressed animosity between the lines – disconcerted Angélique. She suddenly felt chilled to the marrow.

The worthy Yann, guessing from her expression that his master's letter must have been lacking in cordiality – he had noticed that when Joffrey de Peyrac had handed him the letter he had looked extremely angry – tried as tactfully as possible to tone down its effect.

'Monsieur le Comte was very anxious about you, on account of the rumours of war that were going about . . .'

'But . . .' she said.

One thing Yann had said had struck her: 'When Monsieur le Comte heard that you had set out for the English village . . .' but was it not he who had sent her there? She tried hard to call to mind the circumstances of her departure. It had been nearly two weeks ago and the details were beginning to become blurred and vague.

'Monsieur le Comte was quite right too,' Yann commented. 'There was real trouble to the west of the Kennebec. The whole red ant-heap is swarming under the trees, tomahawk and torch in hand.

'Nothing but ashes and blackened beams, and corpses and

wheeling crows ... Luckily there were still a few savages looting at Newehewanik, and they told me that you had set off
south with Piksarett, and not north with the other captives.
After that I was frightened I might be taken for an Englishman,
especially as my hair is on the sandy side like theirs. I had to
keep on hiding ...'

She looked at his haggard, bearded, weary face and regained
possession of herself once more.

'But you must be exhausted, my poor friend! You probably
haven't even managed to eat properly on the way ... Come and
have some refreshment!'

Yann was there, bringing with him the presence of her
people, her faithful friends, of the warm circle of Wapassou, and
it was with an immeasurable nostalgia that she conjured up the
picture of the fort in those distant forest lands, so rustic, and
Honorine ...

It all seemed already like something from another world.

For something had happened to break the magic circle, the
circle of love ... the chalk circle of the ancient Celtic legends.

The evening was drawing in. Angélique found herself assailed
by her old fears. The sound of the sea spoke of her former solitude, of the exhausting battle she had had to wage as a woman
alone, the endless struggle to survive the snares of greedy men,
a struggle from which she had seen no release, no matter which
way she turned: and particularly because of the sound of the
sea, and its harsh breath, coupled with the voices of the pirates
– she thought of the Mediterranean where she had found herself
entirely alone, pursued like a hunted animal.

But she soon managed to overcome this moment of weakness, for the happiness of the past months had strengthened
her.

She felt that she had succeeded in overcoming the obstacles
that had stood in the way of the full blossoming of her personality, and that now she was gradually attaining that inner tranquility of mind that was the prerogative of her years and one of
its greatest attractions. Sure of herself, sure of the love in which
she could take refuge and seek rest, the world now appeared less
hostile and easier to bend to her will.

She must just persevere a little longer and this trying time
would come to an end. Everything would return to normal
once more.

She sought an opportunity for further conversation with Yann, for his open face revealed his astonishment at finding her in the company of these gallows-birds. But whether by chance or as a result of some minor plot she never had a moment alone with him all evening, for the others monopolized him. Although Boulanger and Beaumarchand did their utmost to welcome him as one of them, Count Peyrac's equerry found it impossible to overcome his repulsion for them.

'Eat up, lad,' Hyacinth urged him cordially, serving him a brimming ladleful of soup, and doing his best to give his hideously sinister, swollen face an expression of welcome.

Yann thanked him politely, but remained tense, and from time to time attempted to catch Angélique's eye in the hope of some unspoken explanation.

That night they dined on turtle soup, which Hyacinth had himself put on to simmer. Now turtle soup was the buccaneer's speciality and it had to be admitted that this particular specimen was especially delicious, for, like many other pirates, Hyacinth was an excellent cook.

'I can feel the life flowing back into me,' Aristide said with a smack of the tongue.

'We'll soon have you hopping about like a rabbit,' Angélique agreed as she tucked him up for the night.

By now she had the impression that she was no longer keeping watch over him – rather that he and his companions were watching her.

She nevertheless managed to draw apart with Yann in order to explain the strange company she was in.

'The captain of their ship abandoned them on the coast, probably for insubordination. They are no danger as long as they are sick ... that is, for the time being. But I am anxious for Monsieur de Peyrac to come for us as soon as possible. Cantor must have reached Gouldsboro by now ... Have you any ammunition?'

He had used up what he had in hunting animals to keep alive. All that remained was a little gunpowder at the bottom of his powder horn.

Angélique loaded the musket and laid it beside her.

The heat was unbearable, and the night breeze off the sea did nothing to dispel the feeling of oppression.

As was her custom, Angélique sat down under the tree not far from the sick man. A strange lethargy began to steal over her and soon she found it hard to keep her eyes open.

The last thing she saw was the half moon emerging from the

clouds, as its long, golden shimmer suddenly spread across the silent bay, leaping over the black mounds of the scattered islands.

'That's my moon,' Angélique thought vaguely, 'the moon that makes me amorous . . .' For she knew that she was more easily roused on the night when the moon billowed like a lateen sail across the sky.

Then she fell fast asleep, and had a most disturbing dream: she was surrounded by a crowd of people whose faces she could not make out, for they stood out like so many black shadows against an ice-pink sky.

She gave a sudden shudder. This was no dream, for her eyes were open. SHE WAS SURROUNDED BY A CROWD OF PEOPLE. She could see their dark heavy shapes moving slowly about her, and the sky was pink, for dawn was rising over Casco Bay.

Angélique made to get up. Her body felt like lead. She ran her hand mechanically over her face.

Then she noticed Yann a short distance from her; he was standing, tied to a tree, well and truly bound, his lips tight with fury.

There was Aristide Beaumarchand, sitting up, supported by two unknown sailors, greedily swigging the contents of a fresh bottle of rum.

'So there you are, my pretty one,' he said with a titter. 'It's our turn to have the upper hand now . . .'

A voice said:

'Shut up, you old numbskull, no self-respecting gentleman of adventure would insult his vanquished enemy . . . especially when that enemy is a lovely lady.'

Angélique looked up at the man who had spoken. He seemed young, attractive, and well dressed, as if he had once been a page, to judge by his smile and his manners.

'And who are you?' she asked in a toneless voice.

He raised his broad-brimmed hat with its red feather and bowed gallantly.

'I am François de Barssempuy.'

Then with a second deep bow, his hand on his heart, he added: 'Lieutenant to Captain Gold Beard.'

CHAPTER TWENTY-NINE

IT WAS THEN that she saw that there was a ship lying at anchor in the bay at the foot of the promontory.

The first thing that struck her was that it was a very handsome ship, although on the short side and somewhat old fashioned, with its high poop and forecastle, whose brilliantly coloured ornaments glittered in the dawn light.

It was an argosy rather than a ship, a vessel of considerable dignity, that rocked gently as a boat was lowered from its side into the still waters in which the reflection of the anchor chain formed a sharp angle where it touched the surface ... 'Ha ha!' laughed Hyacinth, 'turtle soup makes one sleep, doesn't it, specially when a little something is added ... I had the pick of all your little bottles ...'

Suddenly Angélique felt wide awake again. She grasped what had happened. She leapt nimbly to her feet and in a flash had hurled herself at Beaumarchand, seizing him by the shoulders and shaking him as if he were a plum tree.

'You wretch! I sewed your belly up for you and you have betrayed me to Gold Beard!'

It took four of them to tear her off while he, badly shaken, was as waxen as a candle and running with sweat.

'It's all going to burst open again!' he moaned, clutching at his stomach.

'And I hope it does,' Angélique replied, furiously.

'Hold on to her,' he begged the others. 'You saw what she did to me? A woman who shakes a sick man about like that, deserves no pity.'

'Idiot!' Angélique shouted at him, and with a gesture that brooked no retort she freed herself from the hands that held her, saying as she did so:

'Take your hands off me!'

Breathing rapidly she stood glowering at Aristide, who was not feeling in good fettle.

He was no Adonis, with his body shrunken within his ill-fitting clothes.

'You are a loathsome creep,' she shouted contemptuously at him, 'the most despicable person I ever met. I could gladly spit on you ...'

'Get her knife,' he begged.

'Let any man dare to come near me,' said Angélique, stepping back, one hand on her dagger.

And the circle of flabbergasted men looked at her as if she were some apparition, with her dazzling hair all blown about by the wind and her pale green eyes that seemed to mirror the sea.

'Madame,' Monsieur de Barssempuy said with great courtesy, 'I'm afraid I must ask you for your weapon.'

'Come and get it.'

'Be careful, Lieutenant!' called Aristide, 'she knows how to use it. That was what ripped me open.'

'And she hurled beehives at our heads,' the buccaneer called Hyacinth added, standing prudently out of range, 'and we still have faces like pumpkins.'

The men looked at him and burst out laughing.

'She's dangerous, I tell you!' Hyacinth yelled indignantly. 'She's a witch, is that woman, you know she is. They told us so in the Bay.'

But the men only laughed the louder.

Angélique sensed that most of them thought pretty poorly of these wretched deserters who had betrayed her so ignominiously.

She pretended to lose interest in the wretched pair and turned to Barssempuy, who at least was a Frenchman and a nobleman to all appearances.

'How did they manage to betray me like this?' she asked, walking up to the man with complete unconcern. 'That wretch had been terribly wounded, and the others were not much better. And we were watching them all the time. How could they have told you that I was here?'

'It was Martinez,' the young man replied. 'He disembarked on one of the islands in the Bay where we were caulking the ship and he told us where you were.'

Martinez? ... The fifth pirate who had left with Cantor and the English? A troublesome fellow whom they had intended to disembark somewhere before leaving Casco Bay. So it had been easy for the cunning wretch to get them to put him down somewhere on an island where he knew his erstwhile companions were resting and cleaning the hull of their vessel.

As bearer of the information that the Countess of Peyrac could be taken prisoner without difficulty a few miles away, the mutineer was certain of a warm welcome.

And all the time that Angélique had been wearing herself

out nursing this evil wretch he, although a desperately sick man had managed to find enough breath to plot and scheme this piece of double-dealing, this back-handed blow of which she was now the victim.

The arival of Yann could scarecely have suited them, but he was alone.

Warned no doubt by distant signals of the arrival of their accomplices the night before they were due to land, the men had put a sleeping-draught into the soup.

She looked round. Where were Adhemar, the old Indian woman and the four English people who had escaped the massacre? A certain amount of noise from the beach led her to think that they had probably already been taken on board as prisoners.

And what about Piksarett? She looked hard in the direction of the forest, but the forest was mute, motionless, and offered her no reprieve. Before her lay the sea, with its horizon tipped by a wisp of mauve mist, and the mouth of the little bay of Maquoit, with its brightly painted ship lying at anchor, as the pink of dawn grew paler, merging little by little into the colourless light of day.

Angélique had regained her composure and her mind was working feverishly. She asked herself what advantages there were in having fallen in with French privateers. The Caribbean buccaneers owed their allegiance half to the French and half to the English. English pirates might well not have bothered about her and would have left her in peace on her rock, but with her compatriots at least she had the advantage of being able to talk things over.

This man Gold Beard, so be it! He wanted war. He was taking her prisoner no doubt to use her as a hostage against Joffrey de Peyrac! So be it! But he would hear her out! He would come to regret this foray of his ... No matter what kind of man he turned out to be, she felt quite sure that she could win him over.

Gold Beard! A name calculated to frighten, the name of a swash-buckler, a braggart who thought that the disguise made the man! Not very clever, in all likelihood, but possibly more civilized and more approachable than many of his kind.

Angélique noticed that the members of the crew surrounding her were better dressed and cleaner than she would have expected, which led her to think that she might be able to come to some kind of understanding with their master. Of course, they were dressed in a somewhat showy and flamboyant manner, like most sailors who, freed from all ties and with pockets full of gold, lead a gay life, unable to resist the temptation of strutting about in borrowed plumes. Within every man who suffers no constraint lies a bragging child. But there was nothing in their manner that she could have regarded as really coarse or disreputable, and she now understood better why the five scoundrels she had found had been set ashore as undesirables on some deserted strand.

All this took Angélique only a few seconds to register, long enough for her heart to regain its normal rhythm and for her to make her plans.

'This Gold Beard, your captain, where is he?'

'He is coming towards us now, Madame.'

François de Barssempuy pointed to the boat that had left the ship's side and was being rowed towards them.

Standing in the prow was a man of giant stature. Seen against the light his figure stood out as a huge black silhouette, and his features could not be perceived – only that he was bearded and long-haired like a Viking, and had a kind of golden, bristling halo all round his head. He wore a sleeved doublet with broad revers sewn with gold braid, and a broad shoulder belt laden with weapons; his riding boots reaching to mid-thigh, emphasizing the strong lines of his robust legs. Standing thus outlined against the dazzling backcloth of the bay, he seemed to Angélique to be a veritable giant.

As they came within a few fathoms of the shore, he suddenly donned a large felt hat with yellow and green parrot feathers, that he had been holding in his hand.

Angélique felt a sudden pang of apprehension. Would the captain in fact be more civilized and reassuring than his crew?

Taking advantage of the fact that everyone seemed to be looking at the new arrival, she sidled imperceptibly closer to Yann, where he stood tied to his tree.

'Get ready,' she whispered. 'I'm going to cut your bonds with my knife. When this man Gold Beard lands, everyone will be busy looking at him and will move forwards to meet him. Run off into the forest as fast as you can ... Run! Run! Go and warn Monsieur de Peyrac and tell him not to worry too much about me. I will do my best to keep the pirate in these waters until help arrives ...'

She spoke in the Indian way, almost without moving her lips, and kept her gaze fixed in the direction of the boat.

It seemed to her that Gold Beard must be a redoubtable captain with a considerable hold over his men, for they all kept their eyes firmly fixed on him and straightened their ranks.

The moment he slipped into the water and began to wade heavily towards the shore, Angélique slipped her knife round behind the tree between Yann's wrists, and with a single cut severed his bonds.

In complete silence, broken only by the sudden screeching of gulls that sent a thrill of anxiety through her heart, the pirate advanced towards the promontory.

In an attempt to draw the others away from Yann, Angélique stepped forward boldly.

Yann bounded off like a wild hare, jumping over bushes, leaping over clefts and hollows, slipping between the tree trunks of the pine woods, scaling rocks as he gradually climbed higher and higher. Using the light from the bay seen through the trees to guide him, he made his way round the inlet until he had reached the other side of the fiord.

Then, panting for breath, he stopped, certain that he had not been followed. When he had got his breath back he made his way towards the edge of the cliff to see where he was.

From this vantage point he could see the whole sweep of the bay, the ship lying at anchor and the beach black with people.

His eyes sought out Madame de Peyrac, but, unable to see her, he leaned still farther out, clutching at the root of a stunted tree growing from the extreme edge of the cliff.

Then he saw . . . HE SAW . . .

His jaw fell, as he gazed in open-eyed surprise, for Yann the sailor, who had seen quite a lot in the course of a harsh life, suddenly felt the world fall to pieces round him as in some cataclysm.

Gold Beard was standing there on the beach with a woman in his arms. A woman who stood looking up at him as if transfigured.

That woman was none other than the wife of Count Peyrac!

There, surrounded by all those men, immobile and almost as astonished as Yann up on his cliff, Gold Beard and Angélique stood gazing at one another, passionately embracing and kissing in front of everyone exactly like two long separated lovers . . .
EXACTLY LIKE TWO LONG SEPARATED LOVERS.

CHAPTER THIRTY

'Colin!' she said.

The room on board his ship to which he had taken her was cool, and through the open poop windows could be seen the sparkling waters of the bay and the dancing reflection of an island.

The ship was still riding at anchor. Silent, drowsy with the heat of the day, it rocked gently, dreamily, and there was no sound but the splashing of wavelets against the hull. The *Heart of Mary* seemed suddenly deserted, its only two remaining occupants being these whom Destiny had brought so dramatically face to face.

'Colin! Colin! she repeated in a dreamy voice.

Angélique was gazing at him with half open lips. She had still not recovered properly from the violent emotional shock composed of mingled surprise, consternation, and intense delight she had felt as this giant of a man had climbed up from the water's edge and she had suddenly recognized ... yes, those broad shoulders, those blue eyes, then, when he saw her, the indescribable expression, the start of surprise that had stopped him in his tracks. She had run towards him. Colin! Colin! My dear friend of the desert!

In the narrow confines of the cabin the huge frame of the man now known as Gold Beard dominated everything else.

He stood facing her in silence.

It was very hot. He removed his crossbelt and laid it on the table, then took off his doublet. Three pistols and a small axe hung from his crossbelt, and she remembered the pain she had felt when he had clasped her to him against all this weaponry. But at the same time he had bent down and laid his lips on hers, which had been a spontaneous, violent and delicious sensation.

Now that the frantic excitement of the moment was dying away, she had begun to see him better as the pirate he had become, and regretted the impulse that had thrown her into his arms.

The white collar of his shirt open on his massive chest and the white sleeves rolled up on his powerful arms stood out as bright splashes of light among the oppressive shadows ...

The last time she had seen him had been at Ceuta,* the Spanish city in a Saracen land.

Four – no five – years had passed since then, and now they were in America.

Angélique was beginning to get her bearings again, to take in what was happening. That morning in the anxious light of dawn she had awaited Gold Beard, a redoubtable pirate, an enemy . . . and the man who had come was Colin Paturel, her companion, her friend . . . her lover of old. A shattering surprise!

But it was true. Somewhat crazy but true. For is it not in the nature of all adventurers, all mariners to do just that: to meet at every point on the globe to which ships are drawn across the seas.

It was chance – of a kind about which she had never even thought – that had brought her face to face with the man in whose company she had escaped from Meknès, with whom she had fled from Barbary . . . But that was on the other side of the globe, and a long time ago. Neither of them knew what the other had been doing in the years since.

That tall, silent presence, similar to and yet different from the one she had remembered, made her more acutely aware of the reality of that time, as if the years had suddenly begun to fill the confined space of the cabin with a heavy, slightly turbid water that held them apart. And now they were growing more distant from each other, recrossing the barrier of time. Time was resuming its shape, and once more becoming a palpable element.

Angélique rested her chin on her hands and forced herself to smile in an attempt to dispel the confusion that had brought fire to her cheeks and made her eyes over bright.

'So it's you,' she said . . . 'You, my dear friend Colin, in the person of the corsair Gold Beard about whom I have heard so much . . . I must confess it was the last thing I was expecting . . . I had not the slightest inkling . . .'

She broke off because he moved. He drew up a stool and sat down to face her, across the table, his arms folded, leaning forward, head sunk slightly into his shoulders as he looked at her unwaveringly with his blue, thoughtful eyes.

And beneath this gaze she knew not what to say, aware that he sought and found each familiar feature, as she herself in this weather-beaten face with its golden beard, in this broad forehead crossed by three pale lines that looked like scars beneath

* See *Angélique and the Sultan*.

his tousled Norman hair, rediscovered, scarcely changed, a familiar, reassuring and beloved face. No doubt an illusion, for during the past years had he not become a criminal?

But she could not help seeing him as he had bent over her when fear had set her trembling. And beneath his incisive glance, she knew that she was holding up to him the face of the woman she had become and that the light from the open windows was casting a pearly sheen over her hair. The features of a woman who did not seek to hide them, full of pride and self-knowledge, with that imperial seal that maturity set upon them; there was a greater purity of line, greater harmony in the bone structure, the line of the nose, the brows, the curve of the mouth, a greater softness, shadow and mystery in her sea-blue gaze, and a perfection in the fulfilment of her whole being that radiated from her and that had been responsible for the enslavement of Pont-Briand to the point of madness.

CHAPTER THIRTY-ONE

AFTER A long pause he said:

'It's astounding! You are even more beautiful than I remembered you.

'And yet,' he went on, 'that memory, God knows how it has haunted me!'

Angélique shook her head in denial.

'There is nothing very miraculous about my being more beautiful today than the poor wreck I was then ... And my hair has gone almost white, look.'

He nodded.

'I remember ... It began to go white as we made our way through the desert ... Too much pain ... Too much suffering ... Poor child! Poor courageous child ...'

She recognized his voice with its hint of peasant accent and that trace of paternal teasing in its deep tones that had so moved her in days gone by. She did not want to feel moved like this, to be unable to find the words she sought.

And her gesture of passing her hand across her forehead, gracefully but a little sadly, to brush back a lock of her golden hair, made him sigh deeply.

Angélique would have preferred to give the whole incident

a lighter tone, to talk and joke with him. She felt as if Colin Paturel's glance penetrated to her innermost depths, overwhelming her, paralysing her.

He had always been serious, and did not easily laugh. But today he seemed still more grave, with a heavy inscrutability that might well mask sadness and cunning.

'So you know that I am Count Peyrac's wife?' she resumed, to break the silence.

'Yes, indeed I do ... That is why I am here. To capture you, for I have an account to settle with the Lord of Gouldsboro, Count Peyrac.'

A smile lit up his features, suddenly giving his rough features a look of gentleness.

'But were I to say that I expected to find you under this name, it would be a lie,' he said. 'And you are here, you, whom I have dreamed of night and day for so many years.'

Angélique began to feel that she was losing her grip on the situation. She realized that the past few days, spent at the extreme tip of a wind-beaten peninsula hoping against hope to be rescued, had worn down her resistance, and that she now found herself defenceless when faced with a situation whose demands exceeded her powers.

'But you are Gold Beard,' she exclaimed as if to protect herself from herself. 'You are no longer Colin Paturel ... You have become a criminal.'

'No, good heavens no, what a notion!' he replied in surprise, but remaining completely calm.

'I am a corsair in the King's name, and I have valid documents to this effect.'

'Was it true that you drew the Spaniards' fire on to the monks when you took Portobello?'

'Oh! That was another story. They had been sent to us by the Governor, thinking that their pious prayers would make us agree to terms, but treachery is always treachery, whether disguised by a monk's robes or not. We had come to vanquish the Spaniard, and vanquish him we did. The Spaniards are not like us people from the North, and they never will be like us. They have too much Moorish blood in their veins ... And that's not the end of it ... The cruelty they practise in the name of Christ, that I cannot stand. The day we made those monks walk ahead of us, there were ten pyres burning on the hills, ten fires lighted at the orders of those pious monks – autos-da-fé being held as sacrifice for victory, with hundreds of Indians burning at the stake, because they had refused to work in the gold mines or to be converted . . .

'Crueller than Moors and greedier than Christians – that's the Spaniards. A frightening mixture of rapacity and fanaticism . . . No, I have not the slightest remorse at having made those monks act as a shield to us in Portobello. It is true, and I have to admit it, my sweet, that I am no longer the good Christian I used to be . . . When I left Ceuta on the *Bonaventure*, I went first to the East Indies.

'There it fell to my lot to save the life of the daughter of the Great Mogul who had been captured by pirates, and the riches he showered upon me as a mark of gratitude made me a wealthy man. Then, by way of the Pacific islands I made my way to Peru, then to New Granada, and finally to the Antilles, where, after fighting with that great English commander, Captain Morgan, against the Spaniards – I was with him in Panama – I followed him to Jamaica where he is Governor. With the money from the Great Mogul and the booty I had won I fitted out a ship as a privateer. That was last year. Yes, I admit it, after my days in Morocco I have ceased to be a good Christian. I've found I could only pray to the Virgin Mary because she was a woman and made me think of you. I know that that was not right either, but I felt that the heart of the Virgin is indulgent to poor men, that she understands everything and especially matters of that kind. So that was why, as soon as I found myself the owner of a ship, I called it the *Heart of Mary*.'

He carefully drew off his leather gloves and laid his two bare hands, palms uppermost, in front of her on the table.

'Do you see,' he said, 'can you see the marks of the nails? They are still there . . .'

She lowered her gaze from his face and saw the purple marks left by the nails that had crucified him. One day at Meknès, the Sultan Moulay Ismael had had him nailed to the New Gate at the entrance to the town, and if he had not died, it was only because nothing could lay low Colin Paturel, the King of the Slaves.

'There was a time when seafaring folk began to call me the Crucified,' he continued. 'I said I would kill anyone who gave me this name, and I had some gloves made. For I knew that I was unworthy of bearing so blessed a name. But I am not a criminal either, only a seaman who, after much fighting, and much plundering, has managed to become his own master . . .

to obtain his freedom, in other words. We alone know that that means more than life.'

He had spoken for a long time. And Angélique's heart had begun to grow calmer and she felt grateful to him for enabling her to take possession of herself once more. The heat outside seemed less trying.

'His own master,' he repeated. 'After twelve years of slavery, and many more of servitude under the orders of captains not worth the rope to hang them with, that is something to delight the heart of man.'

His hands moved towards Angélique's, enveloping them but without clasping them.

'Do you remember,' he asked, 'do you remember Meknès?'

She shook her head and drew her hands away, holding them against herself in a gesture of refusal.

'No, hardly at all, I don't want to remember. Everything is different now. We are in another land now, Colin, and I am the wife of Count Peyrac . . .'

'Yes, yes, I know,' he said with the same faint smile, 'you have already said that.'

But she could see that the statement meant nothing to him, that she would always remain in his eyes that solitary, hunted slave girl whom he had once taken under his protection, his companion in flight, his beloved child of the desert whom he had carried on his back, whom he had possessed on the bare rocky ground of the Rif and tasted in her the most wondrous delights of love.

And then she suddenly remembered that she had borne Colin's child in her womb, and a pang shot through her, as poignant as the pain she had felt on losing the child.

Her eyelids drooped and in spite of herself her head fell back as she relived that demented carriage drive that had carried her off, a prisoner of the King, across the roads of France, then the accident, the terrible shock, the pain, and the blood that had begun to flow ... At that time she had been abandoned by everyone; in a swift moment of reminiscence she had asked herself, wild-eyed, how she had ever managed to escape the crushing pincers of the French King's ban and begin a new life once more. It seemed unbelievable.

The man who sat watching her saw, fleeting across this disturbingly beautiful face, a reflection of pain and distress never revealed ... never avowed. Those secret sorrows that women keep to themselves, for men would never understand ...

The sunlight, now growing pink, gave to Angélique's golden face, with the long shadow of her eyelashes spread across her cheeks, an unearthly beauty, and brought back marvellous memories that had haunted him day and night, memories of this woman asleep beside him, or swooning with pleasure in his arms.

He half stood up and leaned across towards her.

'What is it, my lamb? Are you unwell?'

'It's nothing?' she replied softly.

Colin's deep, troubled voice, so reminiscent of the past, stirred her to the very depths, but this time it was a gentler movement like that of a child within her, and she recognized the feeling, the sweet wave of physical desire that this man's presence made her feel in spite of herself.

'I am so tired,' she murmured. 'All those days waiting by the sea, looking after that miserable wretch ... what was his name now?'

And she ran the palms of her hands nervously over her brow and cheeks, avoiding his gaze.

He stood up straight, came round the table and stood before her. He looked gigantic under this low ceiling. The Herculean figure, all muscle and bone, of Moulay Ismael's strongest slave had, over the course of his seafaring years, filled out with flesh which gave this giant, whom none had ever managed to beat or bend to their will, an impressive stature, square shoulders, a powerful round neck, the brow of a bull, and a chest as broad as a shield.

'Rest,' he said gently. 'I will have you sent some refreshment. You must rest, then you will feel better and we can talk.'

His tone remained calm and assured, a tone that reassured, that relieved her anxiety. But she sensed that he had reached some implacable decision about her and she threw him an almost supplicating look.

A tremor ran through him and his jaws clenched.

She hoped that he would leave her, but suddenly he was kneeling down, and she felt his hot hand grasp her ankle in a grip that nothing could release, as his fingers lifted the hem of her dress up towards her bare knee.

He laid bare her pearly white leg upon which was revealed the twisting bluish furrow of the old scar.

'It's there,' he cried with contained rapture, 'it is still there, the mark of the serpent.' Then leaning down, he suddenly laid his burning lips on the blue scar.

Then almost as swiftly he released her and, with a glance full of passionate longing, left the room.

CHAPTER THIRTY-TWO

SHE REMAINED alone, but the burning sensation of his kiss on the ancient wound that Colin's knife had made so many years ago to save her when she had been bitten by a snake, still remained, and, where his fingers had encircled her ankle, the sensation remained with her, like a tight steel band.

She saw the pink mark of his fingers gradually begin to fade.

He had always been so; this man, this gentle, peace-loving, courageous man who did not know his own strength! He had often hurt people unintentionally, under the stress of emotion, and as he made love to her he had sometimes frightened her, even made her groan, so weak and fragile had she felt in his arms, a creature he could so easily have crushed though inadvertence. Whenever he became aware of his unintentional violence, he would implore: 'Forgive me ... I am a brute, am I not? Tell me I am, tell me I am a brute,' to which she would reply laughing: 'No you aren't; didn't you feel you made me happy?'

Angélique was shaken by a violent trembling and began to pace up and down the narrow cabin, unable to overcome the sensations that tormented her. The heat was unbearable and the evening light had become orange, sulphur-coloured.

Her dress stuck to her shoulder-blades and she felt a tremendous need to change her clothes, and to feel some cool water trickling over her.

Caught off her guard that morning by the pirates, she had been barefooted when captured. And barefooted she had gone down to the beach to where Gold Beard awaited her – how tightly he had clasped her to him! – and she was still barefooted as she strode up and down the wooden floorboards. She went over to the window and shook out her hair in the hope of feeling the freshness of the sea breeze, but the air was still and heavy, with a smell of melted pitch. The sailors were still busy caulking and filling the timbers of the ship ... She felt overpowered at the thought that chance had brought her face to face with a lover from her past life whom she had not realized had made so vivid an impression on her heart. And once again her heart gave a lurch as she felt the sweet wave of desire sweep over her at the recollection of his deep voice saying: 'What is it, my lamb? Are you unwell? . . .'

Simple words, but words which had always moved her to the very depths. Like his possession of her, primitive, but total, so full of power that she submitted to it rather than shared it.

It swept over her, like a wave breaking on top of her, taking her breath away, the drive and ardour of the gigantic Norman, freed from all restraint as soon as her eyes said yes. Her body was revisited by forgotten sensations, the extraordinary delight of that desert lovemaking.

He had always been terribly impatient to possess her. He wanted her right away. He would lay her down on the sand and enter her immediately, without a word of love, without a caress. And yet she had never been offended by his way with her, for every time she had been aware, in the thrust of his powerful loins, in his inexorable invasion of her, the drive of a strength that was prodigious, but serene and generous, a boundless and almost mystical giving of his entire being. He may have been heedless of her, but not of the act itself. A celebrant lost in love, celebrating the offering, the union, the joy of mankind on earth.

Was it sacrilegious to think that Colin Paturel made love as he did everything else, with faith, piety, strength, and violence?

She sometimes thought she would die of his embraces, for her exhausted body was too weakened by privation to be able to bear his raptures and respond to them, and yet this lovemaking had taught her the delights of submission, the savour of being nothing, nothing more than a proffered cup from which he drank his fill, nothing but flesh to provoke his pleasure, nothing but a body, a female body, abandoned and forgotten beneath him, but from which he drew such utter ecstasy.

Abnegation, abdication, which would suddenly find their recompense in an unpredictable flash, at that moment when she sank into oblivion, just as the virile attack was reaching its climax and snatching her from the void, dragging her back to life with a cry of awakening, a cry of rebirth, of renewal, a cry that rose from her innermost depths as she writhed in the ultimate spasm.

She still remembered that irrepressible convulsion as a dazzling wave that radiated in a torrent of sensation through her body, half dead and yet still capable of the pleasure that is the source of all life.

Like the bud that bursts forth suddenly in the light of spring.

By this stirring of her vitals she recognized the strength of life.

'I am alive, I am alive,' she kept on repeating to herself. With his blind passion he seemed to have wrested her from the sleep of death into which she had been sinking, her blood stirred again in her veins, and she wondered at this precious miracle, as wide-eyed, she looked up at Colin's face, close to hers, with its blue, limpid eyes like pools of clear water, and his shadowy mouth glimpsed between the hairs of his golden beard as his panting breath gently brushed her face.

Yes, Colin had not only saved her life: he had given her back life and taught her to love life and not merely survive. And it was essentially thanks to him that she had had the courage and strength to find her husband and children again.

Oh! why now did the movement of the sea and the sound of the tide rushing into the narrow channels along the coast, why did all this have to conjure up so vividly visions of the past? In the woods of Wapassou she would have forgotten Colin.

'I must get out of here,' she told herself, beginning to panic.

She ran to the door and tried to open it. But it had been bolted. Then she noticed her travelling bag on the floor, and a tray of food on a table, some grilled salmon with boiled golden corn, a bowl of salad, and a glass dish containing some slices of preserved citron and pineapple. The wine in the flagon seemed of good quality and the water in the jug was cold.

While she had been daydreaming someone must have come in and left all this, and her thoughts had been so far away that she had not noticed.

She did not touch the food but drank some water.

She opened her bag and noticed that half her things were missing, and this made her impatient. She would go and ask Colin to send those good-for-nothing sailors of his back on land to fetch all her things.

He would do as she bade him. He was her slave. She was the only person who mattered to him. She had seen this as soon as their eyes had met and they had recognized one another.

The only thing he wanted on earth was her, still her, always her. And she had just been restored to him . . .

How could she escape him? How could she escape from herself?

She was on the point of banging on the door and calling loudly, when she changed her mind. No, she did not want to see Colin. The mere thought of the way he looked at her threw her into a state of extreme agitation and she began to feel that things were too much for her.

If only Joffrey would come quickly to fetch her.

'I do hope that Yann hurries!'

She looked outside. The day was drawing to a close. The sun had disappeared behind a bank of cloud from which came the occasional flash of summer lightning, while the rocking of the ship, still riding at anchor, was becoming more pronounced.

Angélique removed her clothes and poured the cold water from the jug over the nape of her neck, letting it run the full length of her body. This made her feel better, and she slipped on a fine lawn shift. She continued to pace up and down the little room, now grown quite dark, like a pale, agitated ghost. The short shift felt pleasant and light on her feverish body and she became aware of the pleasant sensation of a light breeze playing around her bare legs, a still uncertain breeze that had at last sprung up, ruffling the crests of the waves before falling again.

'There is a storm brewing ... That is why the ship is still lying at anchor and has not sailed,' she thought. Colin must have sensed the approach of a storm.

She picked up the piece of printed calico spread over the bunk, wrapped herself in it and lay down. She wanted to sleep.

But a myriad thoughts crowded in her brain. Why had Gold Beard wanted to take her prisoner? What were these title deeds he held to land at Gouldsboro? Why had Joffrey sent her to the English village? She would think all this out later, later!

The thunder burst upon them with a dull roar, awakening echoes on the nearby land. But the following rumble already seemed farther off.

The storm is farther out at sea ...

The rocking motion of the ship was bearing her away, plunging her into a sweet torpor. Colin ... Long ago ... in the desert ...

He only kissed her afterwards, after his body had satisfied its urgent hunger. He only caressed her afterwards ... Their kisses were gentle, hesitant and cautious, for their lips were cracked through lack of water and the burning rays of the sun, and would often bleed ... A thrill ran through her and her body tensed at the memory of Colin's cracked, dry lips on hers, Colin's lips exploring her body . . .

She turned over violently. Then, with nerves at breaking-point, through sheer exhaustion she fell into a deep sleep.

CHAPTER THIRTY-THREE

'No, COLIN, not that, I beg you, not that . . .'

Gold Beard's arms, Colin's muscular arms were lifting her irresistibly, raising her up towards him, and, clasped to his firm naked chest she felt Colin's fingers, there between her breasts, grasping the edge of the fine lawn shift and pulling until the veil was rent without effort in a single wrench, as silent as the dimness of a mist. Colin's hands were on her loins, on her hips, taking hold of her, familiarizing himself once again with her. The man's hand insinuating itself between her legs, there, in that place set apart where the skin is as soft as satin, moving still higher in a caress that seemed never to end.

'No, Colin, not that, I beg you . . . I beg you!'

Black night surrounded her, shot with a glimmer of bronze.

The man had placed a candle on the table behind him, but for Angélique, naked and swooning in Colin's arms, all was night. He was like night himself, a vast abyss of night, a dark shape leaning over her entirely enveloping her in his obscure untamed passion. And as he clasped her to him, still tenaciously caressing her, his mouth sought her lips as she tried to escape him, rolling her head from side to side in a final attempt to resist him.

'My little girl, my little girl!' he whispered, trying to appease her.

This was what he used to call her.

At last he managed to overcome her resistance and she felt his soft, cool lips through the tickling warmth of his beard as they took hold of hers.

Then he remained completely motionless, her head held rigid by his encircling steely arm, and made no attempt to force the barrier of her closed lips. And little by little it was she herself who sought to awaken, to move, and grasp the secret of the man's mouth that lay like a seal upon hers, bidding it come to life, soliciting a response, and finally feeling the lips part. Then she in turn capitulated with a kind of avid, dumb cry, over-whelmed by a sudden hunger, and gave herself up to the mysterious, intimate approach of the kiss.

Unspoken, giddy dialogue, a quest more subtle, more delicate than total possession, hesitant curiosity, recognition, avowal, discovery, a striking spark, its crackling ever renewed, stirring desire and tenderness in the blood, as the sun burnt forth in the head, an endless contact, thirst never slaked, the paradisial taste of oblivion, delicious pulp to stave off hunger, response, response, each time more tender, more total, until the body so desired is nothing more than an immense, impatient offering, a feast of love duly prepared for the celebration of the rites.

Colin's sheer power pushed her down, tilting her back until she was pinned, powerless, to the bed.

'No, Colin! ... please, my love, not that ... Have pity on me, I can't ... I can't ... resist you any more.'

Colin's knees had begun to force their way between her tightly joined legs, trying to part them with one firm thrust, a single, unremitting pressure ...

Then Angélique cried out in protest, almost without hearing it herself:

'If you do, I will hate you! By God, I would hate you, Colin!'

He froze, thunderstruck, listening to the echo of her cry as it cut into him like a blade.

A long minute dragged by in silence, while the flickering flame of the candle cast shadows on the wall, those eternal shadows of human nights, confused shadows, everlastingly re-shaped since time immemorial, the shadows of a man and a woman intertwined in love ...

With a firm twist of her body Angélique freed herself from the imprisoning band of Colin's powerful arms and leapt in such haste and folly from her bunk that she almost tipped the table over, knocking the candle to the floor, where it went out.

She had drawn with her the piece of calico in which she had wrapped herself before going to sleep, and now feverishly wrapped it round her again, while she tried, giving herself many a hard knock in the process, to place the table as a rampart between Colin and herself.

She could not see him, for the darkness was absolute. Out-side the night was moonless, a night of cloud and trailing mists.

But she sensed that the man had gathered himself together again like an animal about to spring.

'Angélique! Angélique!' Colin's voice came to her through

the darkness, and his cry not only told of the anguish of frustrated desire but also spoke of heart-rending despair.

'Angélique!'

He moved forward, staggering, arms outstretched, and stumbled into the table.

'Be quiet!' said Angélique softly, through clenched teeth, 'and go away. I cannot give myself to you, Colin, I am Count Peyrac's wife.'

'Peyrac!' murmured Colin's hoarse voice, and she had the impression he was about to die, 'Peyrac, that outlaw, that gentleman of adventure, playing the prince and the king on the Acadian coast . . .'

'I am his wife!'

'You married him the way all the sluts who knock about the Antilles marry . . . for his gold, for his ships, for the jewels he decked you out in, because he fed you . . . didn't you? What rock did you discover him on? You were knocking about the world looking for a rich corsair, weren't you? And he offered you emeralds and pearls . . . didn't he? Now be honest?'

'I owe you no explanation. I am his wife, and I married him before God.'

'Fiddlesticks! . . . These things are easily forgotten!'

'Don't blaspheme, Colin!'

'I too can offer you emeralds and pearls . . . I could be as rich as him . . . Do you love him?'

'It's not your business whether I love him or not!' she cried in despair. 'I am HIS WIFE and I don't intend to spend my life breaking solemn oaths.'

He flinched, and she added quickly:

'We cannot do that, Colin . . . it's out of the question! That's over . . . You would destroy my life . . .'

His voice was dull as he asked:

'Is it true that you would hate me?'

'Yes, I would! I should hate you. I should hate even the memory of you, even the past . . . You would have become the cause of my unhappiness, my worst enemy . . . the instrument of my worst transgression . . . I should hate myself. I would rather you killed me right now . . . Kill me! Kill me rather than that . . .'

Colin's breath rasped like the bellows of a forge, as if he was in his death agony.

'Leave me alone! Leave me, Colin!'

She spoke softly, but the contained violence of her words

gave each one the strength and cutting edge of a sharp dagger.

'I cannot leave you,' he breathed, 'you belong to me. You belong to me in all my dreams. And now that you are here before me, I will not give you up. Otherwise what would be the point of my having found you again? What would be the meaning of the chance that put you in my path again? . . . I have missed you too much by night and by day . . . I have suffered too much from the memory of you to give you up now . . . I must have you.'

'Then kill me; Kill me right away.'

The heavy darkness was filled with the sound of their broken breathing. And Angélique felt herself faltering as she clung to the table, as the ship rocked back and forth in a giddy, immeasurable movement, a blind vertigo in which her fear of her own weakness was added to her fear of what might happen if ever this inescapable 'thing' which she sensed was returning, ever took place . . . And it was true that at that moment she would have preferred to die.

When she heard Colin move and felt that he was drawing closer, a noiseless cry rose from her innermost depths, a cry such as she had never uttered within her, a cry she did not recognize as an appeal for help to something stronger than her own weakness, something more lucid, more merciful . . .

Then little by little she realized that all had grown still about her, that peace had returned, and she sensed an emptiness, as she realized that once again she was alone.

Colin had left her. Colin had gone.

CHAPTER THIRTY-FOUR

IT WAS A very cruel moment for her, a moment of confusion, of despair, in which the eternal child in woman took the upper hand with all its illogicality, its regrets, its unwillingness to face reality, a moment in which her tormented body and distracted mind struggled in the grasp of an unbearable dilemma. She felt as if she ached to the very tips of her fingers, ached so that she could scream.

Finally her nerves began to calm down and she groped around in vain for the candle. It must have rolled away into some corner, but a glimmering of milky white light came from the moon, slipping between two clouds, and Angélique staggered as if drunk across to the little balcony outside the french windows and leaned against the gilded balustrade.

There she rested her weight on her elbows, and drew a series of deep breaths.

The moon was shining now. The sky, just dappled with clouds, spread out over her head like a pearly shell, filled with the endless roar of the surf and the nostalgic, rather lugubrious cry of the seals along the beaches.

Angélique's eyes strayed, without dwelling on any one thing, but her senses gradually grew calmer, and as a full realization of the terrible danger she had run was borne in on her, her legs almost gave way under her.

'I almost did it,' she told herself, breaking out into a cold sweat.

Then, as the seconds passed, elemental fear crushed and utterly destroyed the dazzling, delightful mirage of temptation.

'If I had done it . . . !'

At that very moment, she told herself, she would have been like one dead . . . like . . . she could no longer find words to describe the sensation of ravishment and total destruction she would have felt, if . . .

Henceforth she would know that desire must be rated among the most terrible of terrestrial cataclysms, equal in force to tidal waves, cyclones, and earthquakes, something that defied reason, that trampled human weakness irresistibly beneath blind physical force.

How had she found the strength to escape him? Horror-struck, she bit her fingers, staring before her into the yawning gulf.

How could I have?

She touched her lips.

'And that kiss . . . I should never . . . I should never have kissed Colin in that way.'

Her tongue against his tongue.

She dropped her face into her hands.

'Unpardonable! Unpardonable! . . .'

Joffrey!

She felt a superstitious fear at calling upon him, as if he were standing there behind her, staring at her with his piercing eyes.

'It was Joffrey who taught me the delights of kissing, it was he who gave me back my taste for it. And I love . . . I so love those endless kisses we share, I could spend my life clasped to his heart, my arms around his neck, and my mouth on his . . . He knows I could. How could I have come so close to betraying him. It is because I am parted from him that I am weak . . .'

Never is a woman more vulnerable than when she feels the need for consolation in her beloved's absence. Men should be aware of this; husbands should know it.

With her discovery that the turmoil she had felt had stemmed from the unbearable emptiness she felt at being alone, far from him, little by little Angélique began to absolve herself from guilt.

'He should never leave me alone . . . and in any case, was it so serious? Even supposing I had? An embrace? . . . Like drinking when one is thirsty. There is no harm in drinking . . . If that is all that is involved when we women are deceived, why all the fuss? A passing desire, a sudden longing . . . so little, in truth. In future I shall be more indulgent when men misbehave. What if Joffrey one day . . . with another woman? . . . No, I couldn't bear it . . . I should die . . . Yes, now I know that it is very serious! Forgive me . . . Why is it that so accidental an act should, ever since the world was created, bring such tragedy in its wake? The spirit is willing but the flesh is weak! Oh yes, how true!

'Why should I have felt with Colin, who is almost a stranger to me, so irresistible a temptation? . . . Is love so physical a thing? Joffrey, in his usual cynical way, tells me it is when he wants to tease me. Love is a question of waves of mutual attraction that emanate from the skin . . . No, not only that! But possibly one of the fundamental conditions? In the past there were some men with whom I found it not, of course, disagreeable, but I knew that there was something missing. The thing I felt from the start with Joffrey, even when he frightened me . . .

And with Colin? . . . There has always been something more with him, something I could not explain . . . With Desgrez too, perhaps. And, now that I think of it, it seems strange, the fat captain at the Chatelet, could I have brought myself to "pay" him thus to save Cantor's life if . . . My memory of him is not as unpleasant as all that . . . But with the King? In that case I understand better . . . There was something lacking . . . Something missing, that strange, weird recognition between flesh and flesh, that exists between certain people without any evident reason.

'Whatever it is exists between Colin and me – and there lies the danger – I must never be alone with him.'

Dreamily, as the ship rose and fell, she let her thoughts wander through the moonlight, and saw in her mind's eye a procession of all the men she had ever known, all so different, among whom suddenly and without her knowing why, she caught sight of the frank, open face of Count Lomenie-Chambord and the distant, noble figure, hieratic yet forbearing of the Abbot of Nieul.*

CHAPTER THIRTY-FIVE

THERE WAS a man trying to hide as he clung to the woodwork beneath the balustrade.

For some moments Angélique had broken off her wandering thoughts about the inconsequence and illogicality of the human race in matters of love, and her memories and companions, in order to observe him.

Her attention caught by a slight noise, she had leaned forward and caught sight of the shadow of a man with hair unkempt and clothes in ribbons, clinging to what were known as the 'galleries', projecting ornaments encircling the two floors of the poop castle.

'Hi! you,' she whispered, 'what are you doing there?'

Seeing himself discovered, the man slithered away to one side and she caught sight of him again a little lower down, this time clinging to the mouldings around the great plaque painted with the allegory of the Heart of Mary surrounded by angels.

The mysterious acrobat gave her a menacing look that nevertheless held a note of supplication.

There were raw, bleeding patches round his wrists.

Angélique understood. Gold Beard's ship had prisoners on board. And this must be one of them trying to escape.

She signalled to him that she had understood and backed away out of sight.

Realizing that she would not raise the alarm, the man took courage and she felt a jerk as he left the ship and heard him dive into the water.

When she looked again all was calm. She sought him in the

* See *Angélique in Revolt.*

water beside the ship but he had already surfaced some way off in the shadow of an island and had begun to swim away.

A terrible nostalgia gripped Angélique. She too wanted to get away, to flee this ship in which she felt trapped by her own weakness. Tomorrow Colin would be there again.

'I must leave this ship at all costs,' she told herself, 'at all costs ...'

CHAPTER THIRTY-SIX

AT THE foot of Mount Desert flows a cool, shady stream, whose limpid waters taste of clay. Pierre du Guast de Monts drank of this water when he came in 1604 to found the first European colony in North America. He was a rich Huguenot nobleman, to whom his friend Henry IV of France, had given the title of Viceroy of the Atlantic Coast of the New World. The geographer Samuel Champlain accompanied him, as did the poet Lescarbot who sang of 'the sweet waters of Acadia'.

Of that first settlement nothing remains but a rotting, half-fallen cross set up by Father Biard the Jesuit, and an old chapel with a silver bell that tinkles in the wind, and is occasionally rung by inquisitive and anxious Redskin children of the Cadillac tribe.* An ancient Indian track finishes there, a track leading from the north, crossing lakes and forests from the distant Mount Katthedin, then from rock to rock and across a short stretch of sea before coming to an end on Mount Desert Island.

That particular spring, the green grass and tender birch shoots had lured back the herds of lowing bison, sombre, ancestral, gigantic bovine creatures with obstinate looking heads and velvety withers.

Seen as dark masses through the golden leaves, they seemed fearsome but they were in fact peaceable, bucolic creatures.

The forest Indians hunted them very little, for they preferred fallow deer, stags, and roe deer. So the herd of bison which was

* During the following century, after one of their great chiefs had distinguished himself in the Franco-English war, the mountain was re-named Mount Cadillac.

In modern times the name of this great Indian chieftain was also given to a make of motorcar.

busy that morning cropping the tall grass at the foot of the mountain showed no anxiety when their delicate nostrils sniffed a passing group of men up wind.

Joffrey de Peyrac, accompanied by Roland d'Urville, the Norman, Gilles, Vanereick, the filibuster from Dunkirk, and Erasmus Baure, the Recollect Father, having left his chebec in the shelter of the harbour on the eastern side of the island, had set off to climb the mountain. This, the highest point in the area, lay less than a league across the sea from Gouldsboro, and was a peak over 1,500 ft in height, composed of huge twin domes of pink granite.

Once through the foliated zone that foamed greenly around the foot of the mountain, all vegetation disappeared save the dark tufts of a few stunted pines and, growing almost flat out of the bare, flesh-coloured rock, a few glossy bilberry bushes and a carpet of dwarf rhododendrons that spread out across the rounded, worn curves of the mountain forming sumptuous carpets of purple and pink.

The close, whispering wind grew more and more cutting and icy as they climbed higher.

The four men, with their escort of sailors, carrying the muskets, climbed, swift and light-footed, without following any particular path. The huge slabs of pinkish or purplish granite were sufficient guide, drawing them up towards the summit like the shallow steps of a well-worn stairway.

In every crevice, every fissure where the wind had blown a handful of arable soil, grew a thousand tiny, precious flowers: white and yellow stonecrop, and various saxifrages delicately spotting the vast expanses of bare rock with patches of intricate embroidery.

Caring little for so much prettiness mingled with such wild grandeur, Count Peyrac pressed on with his head down, anxious to reach the top before some unpredictable mist came down and masked the horizon.

To examine the extensive panorama that would be revealed from the top, to count every island and scrutinize every inlet and promontory, this was his purpose in climbing this mountain.

Every moment mattered. The days were flying past in the hurly-burly of the active season, in the confusion of awakening when the land and its creatures fling themselves ravenously into the tide of summer.

The Indians were coming down to the coast to barter their

goods, white men were arriving for the fishing, men felled timber, planted seed, and did business; and great whirlwinds of activity swept them all along in the feverish hustle and bustle of a too short season.

One event followed hard upon another. Ten days earlier, after parting company from his young ally Baron Castine at Penta-gouet on the Penobscot, Count Peyrac had set off eastwards towards Gouldsboro.

He had lingered a little on the way, for his route lay along a still somewhat inaccessible track, that ran close to a couple of small mines of his that worked silver and sylvanite, an ore in which gold occurs in a black, and therefore invisible form. There he stopped, and had a look at the work going on, and brought cheer to the miners who had spent the winter there, left Clovis as foreman, and set off again. A little farther on he found Saint-Castine's chaplain, a Recollect Father called Baure, with a message from the Baron.

Thus it was that he learnt of the massacres in the west. The Abenakis had unearthed their war hatchet and were laying waste the English colonies in Maine down towards Boston.

'I am managing to keep hold on my tribes,' Saint-Castine wrote. 'So no one will move in our part of the country. I have sent messages to the English traders in Pemaquid and Wis-casset, my neighbours, telling them there is no need for alarm on this occasion and to remain where they are.

'Nevertheless, they have taken refuge on Newagan Island with supplies of food and ammunition. But I am willing to vouch that, with your help, peace will be maintained in our territories.'

Then Peyrac had reached Gouldsboro.

There he learned at one and the same moment that Angél-ique had not reached Gouldsboro after going on board the *Rochelais* in Sabadahoc Bay, as the unknown sailor had told him she had, but that his son Cantor, after sailing a sloop full of English refugees as far as Gouldsboro, had just set off again in the *Rochelais* with its captain Le Gall, to fetch Angélique from Casco Bay, where she had remained, it was said, with the sick and wounded.

Feeling both reassured about his wife's fate and annoyed by these setbacks, these endless to-ings and fro-ings and the incomprehensible behaviour of one and all, Joffrey de Peyrac wondered whether he should not set off after his son, but in view of the feverish agitation that gripped his coastal colony, he decided that he had better bide his time.

His meeting with the man of the 'lambis' pearls along the Kennebec, the man from the ship with the orange flag, still continued to nag at his mind. Who were those people who had lied to him? Perhaps they had just misheard something shouted to them through the fog, from one ship to another?

He would have to wait for Angélique to return with Le Gall in order to sort out the mess. The main thing was that Angélique was safe and sound. And yet he would not feel completely easy until he held her in his arms.

Now all this had taken place four days earlier, and as he climbed hastily up the side of the Desert Mountain, perhaps one motive for his haste was a secret hope that he might be the first to see a reassuring sail in the distance.

Behind him his two companions exchanged banter snatched away by the gusty wind. Gilles Vanereick, a Frenchman by nationality, a Protestant converted to Catholicism, a merry, earthy servant of the King of France who nevertheless preferred to serve him from afar, was wearing a yellow satin doublet with buttons fashioned out of genuine pistoles, plum-coloured silk breeches and green pleated hose. He wore a printed calico scarf round his forehead beneath a hat decked with parrot feathers, and a sash of the same floral print round his slightly protruding abdomen. Agile and alert in spite of his girth, he had the reputation of being a devastating fighter and of never having been wounded. The only scar he bore was a mark on the back of his hand made by the hand-guard of his boarding sword, the result of prolonged use of the weapon, 'day and night', as he said, 'day and night!'

A northerner, from the Low Countries that were for so long subject to Charles V and his descendants, he had dark eyes and a curling, black moustache in the Spanish style superimposed on his good natured, Flemish sensuality.

Count Peyrac had become friendly with him in the Caribbean, and Vanereick had decided to pay him a visit in his northern colony, the time of the year, he reckoned, being too hard for a small-time filibuster from Saint Christopher with all the Spaniards about.

He had arrived at the same time as the *Gouldsboro*, under the command of Erickson, upon its return from Europe.

The *Gouldsboro* was carrying craftsmen and a few Huguenot refugees, whereas the corsair ship had on board more or less dark-skinned women, among them a Hispano-Indian halfcaste of great beauty, who was Vanereicks' mistress. No sooner had she disembarked than she began to dance on the beach to the clicking of the castanets and to the considerable displeasure of Messrs Manigault and Berne, who were responsible for discipline in the port and the morals of their little Protestant community.

The night of the summer solstice had been marked by some rather violent affrays, and although Joffrey de Peyrac's presence had prevented things from getting out of hand, d'Urville the Governor said he had had enough of all these madmen and wanted to resign.

The day after that eventful midsummer night, Peyrac took them up the mountain to cheer them up a bit. And he too felt the need to get away for a while in order to get his bearings. He hoped that a kindly wind would enable him to see from the summit, however far away, the sail on the ship bringing Angélique back to him.

Then he had another idea concerning the suspicious vessel that they had encountered on the banks of the Kennebec, the ship whose orange flag he had seen flying above the treetops. He wanted to test his hypothesis.

Behind him, the small group of his subordinates, lieutenants and friends, were busy chatting together as they clambered nimbly up the large slabs of pink granite.

D'Urville was busy asking Vanereick what had driven him, a filibuster from the Antilles, to try his luck in Massachusetts Bay and Frenchman Bay. And Vanereick made no secret of his reasons.

'I am too small a fish for those enormous Spanish galleons one meets nowadays in the Caribbean, 600 tons and armed to the teeth, with a veritable pack of other vessels to escort them. On the other hand I could trade with Monsieur de Peyrac: sugar, molasses, rum, cotton, in exchange for dried cod and timber for masts . . . and we might even join forces to attack some enemy ships.'

'We shall see . . .' Peyrac replied. 'Meanwhile refit your ship, refresh yourselves in our domains, do as you like, in short. It occurs to me that you might indeed be of assistance to me shortly against Gold Beard, the pirate you must have heard speak of in Jamaica.'

Now they were on the crest of the mountain. The wind cutting like a knife blade across the bare top of Mount Desert assailed them with such violence that they had difficulty in keeping their feet. Vanereick was the first to capitulate, saying that he was used to warm lands, and, chilled to the marrow, he took shelter on the less exposed side of the mountain behind a rocky outcrop. Roland d'Urville soon joined him there, clinging to his felt hat with both hands. Father Erasmus Baure faced the wind long enough to say an Our Father and a Hail Mary, then decided he had had enough, as did Vanereick's sailors.

Enrico Enzi, who was escorting Peyrac, remained stoical, as yellow as a quince, swathed in the Arab style sashes and turbans that made up his habitual Maltese garb.

'Get away with you,' the Count said to him, 'go and shelter somewhere.' He remained alone at the top of Mount Desert, braced against the force of the incessant wind, unable to take his eyes off the panorama spread out beneath him.

There, inscribed in hieroglyphics of land and water, lay all the charm, the vastness and the complexity of a land coming to life in its full vigour, a land with an endless reserve of rare sights to offer.

On all sides lay the sea, pushing its way into the land; on all sides lay the land stretching out in peninsulas and promontories across the blue mottled surface of the turbulent ocean, but which, seen from so high, looked soft and smooth as satin. Islands crowned with ebony-coloured pines, islands dim with the greenish gold of birch trees in their spring growth.

At the far end of the bay he could see an area completely made up of pink and red rocks breaking through the ironstone rock face, ancient ironstone that had turned almost mauve from the compression of vast glaciers in the remote past.

In the gravel of the moraine of rivers younger than the ironstone could be found the prehistoric remains of fur-covered elephants with tusks shaped like hunting horns. Granite surfaces had been rounded by the pressure of the ice and sudden sheer cliffs bore witness to sudden subsidence, as they stood reflecting the starkness of their open wounds in the deep waters of the roadsteads.

And the bays, the islands, the rivers made hazardous by tidal bores, up which one could only sail at high tide, with their endless mists and storms, beaches peopled with seals, forest-covered banks swarming with fur-bearing animals, where you can see black bears catching fish with their paws at the edge of the waves, and Indians swarming everywhere in the hope of trading their furs with visiting ships; all this vast area around Frenchman Bay, like a miniature Mediterranean, its shores new and not ancient, here beaches pink or white, or tinged with blue, even on occasion raspberry red, this desert, this paradise, this witch's cauldron, that narrows as one goes farther up, deeper and deeper into darkness and mist, with the surf roaring all round one, until the very tip of Frenchman Bay is reached, where the four Defours brothers, Marcelline-la-Belle and her ten children, Gontran-le-Jeune, brother-in-law to old Nicolas Parys, and a handful of others flounder about in the Chignecto marshes, selling their baskets of peat to the highest bidding ship, while Father Jean Rousse hurls imprecations at them for their wild, godless lives, this tiny section of the American continent – although gigantic to the wretched creature trying to establish himself on it – already had a history in its image – unknown, cruel, and dispersed over vast expanses and the abysses of lost horizons, a history filled with sadness and pain.*

Joffrey de Peyrac looked down at the oval-shaped sheltered harbour of the island and saw the tiny shape of his chebec with its long, sharp lines.

The boat had been built to his own specification at Kittery in New England, already quite an old seaport, on the Piscataqua river in the state of Massachusetts. What remained now, he wondered, of that busy naval shipyard? Ashes, possibly? The Indian wars, flaring once more, would cause incalculable upheaval for them all.

The birds began to circle noisily up towards the heights, announcing the arrival of one of the lords and masters of the region – fog . . .

Joffrey de Peyrac closed his spyglass and rejoined his companions, who were making the best of the icy conditions with their collars pulled about their noses.

He sat down beside them, wrapped about in his huge cloak. The savage wind laid flat the multicoloured feathers in their hats, and the fog suddenly bore down upon them in silence, rolling its smoke-like waves round the pink flanks of the mountain, wrapped them about and engulfed them in its mystery. So heavily did its breath fall upon them, that the wind had dropped, and fled away with a whisper, and for a while, all was calm, and the white men, alone in an invisible universe, sat as

* Apart from the fighting that took place during the Franco-English war, the history of Acadia was marked, in the years 1620–1640, by bloody rivalry between two Frenchmen, Charles Latour and Pierre d'Aulnay, which assumed truly tragic proportions.

it were in the clouds, above a world that had vanished utterly.

'Well, Monsieur d'Urville, it appears that you are about to hand me your resignation as Governor of Gouldsboro?' said Peyrac.

The gentleman from Normandy blushed, then grew pale and looked at the Count as if he thought he must possess the unnerving faculty of reading men's most hidden thoughts. Yet there was in fact nothing very sinister in this piece of guesswork, for a few days earlier, Peyrac had seen him tearing his hair out over the difficulties facing his administration.

There were too many people in Gouldsboro now, he said. What with the Huguenots, the miners, the pirates and sailors of all nationalities, he could make neither head nor tail of them all, not that he had ever been much good at it anyway. Where had the good old days gone when, as almost the only man in charge of this deserted region, he had been able to devote himself to the lucrative business of fur trading with the Indians and the rare ship that risked entering the harbour, still undeveloped in those days and difficult of access.

But now it was like a continental fair and he, d'Urville, a Norman gentleman from Cape Contentin, no longer even had time to bestow his favours on his lovely Indian wife, the daughter of the local Abenaki-Kakou chieftain, nor to go off, under the pretext of visiting some distant French or English neighbour, to enjoy for a change the pleasures of sailing on the choppy ocean.

'My lord,' he cried, 'pray do not think that I no longer wish to serve you. I shall always be there to obey your orders and help you as best I can, to attack your enemies, and protect your domains at cannon point, nay, even at sword point, to command your soldiers, your sailors, but I have to admit that I am not equipped to deal with situations that involve the Saints, the Devil and the Scriptures. Your Huguenots are hard working, courageous, capable, industrious, and devilish good merchants ... but devilish troublemakers too. They will turn Gouldsboro into a very well-ordered city, but we shall never hear the end of their gas and gab, for we shall never know what laws we are supposed to be following. Whatever was done to them in La Rochelle, those people have been, as it were, mutilated so that they no longer feel themselves subjects of the King of France. Let just one Frenchman come among them with a medallion of the Blessed Virgin about his neck and they begin to kick up a shindy and refuse even to allow him to take on fresh water from their place. We got on quite well with one another this winter, and spent many hours chatting round the fire during the stormy season. I am a bit of an unbeliever myself – begging your pardon, Father – and ran little risk of offending them with my paternosters. And we fought well together when we had to against that pirate Gold Beard. But it is precisely because I know them too well now that I do not feel I am enough of a diplomat to keep the balance between the extraordinary mixture of religions and nationalities and all those pirates as well.'

Joffrey de Peyrac was silent. He was thinking of his friend Captain Jason, the persecuted Huguenot who had been broken in to the Latin temperament on the Mediterranean, a man who would have done wonders in the position that d'Urville was relinquishing. But Jason was dead and so was that admirable scholar the Arab doctor Abd-el-Medrat who might also have helped him in his task. D'Urville, merry and shrewd man that he was, was not abandoning the task out of cowardliness, or even laziness, although a life led under conditions of such complete freedom had bred in him a certain propensity for taking things easy.

The youngest son of his family, he had received no kind of professional training beyond being taught to hold a sword and ride a horse, and, scarce knowing how to read, he was aware of his own shortcomings. He had killed a man in a duel and had fled to America to save his neck from the block under the laws brought in by Cardinal Richelieu. Nothing short of this would have dragged him here, for he had no conception of any kind of life beyond that of the Paris taverns and gambling dens. Fortunately for him he came from the Cotentin peninsula, that snail's horn that stands out from the French coast to peer across at England, almost an island in the solitude of its wild coastlines, copses and its sandy wastes.

Brought up in an old castle on the Cap de le Hague, d'Urville loved and understood the sea that had cradled him in his youth. Today he could do wonders by keeping a tight hold on the little fleet of ships at Gouldsboro, swelled every year by new additions, but Joffrey de Peyrac also realized the necessity of taking from his shoulders burdens he considered beyond him.

'And how about you, Monsieur Vanereick, if you have wearied of venturing out against the Spaniards, would you be tempted by the honours of Viceroy in these latitudes?'

'Possibly! ... But only when I acquire a wooden leg. I think

I would prefer even that to selling turnips and coconuts in the streets of Tortuga ... But joking apart, my coffers are not yet full enough. And one must be rich to impress a population that is a mixture of adventurers and Huguenots. I have already sown scandal among the latter with my Ines. Have you seen Ines?'

'I have seen Ines.'

'Is she not enchanting?'

'She is indeed enchanting.'

'You see I could not possibly give that charming creature up yet. But later ... it seems an interesting idea ... There you have Morgan, the greatest pirate and plunderer of our time, and today he is Governor of Jamaica, and I can assure you that he does not trifle with law and order there, and even princes bare their heads to him ... I feel I am that sort of a man too. Less stupid than I look, you know!'

'That is indeed why I had no hesitation in making you such a proposition ...'

'And I am honoured by it, indeed I am, my dear Count ... But later, later! You see, I have not yet sown my wild oats, even if I have left it a bit late in the day!'

CHAPTER THIRTY-SEVEN

THE FOG began to clear and Joffrey de Peyrac stood up and made his way back to the summit platform.

'Are you hoping to catch a glimpse of Gold Beard, lurking in some corner?' d'Urville asked him.

'Possibly.'

What was he looking for precisely, what did he hope to discover in that labyrinth of water and trees spread out at his feet? It was less a process of logical deduction than a shrewd sixth sense, that had led him to the top of this vantage point.

The man with the 'lambis' pearls ... the man to whom he had given those pink pearls on the banks of the Kennebec, the man who had lied to him, had he been one of Gold Beard's accomplices? And that mysterious ship, had it been the pirate's? And why had someone twice tried to mislead him about what had happened to Angélique?

Were these 'mistakes' just a matter of chance? He did not believe it. It was a rare thing at sea to find messages sent by word of mouth not transmitted with complete accuracy. For the brotherhood that exists between sailors, their very soul and hopes, demand that this should be so ... So why these sudden repeated deceptions? What new danger lay in that direction?

A final gust of wind swept across the bay, clearing the last of the fog as far as the horizon. The clear bluish white sky hovered over the sea like a wing, like a hollow, sonorous shell lined with mother-of-pearl.

Joffrey had to fight his way forward, step by step, leaning against the wind, as if against some contrary force, struggling forward to reach the edge of the plateau, where he stretched out full length to give less of a hold to the wind.

With his spyglass glued to his eye, he systematically examined the island-studded waters.

Here he saw a ship lying at anchor, there a fishing boat, there a flotilla of Indians crossing the straits, there two cod-fishing sloops, and farther off in the lee of an island the cod-fishing boats themselves.

Their crew had gone ashore, and he could see smoke rising as they caulked, cooked food or smoked meat.

As he proceeded with his inspection, he felt the jagged edges of the granite pressing into his chest, causing him a feeling of pain and oppression.

Would he find what he had come to seek on this bare windswept mountain?

Out towards the west, just beginning to appear through gaps in the cloud, the chain of the Blue Mountains stood out against the sky, such a vivid blue that the bay beneath them had been given the same name: Blue Hill Bay.

Was it behind there, somewhere, that Angélique was in danger?'

'Angélique! Angélique! My life!'

As he lay clutching the bare rock, he called to her in a burst of feeling that yearned to cross those fathomless distances. She had suddenly become a distant, faceless entity, but still warm and infinitely alive and attractive in her uniquely charming way.

'Angélique! Angélique! My life!'

With a whistle, the wind lashed all around him, and seemed to be hissing cruelly:

'He will separate you! You will see! You will see!'

The prediction made by Pont-Briand, the man he had killed

for having desired Angélique, whistled in his ears: 'He will separate you . . . you will see!'

Overcome by a sudden sense of anguish, he unconsciously lifted his hand to his breast, then, on second thoughts, he went on:

'But what have I to fear? Tomorrow, or the day after at the latest, she will be here . . . Angélique is no longer a young, helpless inexperienced woman. More than once she has proved to me that life could not cast her down. She could cope with anything, has she not just proved this again – God only knows how! – by managing to escape from that strange ambush at Brunswick-Falls? . . . Yes, she truly is of warrior and knightly stock, my dauntless one! It is almost as if danger makes her stronger, more efficient, more lucid . . . even lovelier . . . as if her incredible vitality thrived on it! . . . Angélique! Angélique! . . . We shall win through, shan't we, my love? Both of us . . . Wherever you are, I know we shall soon be together again . . .'

He gave a start. While he had been thinking, his wandering gaze had chanced to light on an unusual detail among the maze of islands – an orange flag flying from a mast top, half hidden among the trees of one of the islands. He lay motionless for a long time like a hunter sighting game, his eye riveted to his spyglass. Then he got up, pondering on what he had seen.

He had found what he had come to seek at the top of Mount Desert.

CHAPTER THIRTY-EIGHT

'MY LORD! My lord!'

Just as Count Peyrac's chebec was rounding Schoodic Point a voice hailed him from a French cod-fisher that was sailing under the lee a few cables away.

Standing at the poop-rail he recognized Yann le Couennec, whom he had sent from Popham to find Angélique.

Shortly afterwards, when the two ships had cast anchor off the Gouldsboro wharves, the Count hastened to join Yann.

'Speak, man! Speak up quick!'

Yann was not wearing his customary cheerful expression and Joffrey de Peyrac felt his heart grow tense with apprehension.

'Did you find Madame la Comtesse? Why is she not with you? Did you pass the *Rochelais*?'

The unfortunate Yann bowed his head. No, he had not passed the *Rochelais*. Yes, he had managed to join Madame la Comtesse, after crossing the area round the mouth of the Androscoggin which had been burnt and pillaged by the Indians, and had found her stranded at Casco Bay.

'I know all that ... Cantor told us as much. He has gone off to fetch them.'

'But alas! It is already too late!' Yann almost wept. 'Cantor will find her gone, for Gold Beard has taken Madame de Peyrac prisoner as a hostage.' And he added hurriedly, to attenuate the effect of this disturbing news, that he did not consider Madame la Comtesse to be in danger. She knew how to look after herself and this particular pirate seemed to have a respect-able-looking crew. She herself had had sufficient coolness to help him to escape in time, so that he, Yann, could make known what had happened to her.

And he told them of the circumstances of his escape.

'I ran for it, and fortunately they did not give chase. For a whole day I followed the line of the coast, then as I approached a creek that evening I had the good fortune to discover this French cod-fisher moored there. Its crew had put in to fetch water, and they took me on board and agreed to go out of their way in order to get me here as soon as possible.'

Joffrey de Peyrac had gone deathly white and was clench-ing his fists.

'Gold Beard! It's always that bandit! I shall pursue him to the death! He already captured the chief of my mercenaries last month, and now he has my wife! What outrageous impu-dence!'

He thought anxiously of Le Gall and Cantor who must by now have reached the agreed rendezvous only to find it deserted or – worse – still occupied by those dangerous, seafaring bri-gands. Discovering that his mother was now in their hands, might not Cantor be tempted to embark on some premature act of war? But no! The lad was more prudent than that! In the Mediterranean he had learned all the tricks of the corsair's trade, and would undoubtedly be content to keep a close watch on Gold Beard's ship while trying to contact his father.

Unfortunately the *Gouldsboro* would not be in any condi-tion to give chase and do battle for two days. By working on her all night they might possibly be able to put out in her the following evening accompanied by the chebec, to which they would add two cannons, and Vanereick's ship. They would have to hope that the pirate would be sufficiently intimidated by this show of force to be willing to parley.

Then Joffrey de Peyrac swung round and strode back to Yann.

'What else is there that you have not dared tell me? . . . What are you hiding?'

His piercing eyes were riveted to Yann's who, terrified, shook his head in emphatic denial.

'No . . . my lord, I swear it . . . I swear to you on the image of the Virgin and Saint Anne . . . I have told you everything . . . Why? . . . What do you think I am hiding? . . .'

'Has something happened to her? She is wounded, isn't she? . . . Or sick? . . . Speak . . .'

'No, my lord, I would never hide such a disaster from you . . . Madame de Peyrac is in fact in excellent health . . . It is she who is looking after all the others . . . She remained there precisely because of the sick and wounded . . . She even sewed up the belly of one of those foul creatures, the one who betrayed her . . .'

'Yes, I know that too . . .'

Peyrac's keen eyes scrutinized the open face of his sailor who during the past winter had become a companion and friend. No Iroquois had ever made him tremble, nor indeed had the prospect of famine. But now Yann was trembling. Peyrac put his arm round the young man's shoulders.

'What's wrong?'

And Yann felt as if he was about to burst into tears like a child. He bowed his head.

'I have walked a long way,' he murmured. 'And it wasn't easy to keep out of the way of the savages on the warpath.'

'That's true . . . Go and get some rest. There is a kind of inn below the fort, run by Madame Carrère and her daughters. The food is good and as from today they are offering claret which has just arrived from Europe. Go and get your strength back again and be ready to set out with me tomorrow if the weather is favourable.'

Count Peyrac and Roland d'Urville summoned Manigault, Berne, Pastor Beaucaire and the chief Huguenot notables to one of the rooms in the fort that served as a council chamber; they asked Vanereick and his lieutenant to attend, likewise Erikson the captain of the *Gouldsboro*, and Father Baure was also present.

Don Juan Alvarez, the commander of the small Spanish guard, stood behind the Count, a dark, forbidding figure watching over his safety.

Joffrey de Peyrac gave them a brief account of recent events. The fact that his wife, Countess Peyrac, had fallen into the hands of their enemy, made it necessary for them to observe the utmost caution. After years in the Caribbean they knew the ways of these gentlemen of fortune and Gilles Vanereick would bear him out when he said that Madame de Peyrac ran no risk of ill-treatment as long as she had any value as a hostage. Never had any great lady taken prisoner, whether she be Spanish, French, or Portuguese, had cause to complain of her jailers, while she awaited the payment of the generous ransom that would set her free once more. It had even been said that some of them, especially when the pirate was a man of prepossessing appearance, were in no particular hurry to see the end of their captivity. But it was also known that, should they be hunted down, brought to battle, run aground, or disappointed in their hopes of ransom, some of these ruthless brutes did not hesitate to carry out their threats to their hostages.

They must also bear in mind the fact that, if attacked, Gouldsboro would have only land defences. Accordingly, before the departure of the expedition ammunition must be shared out to everyone.

At this point, the Spanish sentry poked a frightened head in a black steel helmet round the door and called out:

'Excelencia, someone is asking for you.'

'Who is it?'

'*Un hombre.*'

'Send him in!'

A man, well built and heavily bearded, dressed only in a pair of tattered sailor's trousers, soaking wet, appeared on the threshold.

'Kurt Ritz!' exclaimed Peyrac.

The newcomer was Gold Beard's 'other' hostage, the Swiss mercenary whom Peyrac had engaged as a recruiting officer during a visit to Maryland. The inhabitants of Gouldsboro also recognized him, for he had come ashore among them in May with the soldiers he had recruited for Count Peyrac. He had been about to set off inland when one evening he had been taken by surprise somewhere along the shore by some of Gold Beard's men who had been lying in wait among the islands preparatory to laying siege to Gouldsboro. This had been shortly before the decisive battle that had forced the pirate to take flight, and it was feared that Kurt Ritz might have been made to pay for this defeat. But here he was, apparently in good health, although obviously tired from a long journey.

Peyrac grasped him cordially by the shoulders.

'Grüs Gott! Wie geht es mit Ihnen, lieber Herr? I was worried about you.'

'I managed at last to make my escape from that damned boat, and that damned pirate, my lord.'

'When was that?'

'Just about three days ago.'

'Three days,' Peyrac repeated thoughtfully. 'Was that when Gold Beard's ship was lying to the north of Casco Bay, near Maquoit Point?'

'Monsieur, you must have second sight! That was indeed the name I heard mentioned by members of the crew. We cast anchor there at dawn ... There was a great deal of coming and going between the ship and the land, a certain amount of confusion. Towards the evening I noticed that the cabin in which I was being held had not been properly locked. The boy who brought me my miserable rations had forgotten to padlock the door, so I waited till dead of night then slipped outside. I was right at the stern under the poop deck and the whole place seemed deserted. I could see fires burning along the beach, and it looked as if the crew was making merry on the shore. There was no moon, so I climbed up the poop and clambered on to the rear deck. Then by clinging to the mouldings, I clambered down as far as the balcony of the main stateroom, and from there I dived and managed to reach a nearby island. I waited until I was sure that no one had given the alarm, then picked out another island farther off and chanced my luck, although I am not much of a swimmer. By dawn I had reached it. There were some English refugees on the west side, but I did not mingle with them. I waited over on the east side where there were cliffs. During the day I saw some Indian canoes go by, Tarrantines, Sebagos, and Etchemins, heading north with scalps hanging at their belts. I signalled to them and showed them the crucifix I wear round my neck. We are Catholics, you know, in the upper Rhône Valley. They took me on board with them and dropped me somewhere near the mouth of the Penobscot. Then I walked day and night and, rather than go round each fiord, I swam across several of them, and nearly got swept away by the currents at high tide ... But anyway, here I am.'

'God be praised!' Peyrac exclaimed. 'Monsieur Berne, you wouldn't have a flagon of good wine by you, would you, to cheer the greatest seawater swimmer of the Waldstaette?'*

'Indeed I have.'

And from a console-table Master Berne drew a flagon of claret and a pewter goblet.

The man drained the wine at a single draught. The salt water had made him thirsty, but he had eaten nothing and the strong wine went to his head and sent the blood rushing to his face.

'Ah! *Es schmeckt prima. Ein feiner Wein! The* waves hage knocked me about so much that my head is spinning.'

'You were lucky,' someone said. 'The equinoxial gales were threatening but did not arrive.'

The Swiss poured himself a second drink and seemed greatly cheered.

'Have you still got my good halberd?' he asked. 'I did not have it with me when I was walking among the rocks and those confounded wretches set upon me.'

'It is still in the arm-rack,' Manigault replied, pointing to the row of hooks along the wall supporting lances of different sizes among which stood a longer pike topped with the admirable steel thistle flower of the Swiss weapon, whose elegant iron-work has for so long disguised its deadly efficacy in the hands of a Swiss – its hooked blade for seizing and hauling in, its sharp cutting edge for severing heads, and its tapering point to pierce bellies and hearts.

Kurt Ritz grasped his pike with a sigh.

'Ah! Here it is at last! How many miserable weeks I have spent biting my nails in frustration on board that ship! And what has happened to my men?'

'They are at Fort Wapassou.'

As they looked at him it occurred to them all that he must have made his escape on the day that Angélique de Peyrac was taken prisoner by Gold Beard. Had he seen her? Had he caught sight of the Count's wife? An indefinable sense of foreboding held them back, as indeed it held back Peyrac himself, from questioning him on this point.

'Did they ill-treat you at all?' Peyrac asked him hesitantly.

'No no! Gold Beard is no ruffian and he is a good Christian. His men held prayers every morning and evening up on deck.

* The old name for the earliest of the Swiss cantons – the Forest States.

But he is out for your blood, Monsieur le Comte, for he says that the lands of Maine where you have established yourself belong to him and that he and his men have come over to found a colony ... The women of Gouldsboro were promised to him and his men, for he was told that they were transportees.'

'What insolence!' Manigault exclaimed.

'So he was very much surprised by the defence we put up, and he only captured me to have an opening for negotiations with you, for he is as stubborn as a mule. After these gentlemen here had fired red-hot cannon balls at him, he went off to repair his ships on an island in Casco Bay, but he will be back.'

Kurt Ritz had another drink. By now he was beginning to feel in splendid fettle.

'Oh! I could tell you a great deal about Gold Beard. I talked to the sailors and also to Gold Beard himself, for he is a rough, but honest man, yes, honest. Seen from a distance, he frightens people, but his intentions are honourable. And there's a woman in all this ... his mistress ... It was she who joined him at Maquoit Point. It was she who must have engineered the whole thing for she looks a regular hussy. One of those women who will tot up figures on a sheet of parchment without a single mistake, fill their money bags, and send a chap off to war to fill them yet again. But they've got what it takes to pay for it, the jades. As lovely as Venus and intelligent too. Any man who wouldn't willingly give his life for them, must love neither life nor love. Gold Beard's mistress is that kind of woman ... and lovely too ... The whole ship was seething with excitement at the sight of her coming on board. She's a Frenchwoman. She had been waiting there for him, at Maquoit. Her eyes are like pools of water bubbling from the rock, and her hair is like a sunbeam. It was thanks to her that I was able to make my escape that night, for Gold Beard had given every man three pints of rum to celebrate the occasion ... and as for him ...'

Kurt Ritz threw back his head in a silent laugh, then downed another glass of wine.

'Him ... I would never have thought it ... He's crazy about her ... I saw them through the cracks in the boards of my cabin, as they crossed the poop deck; he was holding her arm and looking at her ... looking at her ...'

The wine was going to his head and he babbled on, not the least surprised at their silence, in no way disconcerted that he saw them, as through a mist, standing rooted to the ground, without a smile, their faces hard and frozen.

'And the woman's name?' snapped the Count, his voice seeming to come from some cotton-wool universe, muffled and far away. Every man present was seized with panic and a desperate desire to run away. Kurt Ritz's head rocked from side to side.

'*Weiss nicht!* All I know is that she is French ... and that she's beautiful, that I do know! And that he's got her under his skin, has Gold Beard, fit to bust ... I SAW THEM ... That night in the stateroom, though the poop window ... The window was open ... I had climbed down that far so I glanced in ... There was a candle burning on the table and I saw them ... The woman was naked in Gold Beard's arms ... the body of a goddess ... with her hair spread out over her shoulders ... In the sunlight I had thought her hair was golden but there I saw it was the colour of moonlight ... A sheet of silvery gold ... like a fairy ... There was something about that woman which is like no one else, something marvellous ... I can quite understand his being crazy about her, that pirate. I didn't dare to dive because of the open window ... Even people making love may have sharp eyes ... and Gold Beard is a captain, always on the alert ... I had to wait a while ...'

He talked on and on. By now he was quite drunk and went on without showing the slightest astonishment at the crushing silence that surrounded him, without realizing that there was anything odd about his being allowed to go on this way describing and dwelling on every detail of the love scene.

He went on, his head wagging from side to side:

'Where does she come from, this woman? I don't know. She met him over there ... Her name ... wait a minute, I think it's coming back to me. While he was making love to her I heard him call her "Angélique! Angélique!" It's a name that suits her.'

There was a terrible silence then suddenly Kurt Ritz's halberd slid from his fingers, and he staggered back until he found himself leaning against the wall, suddenly sober again, his face deathly white and his eyes starting out of his head as he stared at Peyrac.

'Don't kill me, Monsieur!'

And yet not a soul had moved. Not even Count Peyrac, who stood there as erect and immutable as ever. But it was the terrible black look in his eyes in which Kurt Ritz had seen the flash of death. As a man familiar with the battlefield, he had known that death was upon him, and now, completely sober, without understanding why, he looked at Peyrac and knew that he was in mortal danger.

At the same moment with a horrified prescience, he realized that every one of the participants in what was for him an incomprehensible drama, all those who stood there like ghosts in a unearthly silence, would have rather been deaf, dumb, blind, or six feet under ground, than have to live through this moment between those four walls.

He swallowed hard.

'What is the matter, gentlemen?' he groaned. 'What have I said?'

'Nothing!'

The word fell like a cleaver from Peyrac's lips.

Once again his master's voice seemed to come from another world.

'Nothing for you to reproach yourself with, Ritz ... Come now, you need rest ... In a few days' time you will have to rejoin your men in the Appalachians at Fort Wapassou.'

The man staggered across to the door and when he had gone the others hastened to take their leave in silence, each man bowing low to the master of Gouldsboro as he went, as they would have done when taking leave of the King of France.

Once outside, they donned their hats and went off home in silence, all except Gilles Vanereick who drew d'Urville to one side and said: 'Please explain ...'

CHAPTER THIRTY-NINE

THEN JOFFREY DE PEYRAC turned to Juan Fernandez.

'Send Yann le Couennec to me here.'

When Yann entered the council chamber, the Count was alone, bending over a map which he appeared to be studying with care.

His thick hair, with its trace of silver at the temples, half hid his face, as he pored over the map, and his lowered eyelids veiled his gaze.

But when he stood up and his glance fell on Yann, the lad gave a shudder, conscious of anxiety coiling within him like a cold snake.

'What is the matter? What is the matter with my master?'

he thought. 'Is he ill, is he wounded, has he received some blow? ... It is as if he had received some inner blow ... a death blow.'

Joffrey de Peyrac went round the table and came towards Yann, appearing so calm and walking so straight that Yann began to think he must have been mistaken.

'No, there is nothing wrong ... What will I imagine next?'

Joffrey examined him with penetrating attention. Yann was of medium height and reached to Joffrey's shoulder, a well set up young man, with a lively, bold expression, who still looked younger than his thirty years, although his eventful life had made an old campaigner of him, a man ready for anything. But where Joffrey de Peyrac was concerned, that French Celtic face would never hold any secrets, for he could read it like an open book.

'And now, Yann,' he said softly, 'tell me what it was you did not dare say before.'

The Breton paled and took a step back, as he searched his head for vain denials. Terrified, he knew there was no escape, for he had already seen Joffrey de Peyrac at work once he had set himself a goal, once he had determined to discover the truth about something his diabolical sixth sense had revealed to him. He was like a hunter who never lost the scent until his quarry was brought to bay.

'What is the matter with you? What is it that you are unable to tell me? Do you think I cannot see how disturbed you are? Tell me, what happened? It was something that happened at Maquoit, wasn't it, where you left the Countess? What was it you say, what was it you happened on that could have upset you as much as this?'

'But ... I didn't' – Yann gave a helpless shrug – 'I told you everything that happened, my lord.'

'It was there, wasn't it? Answer me, it happened over there?'

The poor lad nodded, then let his face fall into his hands.

'What did you see? What was it? Was it before you made your escape? ...'

Yann shook his head in misery.

'Well, was it after you ran off? You told me you ran away. You were running, and you turned round, and you saw something ... That's it, isn't it? Something strange, something inconceivable.'

How could he have guessed? It was diabolical. Yann was beginning to falter.

'What was it you saw?' the implacable voice repeated. 'What was it you saw when you looked back at the beach where you had left her? What did you see?'

Then suddenly Yann felt a hand clamp down like a vice on the back of his neck, a terrible hand that gripped him as if it would snap him in two.

'Now tell me,' came the voice, soft and menacing.

Then, realizing that the young man was suffocating and had turned purple in the face, the Count relaxed his grip in an effort to control himself, and a poignant gentleness vibrated in his persuasive voice.

'Tell me, my boy . . . I beg you!'

Then Yann's resistance broke, and he fell to his knees, clutching at Joffrey de Peyrac's doublet with the distraught gesture of a blind man.

'Forgive me, my lord. Forgive me!'

'Tell me about it . . .'

'I was running . . . I was running . . . I had made my escape just as Gold Beard reached the shore . . . taking advantage of the fact that everyone was looking at him . . . Madame la Comtesse had suggested I should choose that moment . . . I ran, I ran, and then I turned round to see if I was being followed . . . I turned towards the beach . . .'

He looked up at Peyrac in agony.

'She was in his arms, Monsieur!' he cried, clutching the Count as if he himself was being struck these terrible blows. 'She was in Gold Beard's arms . . . and they were kissing, oh! forgive me, my lord, kill me . . . They were kissing one another like lovers . . . like long-separated lovers . . .'

JEAN PLAIDY

'One of England's foremost historical novelists'—*Birmingham Mail*

The reign of Henry VIII
MURDER MOST ROYAL 30p (6/–)
ST. THOMAS'S EVE 30p (6/–)
THE SIXTH WIFE 30p (6/–)

The story of Margaret Stuart
ROYAL ROAD TO FOTHERINGAY 30p (6/–)
THE CAPTIVE QUEEN OF SCOTS
30p (6/–)

The infamous Borgia family
MADONNA OF THE SEVEN
HILLS   30p (6/–)
LIGHT ON LUCREZIA
30p (6/–)

Life and loves of
Charles II
THE WANDERING
PRINCE 30p (6/–)
A HEALTH UNTO HIS
MAJESTY   30p (6/–)

HERE LIES OUR
SOVEREIGN LORD
30p (6/–)

JEAN PLAIDY

'One of England's foremost historical novelists'—*Birmingham Mail*

The story of Henry of Navarre
EVERGREEN GALLANT 30p (6/–)

The Story of Jane Shore
THE GOLDSMITH'S WIFE 30p (6/–)

The persecution of witches and puritans in the 16th & 17th centuries
DAUGHTER OF SATAN
30p (6/–)

The story of Margaret Tudor and James IV
THE THISTLE AND THE ROSE
30p (6/–)

The Tudor novels
THE SPANISH BRIDEGROOM
30p (6/–)
GAY LORD ROBERT
30p (6/–)